KU-748-271

Fellow Mortals

I said in mine heart concerning the estate of the sons of men, that God might manifest them, and that they might see that they themselves are beasts. For that which befalleth the sons of men befalleth beasts; even one thing befalleth them; as the one dieth, so dieth the other; yea, they have all one breath; so that a man hath no preeminence above a beast . . .

Ecclesiastes

TO
DAVID SUTHERLAND

Foreword

It was David Attenborough who said, on the occasion of the 20th Anniversary of the World Wildlife Fund, "If we do nothing, our grandchildren will not inherit our world."

Many people, confronted with this statement, will shrug their shoulders in disbelief. Not because they necessarily believe the statement to be untrue, but because they cannot grasp the enormity of the problem facing our world today. They do not appreciate that the increasing pressure by mankind on the natural environment, which we call earth, is eroding all too rapidly its capacity to sustain human, animal and plant life.

Many words have been written and spoken about these problems in both prose and poetry, in scientific journals and in newspapers, on film and in books. The increasing impact that environmentalists are obtaining on political decisions around the world is evidence that these words are beginning to have some effect.

However, much more needs to be done. This anthology, chosen by Roy Fuller, bringing together old and modern verse on animals, is another step in the right direction.

The art forms of verse and illustration complement each other and together make *Fellow Mortals* a volume that is not only a delight to possess, but one which will inspire the reader to ponder on the relationship between animals and humans. And, perhaps more people will realise that without animals, without the habitat in which they live and thrive, mankind itself cannot survive.

Acceptance of this fundamental concept will surely help in creating a wider public appreciation of the tasks that must be undertaken if we are to leave to our grandchildren an earth they will enjoy.

London, 1981   GEORGE MEDLEY
                        Director, World Wildlife Fund — UK

Contents

CONTENTS

CONTENTS

CONTENTS

CONTENTS

CONTENTS

CONTENTS

CONTENTS

Acknowledgments

The Editor and Publishers desire to make grateful acknowledgement for permission to include copyright material as follows.

"Epistle II: To a Socialist in London" from *The Poetical Works of Robert Bridges*, (Oxford Standard Authors edition, 1936). Reprinted by permission of Oxford University Press.

"The Wild Swans at Coole" and "To a Squirrel at Kyle-Na-No" from the *Collected Poems of W. B. Yeats*, with the permission of M. B. Yeats, Miss Anne Yeats and the Macmillan Co. of London and Basingstoke. US: copyright 1919 by Macmillan Publishing Co., Inc., renewed 1947 by Bertha Georgie Yeats.

"The Undertaker's Horse" from *Departmental Ditties* by Rudyard Kipling, with the permission of the National Trust of Great Britain and Eyre Methuen Ltd.

"My dog Ponto" from *The Great Valley* by Edgar Lee Masters, published by Macmillan Publishing Co., Inc., New York.

"The song called 'His Hide is Covered with Hair' " by Hilaire Belloc, reprinted by permission of A. D. Peters & Co. Ltd.

"I had a duck" by A. Stodart-Walker, from *The Moxford Book of English Verse* 1340-1913, published by Cecil Palmer Ltd.

"Eyes", "The Last Years" and "To a Butterfly", by W. H. Davies. By permission of the Executors of the W. H. Davies Estate. US: copyright

ACKNOWLEDGMENTS

© 1963 by Jonathan Cape Ltd, reprinted from *The Complete Poems of W. H. Davies* by permission of Wesleyan University Press.

"Summer Evening", "The Tomtit" and "Tat for Tit", by Walter de la Mare, by permission of The Literary Trustees of Walter de la Mare and the Society of Authors as their representative.

"To a Bull-dog" and "A Dog's Death" by J. C. Squire from *Collected Poems of J. C. Squire* by permission of the Macmillan Co. of London and Basingstoke.

"The Dead Bird", "The Dead Crab", "The Dead Sheep", "A Dead Mole" and "The Young Martins" by Andrew Young from *Complete Poems* by Andrew Young, edited by Leonard Clark, published by Martin Secker and Warburg Ltd.

"Tortoise Shell" and "The Blue Jay" by D. H. Lawrence. With permission of William Heinemann Ltd. from *The Complete Poems of D. H. Lawrence* and of Lawrence Pollinger Ltd. and the Estate of the late Mrs Frieda Lawrence. US: From *The Complete Poems of D. H. Lawrence* edited by Vivian de Sola Pinto and F. Warren Roberts, copyright © 1964, 1971 by Angelo Ravagli and C. M. Weekley, Executors of the Estate of Frieda Lawrence Ravagli; reprinted by permission of Viking Penguin Inc.

"Night Song", "Daybreak" and "The Herd" by Frances Cornford from *Collected Poems* by Frances Cornford, published by the Cresset Press, reproduced by permission of the publisher.

"Pelicans" by Robinson Jeffers. Copyright 1951 by Robinson Jeffers, reprinted by permission of Donnan and Garth Jeffers.

"Bird-witted" by Marianne Moore. Reprinted by permission of Faber and Faber Ltd. from *The Complete Poems of Marianne Moore*. US and Canada: copyright 1941 by Marianne Moore, renewed 1969 by Marianne Moore.

"The Wolf and the Stork" and "The Fox and the Grapes" by Marianne Moore, from *The Fables of La Fontaine* by permission of the Estate of Marianne Moore, L. Brinn and L. Crane, Executors. US and Canada: from *The Fables of La Fontaine* translated by Marianne Moore, copyright 1952, 1953, 1954 © 1964 by Marianne Moore; all rights reserved; reprinted by permission of Viking Penguin Inc.

"The Ad-dressing of Cats" by T. S. Eliot, reprinted by permission of Faber and Faber Ltd. from *Old Possum's Book of Practical Cats* by T. S. Eliot. US: from *Old Possum's Book of Practical Cats* by T. S. Eliot, copyright 1939 by T. S. Eliot: copyright 1967 by Esmé Valerie Eliot; reprinted by permission of Harcourt Brace Jovanovich, Inc.

ACKNOWLEDGMENTS

"Variation on a Sentence" and "Animal, Vegetable and Mineral" by Louise Bogan from *The Blue Estuaries* by Louise Bogan. Copyright © 1936, 1968 by Louise Bogan. Reprinted with the permission of Farrar, Straus & Giroux, Inc.

"The Bat" and "Dun-coloured" by Ruth Pitter from *Poems 1926-1966* by Ruth Pitter, published by Barrie & Rockcliff/The Cresset Press, by permission of the publisher.

Introduction

When I was asked to make an anthology of animal poetry a number of limits at once occurred, to render manageable what seemed to an unpractised anthologist a stiff task. Those relevant to the reader I will mention here. By contrast, as it were, I always intended "animal" to take in the entire animal kingdom, excluding humans — though of course, humans play a part because of the poets themselves and the human characters who come into some of the poems.

I never seriously considered any arrangement other than the chronological one of the poets' birth dates. The Noah's Ark or animal by animal principle has been behind some amusing collections, but I was interested in man's changing attitude to animals the historical arrangement would be bound to reveal. The problem was where to start and stop. The King James Bible struck me as a good beginning, itself starting with the Creation (though since Chapter 1 of Genesis is apparently not in verse I have prefaced the anthology with Milton's Creation). It leads one on to the Elizabethan poets, still readable without too many difficulties of vocabulary and scansion for the general reader, that mythical figure the anthology's subject prompted me to have constantly in mind. So Chaucer and Skelton (*inter alia*) are missing — with regret; reading the former's brilliant catalogue in *The Parlement of Foules* almost made me revise my decision (an attempt at a translation follows the quotation):

The crane, the geaunt, with his trompes soun;
The thef, the chough; and ek the janglynge pye;
The skornynge jay; the eles fo, heroun;
The false lapwynge, ful of trecherye;
The stare, that the conseyl can bewrye;
The tame ruddok, and the coward kyte;
The kok, that orloge is of thorpes lyte;

The sparwe, Venus sone; the nyghtyngale,
That clepeth forth the grene leves newe;
The swalwe, mortherere of the foules smale
That maken hony of floures freshe of hewe;
The wedded turtil, with hire herte trewe;
The pekok, with his aungels fetheres bryghte;
The fesaunt, skornere of the cok by nyghte;

The waker goos; the cukkow ever unkynde;
The popynjay, ful of delicasye;
The drake, stroyere of his owene kynde;
The stork, the wrekere of avouterye;
The hote cormeraunt of glotenye;
The raven wys; the crowe with vois of care;
The throstil old; the frosty feldefare.

The crane, the giant, with his trumpet peals;
That thief, the chough; also the mocking jay;
The quarrelling magpie; heron, foe of eels;
The feigning lapwing, full of trickery;
The starling that the secret can betray;
The fearless robin, and the coward kite;
The cock, to villages the clock of light;

The sparrow, Venus' son; the nightingale,
That summons forth the foliage green and new;
The swallow, killer of that tiny fowl
That honey makes from flowers fresh of hue;
The wedded turtle-dove, with her heart true;
The peacock, with his angel's feathers bright;
The pheasant, scorner of the cock by night;

The watchful goose; the cuckoo so perverse;
The parrot, full of comicality;
The drake, of his own kind a murderer;
Stork, the avenger of adultery;
The cormorant, byword for gluttony;
The raven wise; the crow with anxious voice,
The long-lived thrush; the fieldfare of the snows.

As for a terminal date, I confess I was daunted at the prospect of foraging among the work of recent years, copious and available and full of animals. In the absence of time's own anthologising process, it seemed recent poetry might swamp or blur the poetry of the past, for despite urbanisation (possibly, indeed, prompted by it), modern verse has intensified the particularly Wordsworthian tradition of seeking inspiration in the animal world. Moreover, qualities such as wit and sophistication, which the moderns are so good at, might detract or divert attention from gentler and more tenuous features in older poetry. It occurred to me that I could end where some anthologies of modern verse begin, with Thomas Hardy. Then, as I began to put poems together, I saw that the 1914-1918 War was a barrier I might conveniently stay on the earlier side of. But this would have virtually ruled out products of the poetic revolution of 1909-1910, and finally I drew the line under poets born before 1900.

This fits in with the overall chronological scheme, admits the modern sensibility, but does not allow it to dominate. Perhaps in any case certain celebrated modern animal poetry may be found not to stand up too well to anthologising examination. For example, re-reading D. H. Lawrence's *Birds, Beasts and Flowers* after nearly fifty years, I often found the free verse disagreeably slack and repetitive, and the manner too knowing. Readers should accordingly not be over-disappointed at the disqualification, under my time rule, of more recent work.

I do not intend to try to advance on behalf of the anthology any generalisations of historical or sociological kind, such as an illustration of the great age of British field sports from the Tudors to George II, or the increase in song birds through the planting of hedges after the first

Enclosure Acts that marked the end of the flourishing age just referred to. Still, one notes that the comparative spareness of poetic examples in the earliest period covered no doubt emphasises that the Elizabethans, like adolescents, were interested in themselves more than in Nature. Then the Metaphysicals seized on animals for metaphor, as they seized on everything. In the early eighteenth century the animal appears in generalised or anthropological guise as a character in a moral fable, and subsequently, during that century, there is a large increase of sympathy for the animal kingdom, marked by closer observation; paving the way for the finding by the Romantics of eternal profundities in that area. The growth of science and of general interest in science played a part in this, but development was also shaped by the increase in women poets (one of women's ways of sharing in the liberatory forces of the century) whose animal subject matter was determined not only by circumscribed lives but also by tender and civilised hearts. During the Victorian epoch the naturalism of the Romantics was built on in an extraordinarily varied way. There may be a lot of dead pets, particularly dogs, in nineteenth century verse, but additionally there is adroit narrative, fun, poignancy and occasional exoticism. A poet like Clare set a remarkable standard of observation, which some of the most modern poets here combine with a return to the Metaphysical style—"Rocks, rising, showed that they were sheep". And I could not resist including a couple of Marianne Moore's quirky translations from La Fontaine to show that the eclectic moderns can even go sympathetically back to the animal moral tale.

Needless to say, these chronological characteristics are by no means neat and tidy. The Elizabethan, Michael Drayton, is a close observer, despite his backward-looking taste for medieval list-making; Cowley's beasts are not mere images; the Duchess of Newcastle shows great compassion in the middle of the *seventeenth* century; and in Pope there are touches as vivid and realistic as anything elsewhere. It may be, delighted to find premonitory virtues, that I have been somewhat lenient with the older poets. For instance, the little piece by Stephen Duck (whose reputation has come down to us with ludicrous overtones, not all on the account of his surname) undoubtedly tails off, but who could resist the sharp eye and language (and enterprising subject) before the rather trite moral is reached? And later in the book I may have slightly dropped my guard in surprise in the face, say, of something out of the way, like a sonnet about a sloth by a scientist. Nevertheless, poetic value has been the overriding determining factor in selection throughout. For that reason I have not eschewed a good few old favourites.

What I have said so far has had mainly English poets in mind. It is somewhat disappointing that American poetry does not exploit as thoroughly as one might expect the wild life that across the Atlantic survived into the English pet dog era and beyond. By the time the anthology starts, the beaver and (despite H. C.'s poem from *England's Helicon*) the wolf had already disappeared from England, and the boar was on its way out. In America such veritable wild beasts lasted much longer but of course there were fewer English-speaking poets to observe and celebrate and draw lessons from them.

On the whole, animal verse tends to be "light" verse. Even with the great mammals, even in cases of affection and loss, there is usually on the poet's part a somewhat distancing irony, a freedom of comparison, even an underlying sense of amusement--rather as in a serious man's dealings with children. This has an excellent effect on most poets, a race tending to take itself too solemnly. Though their animal poems may sometimes have to be sought in the "uncollected" or "fragments" sections of their complete works, the pieces in question are often alive and effective beyond much of their authors' ostensibly more ambitious verse. Even in the case of the admired Coleridge, how pleasantly startling it is to come across (in the volume of the Oxford edition devoted mainly to the dramas) his description of the yellow-hammer's song. Also, good animal poems may be found in stretches of an author's work generally stigmatised as below par. For example,

Wordsworth's late poems are usually considered uniform stodge, but I have included several here, at the heart of them being some animal interest or observation that has leavened the lump, like the owlet's "unexpected scream" in the excellent set of couplets he wrote probably as late as 1834. Matthew Arnold's active poetic life was actually prolonged, not unimpressively, by the death of a brace of dogs and a canary: the earliest poem here,"Geist's Grave", seems to have been written no less than thirteen years after previous poems of any moment. What a pity copious and serious poets like Milton and Browning did not leave bits and pieces behind as Thomas Gray and D. G. Rossetti did.

Nevertheless, the reader will find some poems in the high style, usually brought off, I think, by the poet elaborating the emblematic aspect of the animal without losing the concept of its actuality, like the stunning effect in the middle of Coleridge's "The Nightingale" of:

> ... On moonlight bushes,
> Whose dewy leaflets are but half-disclosed,
> You may perchance behold them on the twigs,
> Their bright, bright eyes, their eyes both bright and full,
> Glistening ...

And in "The Cricket" by the American F. G. Tuckerman (whose deserved re-discovery is quite recent), the elaborations of stanza and myth do not forget the actual insect's "vibrance crisp and shrill". Sometimes the technicalities, as it were, of the subject—the descriptive, the ecological, the natural history sides—prompt the poet to an especial splendour or idiosyncrasy. This will be discovered *passim*, but nowhere more astonishingly than in the extract from Dryden's translation of Ovid. Dryden is often thought to be a plain, muscular poet, like a policeman in uniform, but lines such as the following persuaded me to break my general rule of not including translations (there are a few other breaches for the same or analogous reasons, as already mentioned apropos Marianne Moore):

Cut from a Crab his crooked Claws, and hide
The rest in Earth, a Scorpion thence will glide
And shoot his Sling, his Tail in Circles toss'd
Refers the Limbs his backward Father lost.
And Worms, that stretch on Leaves their filmy Loom,
Crawl from their Bags, and Butterflies become.

Such intense poeticality, with strong elements of
imaginative fantasy and verbal felicity, underpinned
nonetheless by links with the natural world, brings me to a
point that was repeatedly borne in on me as the poems
accumulated, namely that in verse about animals the
subject may unite author and reader in a genuine, everyday, but often remarkable way. A large common experience shared by poet and public, particularly with garden
and domestic creatures, is a way into poetry in an age
when for various reasons the mass of the public has been
alienated from it. For the ordinary reader, subject matter
in poetry is normally more important than for the poet:
the former wants to learn or be directed, to have experience and emotion confirmed, to be comforted, given
enlightenment about living. These days, few poets would
include any such categories in their poetic aims; and
modern criticism would not emphasise them in the poetry
of the past. But many of the poems that follow, from all
periods, initially prompt quite down-to-earth questions
and reflections and responses that yet may lead the reader
on to a real and rich poetic experience as he comes to see
and appreciate the poet's often askew or penetrating
glance at a world of events and feelings more often than
not quite familiar. In particular, I think children may
thus be drawn into deep or complex, even ancient or
crabbed, poems: one need only instance the brilliant little
mystery of presentation used by Hardy in "Why She
Moved House", where the profundity of human death and
interment may be opened up to the young reader, since
the "I" of the poem is, like him or herself, a being of
limited but acute understanding. This is the place to say,
too, that though I have not sought them out I have not
excluded poems written specially for children. There are

not many of them but I judge them to fit in quite well: Jane Taylor's moral pig poem is an exemplar.

I should add, thinking of this common ground (especially in the domestic pet area), that though the sentimental to me indicates bad verse, and so to be avoided, I may have drawn too close to it for some tastes. It is an interesting question *vis-à-vis* animals. I wonder what the present-day reader will think about J. C. Squire's "To a Bull-Dog", once a famous anthology piece, now perhaps a test case. On the whole it seems a remarkably intense expression of worthy emotions widely possessed. As one moves farther back in time the tendency to sentimentality may take on quite engaging features where there are counter-balancing virtues, as I hope are shown by the poems of, say, "foetid" Buchanan, as Ezra Pound devastatingly tagged him. No doubt, the animals in general come out well: I believe justly. Working on the collection, I was often reminded of J. R. Ackerley, author of the classic *My Dog Tulip* (unfortunately not in verse), who late in life, after two virtual love affairs with an Alsatian bitch and a tame sparrow, found and took as his own motto the quotation from Ecclesiastes I have used as my epigraph; though having become more than a bit of a misogynist he used only the tendentious words "a man hath no pre-eminence above a beast".

There is a further important literary characteristic illustrated by the anthology in a modest but vital way: poetry's echoes. Sometimes these are simple: Coleridge writes about Donne's flea. Sometimes there is coincidence: Scott and Wordsworth tell the same anecdote about a faithful dog. But there are more sophisticated allusions, such as Arnold's imitation, in "Kaiser Dead", of Burns's "The Death and Dying Words of Poor Mailie". However, I will not give the whole plot away by quoting more examples, except to say that because of later gnat references it would have been nice to include Spenser's adaptation of the pseudo-Vergilian poem *Culex*, but it was too long, and truncation would have been unsatisfactory. A reverberation from classical literature would thus also have been demonstrated. And, as will be seen, the phrase "fellow mortals" is used by both William King and Burns: it accordingly seemed an apt title for the anthology.

So far as the text is concerned, scholarship must not be expected. I have gone for convenient texts. Readers have become much more tolerant of old spelling and printing usages, so I have not modernised, except in a few cases to avoid ambiguities; nor have I regularised such former practices as italicising nouns, and liberality with capital letters. By contrast, perhaps illogically but seeming all right to me, I have used modernised texts in such cases as the Bible, Shakespeare and Milton. Readers quite unused to unmodernised texts I believe will soon grow accustomed (helped by familiarity with the subject matter), particularly if they start in the eighteenth century and work backwards. Wholly raw texts, though undeniably a nuisance, have their reasons: in the case of Clare, for instance, to begin to punctuate would be to begin to lose some of the *echt*-Clare, as his latest editors, Eric Robinson and Geoffrey Summerfield, have pointed out. Cotton's "On my pretty *Marten*" confirmed me in my simplistic editorial approach. Here, I happened to have been presented with a xerox copy of the 1689 edition, which has "peaknils", not in the OED, and seeming an obvious misprint for "peakrils" (peakril: an inhabitant of the Peak district in Derbyshire), a word Cotton also uses in one of his Epistles. The correction was not made by John Beresford in his 1923 edition of Cotton's poems, though I have adopted a couple of his other emendations, one of them, "Down" for "Dawn", with hesitation—surely right, but less poetic! The poem by Robert Bridges was written according to the system of classical prosody laid down by William Johnson Stone. I have removed from the extracts here certain marks placed by Bridges to show where he disagreed with Stone's syllabic values. This omission is unlikely to affect a reader adversely.

I have admitted extracts from long or longish poems; though sparingly, for the business is not fair to the poet and is apt to tantalise the reader. Three asterisks are used to make clear divisions between bleeding chunks. If I had been even more lenient about extracts, choosing a few lines here and there which referred to animals in wider contexts—or even more leniently had admitted as "animal poems" those where really the human dominated—I suppose the anthology would have illustrated more explicitly the divine or (as I would put it myself) the evolutionary mystery and marvel of living creation. The book as a whole, too, would no doubt have been rather more elevated.

> And bats went round in fragrant skies
> And wheeled or lit the filmy shapes
> That haunt the dusk, with ermine capes
> And woolly breasts and beaded eyes

— one was tempted by such things as the marvellous section of *In Memoriam* which includes this stanza, yet in the end I decided that the lines did not belong here either by themselves or with the other, mainly non-animal, fellow quatrains. And, after all, the great questions are probably sufficiently raised: much to my taste is the half-ironic line by Louise Bogan, after a poem of strict particularities:

> What Artist laughs? What clever Daemon thinks?

The sparse notes and glossaries I have kept by the poems to which they relate: I fear the amount of explication is rather inconsistent; a decent dictionary will still be needed but help with a word or fact may be there when a reader is likely to be initially baulked. A classical dictionary will also add enjoyment: writing about animals does not lessen a poet's reliance on myth.

I have kept my eyes averted from rival collections, though remembrance of the anthologising work of others could not be avoided, of course. Thus I owe the poems by the admirable Thomas Heyrick to Dame Helen Gardner and Mr George MacBeth. I did not canvass in any real sense but warmly thank those who helped in various ways. The London Library has been indispensable, as in other departments of a writer's life; the open shelves providing such windfalls as the Romanes poem.

INTRODUCTION

The growth of compassion for brute creation, as here revealed, must be accounted a considerable virtue, especially over a period when man has done much damage to his own kind. Like Ackerley, as man grows older it seems the attractive qualities of the non-human and the grave drawbacks of the human are strongly brought home to him. Nevertheless, the business should not be exaggerated: some poems here help to maintain right perspectives, not least the song by Belloc. Other more devilish poems, like the parody of Keats, are possibly less defensible.

Yet, even reminding ourselves that it took a human to compose the Ninth Symphony, and all that, the anthology must be seen as a prolonged illustration of the irony of the Sixth Day of the Creation, so poignantly anatomised at the point where I have broken off the prefatory quotation from *Paradise Lost*: "There wanted yet the master work" —the work of genius to come being man. It is man who has fallen, not the beasts: that is the message even for the irreligious, and to some extent salvation can be measured by his very treatment of them. Unhappily, the cruelty of chemicals has succeded the cruelty of the chase; and in nuclear weapons man offers an even worse threat to the rest of mortality.

August, 1981   ROY FULLER

Fellow Mortals

Creation of the Animals

    And God said, Let the waters generate
Reptile with spawn abundant, living soul:
And let fowl fly above the earth, with wings
Displayed on the open firmament of heaven.
And God created the great whales, and each
Soul living, each that crept, which plenteously
The waters generated by their kinds,
And every bird of wing after his kind;
And saw that it was good, and blessed them, saying,
Be fruitful, multiply, and in the seas
And lakes and running streams the waters fill;
And let the fowl be multiplied on the earth.
Forthwith the sounds and seas, each creek and bay
With fry innumerable swarm, and shoals
Of fish that with their fins and shining scales
Glide under the green wave, in schools that oft
Bank the mid sea: part single or with mate
Graze the sea weed their pasture, and through groves
Of coral stray, or sporting with quick glance
Show to the sun their waved coats dropped with gold,
Or in their pearly shells at ease, attend
Moist nutriment, or under rocks their food
In jointed armour watch: on smooth the seal,
And bended dolphins play: part huge of bulk
Wallowing unwieldy, enormous in their gait
Tempest the ocean: there leviathan
Hugest of living creatures, on the deep
Stretched like a promontory sleeps or swims,
And seems a moving land, and at his gills
Draws in, and at his trunk spouts out a sea.
Mean while the tepid caves, and fens and shores
Their brood as numerous hatch, from the egg that soon
Bursting with kindly rupture forth disclosed
Their callow young, but feathered soon and fledge
They summed their pens, and soaring the air sublime
With clang despised the ground, under a cloud
In prospect; there the eagle and the stork
On cliffs and cedar tops their eyries build:

Part loosely wing the region, part more wise
In common, ranged in figure wedge their way,
Intelligent of seasons, and set forth
Their airy caravan high over seas
Flying, and over lands with mutual wing
Easing their flight; so steers the prudent crane
Her annual voyage, borne on winds; the air
Floats, as they pass, fanned with unnumbered plumes:
From branch to branch the smaller birds with song
Solaced the woods, and spread their painted wings
Till even, nor then the solemn nightingale
Ceased warbling, but all night tuned her soft lays:
Others on silver lakes and rivers bathed
Their downy breast; the swan with arched neck
Between her white wings mantling proudly, rows
Her state with oary feet: yet oft they quit
The dank, and rising on stiff pennons, tower
The mid aerial sky: others on ground
Walked firm; the crested cock whose clarion sounds
The silent hours, and the other whose gay train
Adorns him, coloured with the florid hue
Of rainbows and starry eyes. The waters thus
With fish replenished, and the air with fowl,
Evening and morn solemnised the fifth day
    The sixth, and of creation last arose
With evening harps and matin, when God said,
Let the earth bring forth soul living in her kind,
Cattle and creeping things, and beast of the earth,
Each in their kind. The earth obeyed, and straight
Opening her fertile womb teemed at a birth
Innumerous living creatures, perfect forms,
Limbed and full grown: out of the ground up rose
As from his lair the wild beast where he wons
In forest wild, in thicket, brake, or den;
Among the trees in pairs they rose, they walked:
The cattle in the fields and meadows green:
Those rare and solitary, these in flocks
Pasturing at once, and in broad herds upsprung.
The grassy clods now calved, now half appeared
The tawny lion, pawing to get free
His hinder parts, then springs as broke from bonds,
And rampant shakes his brinded mane; the ounce,

CREATION OF THE ANIMALS

The libbard, and the tiger, as the mole
Rising, the crumbled earth above them threw
In hillocks; the swift stag from underground
Bore up his branching head: scarce from his mould
Behemoth biggest born of earth upheaved
His vastness: fleeced the flocks and bleating rose,
As plants: ambiguous between sea and land
The river horse and scaly crocodile.
At once came forth whatever creeps the ground,
Insect or worm; those waved their limber fans
For wings, and smallest lineaments exact
In all the liveries decked of summer's pride
With spots of gold and purple, azure and green:
These as a line their long dimension drew,
Streaking the ground with sinuous trace; not all
Minims of nature; some of serpent kind
Wondrous in length and corpulence involved
Their snaky folds, and added wings. First crept
The parsimonious emmet, provident
Of future, in small room large heart enclosed,
Pattern of just equality perhaps
Hereafter, joined in her popular tribes
Of commonalty: swarming next appeared
The female bee that feeds her husband drone
Deliciously, and builds her waxen cells
With honey stored: the rest are numberless,
And thou their natures know'st, and gavest them names,
Needless to thee repeated; nor unknown
The serpent subtlest beast of all the field,
Of huge extent sometimes, with brazen eyes
And hairy mane terrific, though to thee
Not noxious, but obedient at thy call.
Now heaven in all her glory shone, and rolled
Her motions, as the great first mover's hand
First wheeled their course; earth in her rich attire
Consummate lovely smiled; air, water, earth,
By fowl, fish, beast, was flown, was swam, was walked
Frequent; and of the sixth day yet remained;
There wanted yet the master work . . .

John Milton, from *Paradise Lost,* Book VII, 387-505

THE KING JAMES BIBLE
From *The Book of Job*
God speaks

Wilt thou hunt the prey for the lion?
Or fill the appetite of the young lions,
When they couch in their dens,
And abide in the covert to lie in wait?
Who provideth for the raven his food?
When his young ones cry unto God,
They wander for lack of meat.
Knowest thou the time when the wild goats of the
    rock bring forth?
Or canst thou mark when the hinds do calve?
Canst thou number the months that they fulfil?
Or knowest thou the time when they bring forth?
They bow themselves, they bring forth their young
    ones,
They cast out their sorrows.
Their young ones are in good liking, they grow up
    with corn;
They go forth, and return not unto them.

Who hath sent out the wild ass free?
Or who hath loosed the bands of the wild ass?
Whose house I have made the wilderness,
And the barren land his dwellings.
He scorneth the multitude of the city,
Neither regardeth he the crying of the driver.
The range of the mountains is his pasture,
And he searcheth after every green thing.
Will the unicorn be willing to serve thee,
Or abide by thy crib?
Canst thou bind the unicorn with his band in the
    furrow?
Or will he harrow the valleys after thee?
Wilt thou trust him, because his strength is great?
Or wilt thou leave thy labour to him?
Wilt thou believe him, that he will bring home thy
    seed,
And gather it into thy barn?

Gavest thou the goodly wings unto the peacocks?
Or wings and feathers unto the ostrich?

Which leaveth her eggs in the earth,
And warmeth them in dust,
And forgetteth that the foot may crush them,
Or that the wild beast may break them.
She is hardened against her young ones as though
    they were not her's:
Her labour is in vain without fear;
Because God hath deprived her of wisdom,
Neither hath he imparted to her understanding.
What time she lifteth up herself on high,
She scorneth the horse and his rider.

    Hast thou given the horse strength?
Hast thou clothed his neck with thunder?
Canst thou make him afraid as a grasshopper?
The glory of his nostrils is terrible.
He paweth in the valley, and rejoiceth in his strength:
He goeth on to meet the armed men.
He mocketh at fear, and is not affrighted;
Neither turneth he back from the sword.
The quiver rattleth against him,
The glittering spear and the shield.
He swalloweth the ground with fierceness and rage:
Neither believeth he that it is the sound of the
    trumpet.
He saith among the trumpets, Ha, ha;
And he smelleth the battle afar off,
The thunder of the captains, and the shouting.

    Doth the hawk fly by thy wisdom,
And stretch her wings towards the south?
Doth the eagle mount up at thy command,
And make her nest on high?
She dwelleth and abideth on the rock,
Upon the crag of the rock, and the strong place.
From thence she seeketh the prey,
And her eyes behold afar off.
Her young ones also suck up blood:
And where the slain are, there is she.

From *The Book of the Prophet Isaiah*
God's Rule

The wolf also shall dwell with the lamb,
And the leopard shall lie down with the kid;
And the calf and the young lion and the fatling
    together;
And a little child shall lead them.
And the cow and the bear shall feed;
Their young ones shall lie down together;
And the lion shall eat straw like the ox.
And the sucking child shall play on the hole of the
    asp,
And the weaned child shall put his hand on the
    cockatrice' den.
They shall not hurt nor destroy in all my holy
    mountain:
For the earth shall be full of the knowledge of the Lord,
As the waters cover the sea.

God's Vengeance

For it is the day of the Lord's vengeance,
And the year of recompense for the controversy
    of Zion.
And the streams thereof shall be turned into pitch,
And the dust thereof into brimstone,
And the land thereof shall become burning pitch.
It shall not be quenched night nor day;
The smoke thereof shall go up for ever:
From generation to generation it shall lie waste;
None shall pass through it for ever and ever.
But the cormorant and the bittern shall possess it;
The owl also and the raven shall dwell in it:
And he shall stretch out upon it the line of confusion,
And the stones of emptiness.
They shall call the nobles thereof to the kingdom,
But none shall be there,
And all her princes shall be nothing.
And thorns shall come up in her palaces,
Nettles and brambles in the fortresses thereof.

And it shall be an habitation of dragons,
And a court for owls.
The wild beasts of the desert shall also meet with the
    wild beasts of the island,
And the satyr shall cry to his fellow;
The screech owl also shall rest there,
And find for herself a place of rest.
There shall the great owl make her nest, and lay,
And hatch, and gather under her shadow:
There shall the vultures also be gathered,
Every one with her mate.

HENRY CONSTABLE
(1562-1613)

(The following poem, printed above the initials "H.C." in *England Helicon* (1600), has also been attributed to Henry Chettle (d. 1607?).

To his Flocks

Feede on my Flocks securely,
Your Sheepherd watcheth surely,
Runne about my little Lambs,
Skip and wanton with your Dammes,
    Your loving Heard with care will tend ye:
Sport on faire flocks at pleasure,
Nip *Vestaes* flowring treasure,
I myself will duely harke,
When my watchfull dogge dooth barke,
    From Woolfe and Foxe I will defend ye.

MICHAEL DRAYTON
(1563-1631)

From *Poly-Olbion*

(From *Fourteenth Song*)

    And, now that every thing may in the proper place
Most aptly be contriv'd, the sheepe our wold doth
      breed
(The simplest though it seeme) shall our description
      need,
And shepheard-like, the Muse thus of that kind doth
      speak;
No browne, nor sullyed black the face or legs doth
      streak,
Like those of Moreland, Cank, or of the Cambrian
      hills
That lightly laden are: but Cotswold wisely fills
Her with the whitest kind: whose browes so woolly be,
As men in her faire sheepe no emptiness should see.

8

The staple deepe and thick, through, to the very
    graine,
Most strongly keepeth out the violentest raine:
A body long and large, the buttocks equall broad;
As fit to under-goe the full and weightie load.
And of the fleecie face, the flanke doth nothing lack,
But every-where is stor'd; the belly, as the back.
The faire and goodly flock, the shepheards onely
    pride,
As white as winters snowe, when from the rivers side
He drives his new-washt sheepe; or on the sheering
    day,
When as the lusty ram, with those rich spoyles of May
His crooked hornes hath crown'd; the bell-weather,
    so brave
As none in all the flock they like themselves would
    have.

(*Poly-Olbion:* having many blessings.)

(From *Five-and-Twentieth Song*)

The Duck, and Mallard first, the falconers onely
    sport,
(Of river-flights the chiefe, so that all other sort,
They onely green-fowle tearme) in every mere
    abound,
That you would thinke they sate upon the very
    ground,
Their numbers be so great, the waters covering quite,
That rais'd, the spacious ayre is darkened with their
    flight;
Yet still the dangerous dykes, from shot doe them
    secure,
Where they from flash to flash, like the full epicure
Waft, as they lov'd to change their diet every meale;
And neere to them ye see the lesser dibling Teale
In bunches, with the first that flie from mere to mere,
As they above the rest were lords of earth and ayre.
The Gossander with them, my goodly fennes doe
    show
His head as ebon blacke, the rest as white as snow,

With whom the Widgeon goes, the Golden-Eye, the
    Smeath,
And in odde scattred pits, the flags, and reeds
    beneath;
The Coot, bald, else cleane black, that whitenesse it
    doth beare
Upon the forehead star'd, the Water-Hen doth weare
Upon her little tayle, in one small feather set.
The Water-woosell next, all over black as jeat,
With various colours, black, greene, blew, red, russet,
    white,
Doe yeeld the gazing eye as variable delight,
As doe those sundry fowles, whose severall plumes
    they be.
The diving Dob-chick, here among the rest you see,
Now up, now downe againe, that hard it is to proove,
Whether under water most it liveth, or above:
With which last little fowle, (that water may not
    lacke;
More then the Dob-chick doth, and more doth love
    the brack)
The Puffin we compare, which comming to the dish,
Nice pallats hardly judge, if it be flesh or fish.

From *The Owle*

And every bird shew'd in his proper kind,
What vertue, nature had to him assign'd.
The prettie Turtle, and the kissing Dove,
Their faiths in wedlock, and chaste nuptiall love:
The hens (to women) sanctitie expresse,
Hallowing their egges: the Swallow cleanlinesse,
Sweeting her nest, and purging it of doung
And every houre is picking of her young.
The Herne, by soaring shewes tempestuous showres,
The princely Cocke distinguisheth the houres.
The Kite, his traine him guiding in the ayre,
Prescribes the helme, instructing how to stere.
The Crane to labour, fearing some rough flaw,
With sand and gravell burthening his craw:
Noted by man, which by the same did finde
To ballast ships for steddinesse in winde.

10

And by the forme and order in his flight,
To march in warre, and how to watch by night.
The first of house that ere did groundsell lay,
Which then was homely of rude lome and clay,
Learn'd of the Martin: Philomel in spring,
Teaching by art her little one to sing;
By whose cleere voice sweet musike first was found,
Before Amphyon ever knew a sound.
Covering with mosse the deads unclosed eye,
The little Red-breast teacheth charitie:
So many there in sundry things excell,
Time scarce could serve their properties to tell.

WILLIAM SHAKESPEARE
(1564-1616)

From *Venus and Adonis*

But lo from forth a copse that neighbours by,
A breeding jennet, lusty, young and proud,
Adonis' trampling courser doth espy,
And forth she rushes, snorts and neighs aloud:
　　The strong-neck'd steed being tied unto a tree,
　　Breaketh his rein, and to her straight goes he.

Imperiously he leaps, he neighs, he bounds,
And now his woven girths he breaks asunder;
The bearing earth with his hard hoof he wounds,
Whose hollow womb resounds like heaven's thunder;
　　The iron bit he crusheth 'tween his teeth,
　　Controlling what he was controlled with.

His ears up-prick'd, his braided hanging mane
Upon his compass'd crest now stand on end;
His nostrils drink the air, and forth again
As from a furnace, vapours doth he send;
　　His eye which scornfully glisters like fire
　　Shows his hot courage and his high desire.

11

WILLIAM SHAKESPEARE

Sometime he trots, as if he told the steps,
With gentle majesty and modest pride;
Anon he rears upright, curvets and leaps,
As who should say "Lo thus my strength is tried:
    And this I do to captivate the eye
    Of the fair breeder that is standing by."

What recketh he his rider's angry stir,
His flattering "holla" or his "Stand, I say"?
What cares he now for curb or pricking spur,
For rich caparisons or trappings gay?
    He sees his love, and nothing else he sees,
    For nothing else with his proud sight agrees.

Look when a painter would surpass the life
In limning out a well-proportion'd steed,
His art with nature's workmanship at strife,
As if the dead the living should exceed:
    So did this horse excel a common one,
    In shape, in courage, colour, pace and bone.

Round-hoof'd, short-jointed, fetlocks shag and long,
Broad breast, full eye, small head, and nostril wide,
High crest, short ears, straight legs and passing strong,
Thin mane, thick tail, broad buttock, tender hide:
    Look what a horse should have he did not lack,
    Save a proud rider on so proud a back.

Sometime he scuds far off, and there he stares;
Anon he starts at stirring of a feather.
To bid the wind a base he now prepares,
And where he run or fly, they know not whether,
    For through his mane and tail the high wind sings,
    Fanning the hairs, who wave like feather'd wings.

He looks upon his love, and neighs unto her:
She answers him, as if she knew his mind.
Being proud, as females are, to see him woo her,
She puts on outward strangeness, seems unkind,
    Spurns at his love, and scorns the heat he feels,
    Beating his kind embracements with her heels.

Then like a melancholy malcontent,
He vails his tail that like a falling plume
Cool shadow to his melting buttock lent;
He stamps, and bites the poor flies in his fume.
   His love perceiving how he was enrag'd,
   Grew kinder, and his fury was assuag'd.

His testy master goeth about to take him,
When lo the unback'd breeder, full of fear,
Jealous of catching, swiftly doth forsake him;
With her the horse, and left Adonis there:
   As they were mad unto the wood they hie them,
   Outstripping crows that strive to overfly them.

Venus speaks to Adonis

"Thou hadst been gone," quoth she, "sweet boy, ere this,
   But that thou told'st me, thou wouldst hunt the boar.
   Oh be advis'd, thou know'st not what it is,
   With javelin's point a churlish swine to gore,
      Whose tushes never sheath'd he whetteth still,
      Like to a mortal butcher, bent to kill.

"On his bow-back he hath a battle set
   Of bristly pikes that ever threat his foes;
   His eyes like glow-worms shine when he doth fret,
   His snout digs sepulchres where'er he goes;
      Being mov'd, he strikes whate'er is in his way,
      And whom he strikes his crooked tushes slay.

"His brawny sides with hairy bristles armed
   Are better proof than thy spear's point can enter;
   His short thick neck cannot be easily harmed;
   Being ireful, on the lion he will venture.
      The thorny brambles and embracing bushes,
      As fearful of him, part; through whom he rushes.

"Alas, he naught esteems that face of thine,
   To which love's eyes pays tributary gazes;
   Nor thy soft hands, sweet lips and crystal eyne,
   Whose full perfection all the world amazes:
      But having thee at vantage—wondrous dread!—
      Would root these beauties as he roots the mead."

    *   *   *

"But if thou needs wilt hunt, be rul'd by me:
Uncouple at the timorous flying hare,
Or at the fox which lives by subtlety,
Or at the roe which no encounter dare;
    Pursue these fearful creatures o'er the downs,
    And on thy well-breath'd horse keep with thy hounds.

"And when thou hast on foot the purblind hare,
Mark the poor wretch, to overshoot his troubles,
How he outruns the wind, and with what care
He cranks and crosses with a thousand doubles;
    The many musits through the which he goes
    Are like a labyrinth to amaze his foes.

"Sometime he runs among a flock of sheep,
To make the cunning hounds mistake their smell;
And sometime where earth-delving conies keep,
To stop the loud pursuers in their yell;
    And sometime sorteth with a herd of deer:
    Danger deviseth shifts, wit waits on fear.

"For there his smell with others being mingled,
The hot scent-snuffing hounds are driven to doubt,
Ceasing their clamorous cry, till they have singled
With much ado the cold fault cleanly out;
    Then they do spend their mouths: echo replies,
    As if another chase were in the skies.

"By this, poor Wat, far off upon a hill,
Stands on his hinder-legs with list'ning ear,
To hearken if his foes pursue him still.
Anon their loud alarums he doth hear;
    And now his grief may be compared well
    To one sore sick, that hears the passing bell.

"Then shalt thou see the dew-bedabbled wretch
Turn, and return, indenting with the way.
Each envious briar his weary legs do scratch,
Each shadow makes him stop, each murmur stay:
    For misery is trodden on by many,
    And being low, never reliev'd by any."

JOHN DONNE
(1572-1631)

The Flea

Marke but this flea, and marke in this,
How little that which thou deny'st me is;
It suck'd me first, and now sucks thee,
And in this flea, our two bloods mingled bee;
Thou know'st that this cannot be said
A sinne, nor shame, nor losse of maidenhead,
  Yet this enjoyes before it wooe,
   And pamper'd swells with one blood made of two,
   And this, alas, is more than wee would doe.

Oh stay, three lives in one flea spare,
Where wee almost, yea more than maryed are.
This flea is you and I, and this
Our mariage bed, and mariage temple is;
Though parents grudge, and you, w'are met,
And cloystered in these living walls of Jet.
  Though use make you apt to kill mee,
   Let not to that, selfe murder added bee,
   And sacrilege, three sinnes in killing three.

Cruell and sodaine, hast thou since
Purpled thy naile, in blood of innocence?
Wherein could this flea guilty bee,
Except in that drop which it suckt from thee?
Yet thou triumph'st, and saist that thou
Find'st not thy selfe, nor mee the weaker now;
  'Tis true, then learne how false, feares bee;
   Just so much honor, when thou yeeld'st to mee,
   Will wast, as this flea's death tooke life from thee.

BEN JONSON
(1573-1637)

Satyres Catch

from *Oberon*

Buz, quoth the blue Flie,
    Hum, quoth the Bee:
Buz, and hum, they crie,
    And so doe wee.
In his eare, in his nose,
    Thus, doe you see?
He eat the dormouse,
    Else it was hee.

From *To Penshurst*

Thy copp's, too, nam'd of Gamage, thou hast there,
That never failes to serve thee season'd deere,
When thou would'st feast, or exercise thy friends.
The lower land, that to the river bends,
Thy sheepe, thy bullocks, kine, and calves doe feed:
The middle grounds thy mares, and horses breed.
Each banke doth yeeld thee coneyes; and the topps
Fertile of wood, Ashore, and Sydney's copp's,
To crowne thy open table, doth provide
The purpled pheasant, with the speckled side:
The painted partrich lyes in every field,
And, for thy messe, is willing to be kill'd.
And if the high swolne Medway faile thy dish,
Thou hast thy ponds, that pay thee tribute fish,
Fat, aged carps, that runne into thy net.
And pikes, now weary their owne kinde to eat,
As loth, the second draught, or cast to stay,
Officiously, at first, themselves betray.
Bright eeles, that emulate them, and leape on land,
Before the fisher, or into his hand.

(*Penshurst:* the estate in Kent of the Sidneys.)

Charme

From *The Masque of Queenes*
(Spoken by one of the witches)

The owle is abroad, the bat, and the toad,
   And so is the cat-a-mountayne,
The ant, and the mole sit both in a hole,
   And frog peepes out o'the fountayne;
The dogs, they doe bay, and the timbrels play,
   The spindle is now a turning;
The moone it is red, and the starres are fled,
   But all the skie is a burning:
The ditch is made, and our nayles the spade,
With pictures full, of waxe, and of wooll;
Their livers I sticke, with needles quicke;
There lacks but the bloud, to make up the floud.
   Quickly, Dame, then, bring your part in,
Spurre, spurre, upon little Martin,
Merrily, merrily, make him saile,
A wormc in his mouth, and a thorne in's taile,
Fire above, and fire below,
With a whip i'your hand, to make him goe.

(*Martin:* goat on which witches ride to their meetings.)

ROBERT HERRICK
(1591-1674)

Upon his Spaniell *Tracie*

Now thou art dead, no eye shall ever see,
For shape and service, *Spaniell* like to thee.
This shall my love doe, give thy sad death one
Teare, that deserves of me a million.

His Grange, or private wealth

Though Clock,
To tell how night drawes hence, I've none,
A Cock,
I have, to sing how day drawes on.
I have
A maid (my *Prew*) by good luck sent,
To save
That little, Fates me gave or lent.
A Hen
I keep, which creeking day by day,
Tells when
She goes her long white egg to lay.
A goose
I have, which, with a jealous eare,
Lets loose
Her tongue, to tell what danger's neare.
A Lamb
I keep (tame) with my morsells fed,
Whose Dam
An Orphan left him (lately dead.)
A Cat
I keep, that playes about my House,
Grown fat,
With eating many a miching Mouse.
To these
A *Trasy* I do keep, whereby
I please
The more my rurall privacie:
Which are
But toyes, to give my heart some ease:
Where care
None is, slight things do lightly please.

(*Trasy:* spelt Tracie in the preceding poem — the poet's spaniel.)

Upon a Flie

A golden Flie one shew'd to me,
Clos'd in a Box of Yvorie:
Where both seem'd proud; the Flie to have
His buriall in an yvory grave:
The yvorie tooke State to hold
A Corps as bright as burnisht gold.
One fate had both; both equall Grace;
The Buried, and the Burying-place.
Not *Virgils Gnat*, to whom the Spring
All Flowers sent to'is burying.
Not *Marshals Bee,* which in a Bead
Of *Amber* quick was buried.
Nor that fine Worme that do's interre
Her selfe i'th' *silken Sepulchre.*
Nor my rare *Phil*, that lately was
With Lillies Tomb'd up in a Glasse;
More honour had, then this same *Flie;*
Dead, and clos'd up in *Yvorie*.

(*Phil:* the poet's pet sparrow, as appears from the next poem; *Marshal:* Martial.)

Upon the Death of his Sparrow
An Elegie

Why doe not all fresh maids appeare
To work Love's Sampler onely here,
Where spring-time smiles throughout the yeare?
And not here *Rose-buds, Pinks,* all flowers,
Nature begets by th'Sun and showers,
Met in one Hearce-cloth, to ore-spred
The body of the under-dead?
Phill, the late dead, the late dead Deare,
O! may no eye distill a Teare
For you once lost, who weep not here!
Had *Lesbia* (too-too-kind) but known
This Sparrow, she had scorn'd her own:
And for this dead which under-lies,
Wept out her heart, as well as eyes.

But endlesse Peace, sit here, and keep
My *Phill*, the time he has to sleep,
And thousand Virgins come and weep,
To make these flowrie Carpets show
Fresh, as their blood; and ever grow,
Till passengers shall spend their doome,
Not *Virgil's* Gnat had such a Tomb.

JOHN MILTON
(1608-1674)

From *Paradise Lost, Book IX*

So spake the enemy of mankind, enclosed
In serpent, inmate bad, and toward Eve
Addressed his way, not with indented wave,
Prone on the ground, as since, but on his rear,
Circular base of rising folds, that towered
Fold above fold a surging maze, his head
Crested aloft, and carbuncle his eyes;
With burnished neck of verdant gold, erect
Amidst his circling spires, that on the grass
Floated redundant: pleasing was his shape,
And lovely, never since of serpent kind
Lovelier, not those that in Illyria changed
Hermione and Cadmus, or the god
In Epidaurus; not to which transformed
Ammonian Jove, or Capitoline was seen,
He with Olympias, this with her who bore
Scipio the height of Rome. With tract oblique
At first, as one who sought access, but feared
To interrupt, sidelong he works his way.
As when a ship by skilful steersman wrought
Nigh river's mouth or foreland, where the wind
Veers oft, as oft so steers, and shifts her sail;
So varied he, and of his tortuous train
Curled many a wanton wreath in sight of Eve,
To lure her eye; she busied heard the sound
Of rustling leaves, but minded not, as used
To such disport before her through the field,
From every beast, more duteous at her call,
Than at Circean call the herd disguised,

He bolder now, uncalled before her stood;
But as in gaze admiring: oft he bowed
His turret crest, and sleek enamelled neck,
Fawning, and licked the ground whereon she trod.

JOSEPH BEAUMONT
(1616-1699)

The Gnat

One Night all tired with the weary Day,
And with my tedious selfe, I went to lay
    My fruitlesse Cares
    And needlesse feares
      Asleep.
The Curtaines of the Bed, and of mine Eyes
Being drawne, I hop'd no trouble would surprise
    That Rest which now
    'Gan on my Brow
      To creep.

When loe a little flie, lesse than its Name
(It was a Gnat) with angry Murmur came.
    About She flew
    And louder grew
      Whilst I
Faine would have scorn'd the silly Thing, and slept
Out all its Noise; I resolute silence kept,
    And laboured so
    To overthrow
      The Flie.

But still with sharp Alarms vexatious She
Or challenged, or rather mocked Me.
    Angry at last
    About I cast
      My Hand.
'Twas well Night would not let me blush, nor see
With whom I fought; And yet though feeble She
    Nor Her nor my
    Owne Wrath could I
      Command.

Away She flies, and Her owne Triumph sings
I being left to fight with idler Things,
    A feeble pair
    My Selfe and Aire.
        How true
A worme is Man, whom flies their sport can make!
Poor worme; true Rest in no Bed can he take,
    But one of Earth
    Whence He came forth
        And grew.

For there None but his silent Sisters be,
Wormes of as true and genuine Earth as He,
    Which from the same
    Corruption came:
        And there
Though on his Eyes they feed, though on his Heart,
They neither vex nor wake Him; every part
    Rests in sound sleep,
    And out doth keep
        All feare.

GEORGE DANIEL
(1616-1657)

The Robin

Poore bird! I doe not envie thee;
Pleas'd in the gentle Melodie
    Of thy owne Song.
Let crabbed winter Silence all
The winged Quire; he never shall
    Chaine up thy Tongue:
        Poor Innocent!
When I would please my selfe, I looke on thee;
And guess some sparkes of that Felicitie,
    That Selfe-Content.

When the bleake Face of winter Spreads
The Earth, and violates the Meads
   Of all their Pride;
When Sapless Trees and Flowers are fled,
Back to their Causes, and lye dead
   To all beside:
     I see thee Set,
Bidding defiance to the bitter Ayre,
Upon a wither'd Spray; by cold made bare,
    And drooping yet.

There, full in notes, to ravish all
My Earth, I wonder what to call
   My dullness; when
I heare thee, prettie Creature, bring
Thy better odes of Praise, and Sing,
   To puzzle men:
    Poore pious Elfe!
I am instructed by thy harmonie,
To sing the Time's uncertaintie,
    Safe in my Selfe.

Poore Redbreast, caroll out thy Laye,
And teach us mortalls what to saye.
   Here cease the Quire
Of ayerie Choristers; noe more
Mingle your notes; but catch a Store
From her Sweet Lire;
    You are but weake,
Mere summer Chanters; you have neither wing
Nor voice, in winter. Prettie Redbreast, Sing,
    What I would speake.

ABRAHAM COWLEY
(1618-1667)

(From *Anacreontiques: or, some copies of verses translated paraphrastically out of Anacreon*)

The Grashopper

Happy *Insect*, what can be
In happiness compar'd to Thee?
Fed with nourishment divine,
The dewy *Mornings* gentle *Wine*!
Nature waits upon thee still,
And thy verdant Cup does fill,
'Tis fill'd where ever thou dost tread,
Nature selfe's *thy Ganimed*.
Thou dost drink, and dance, and sing;
Happier then the happiest *King*!
All the *Fields* which thou dost see,
All the *Plants* belong to *Thee*,
All that *Summer Hours* produce,
Fertile made with early juice.

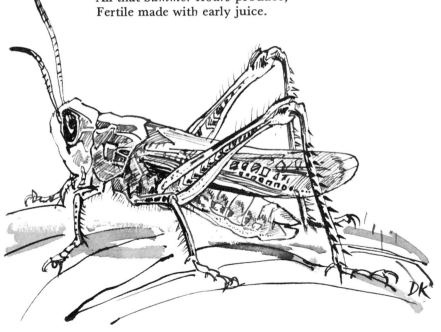

Man for thee does sow and plow;
Farmer He, and *Land-Lord Thou*!
Thou doest innocently joy;
Nor does thy *Luxury* destroy;
The *Shepherd* gladly heareth thee,
More *Harmonious* then *He*.
Thee Country Hindes with gladness hear,
Prophet of the ripened year!
Thee *Phœbus* loves, and does inspire;
Phœbus is himself thy *Sire*.
To thee of all things upon earth,
Life is no longer then thy *Mirth*.
Happy *Insect*, happy Thou,
Dost neither *Age*, nor *Winter* know.
But when thou'st drunk, and danc'd, and sung,
Thy fill, the flowry Leaves among
(*Voluptuous*, and *Wise* with all,
Epicuræan Animal!)
Sated with thy *Summer Feast*,
Thou retir'est to endless *Rest*.

The Swallow

Foolish *Prater*, what do'st thou
So early at my window do
With thy tuneless *Serenade*?
Well t'had been had *Tereus* made
Thee as *Dumb* as *Philomel*;
There his Knife had done but well.
In thy undiscover'ed Nest
Thou dost all the winter rest,
And dreamest o're thy summer joys
Free from the stormy seasons noise:
Free from th'Ill thou'st done to me;
Who disturbs, or seeks out *Thee*?
Had'st thou all the charming notes
Of the woods *Poetick Throats*,
All thy art could never pay
What thou'st ta'ne from me away;

Cruel *Bird*, thou'st ta'ne away
A *Dream* out of my arms to day,
A *Dream* that ne're must equall'd be
By all that *waking Eyes* may see.
Thou this damage to repair,
Nothing half so sweet or fair,
Nothing half so good can'st bring,
Though men say, *Thou bring'st the Spring.*

ANDREW MARVELL
(1621-1678)

The Nymph complaining for the death of her Faun

The wanton Troopers riding by
Have shot my Faun and it will dye.
Ungentle men! They cannot thrive
To kill thee. Thou neer didst alive
Them any harm: alas nor cou'd
Thy death yet do them any good.
I'me sure I never wisht them ill;
Nor do I for all this; nor will:
But, if my simple Pray'rs may yet
Prevail with Heaven to forget
Thy murder, I will Joyn my Tears
Rather then fail. But, O my fears!
It cannot dye so. Heavens King
Keeps register of every thing:
And nothing may we use in vain.
Ev'n Beasts must be with justice slain;
Else Men are made their *Deodands.*
Though they should wash their guilty hands
In this warm life blood, which doth part
From thine, and wound me to the Heart,
Yet could they not be clean: their Stain
Is dy'd in such a Purple Grain.

There is not such another in
The World, to offer for their Sin.
    Unconstant *Sylvio*, when yet
I had not found him counterfeit,
One morning (I remember well)
Ty'd in this silver Chain and Bell,
Gave it to me: nay and I know
What he said then; I'me sure I do.
Said He, look how your Huntsman here
Hath taught a Faun to hunt his *Dear*.
But *Sylvio* soon had me beguil'd.
This waxed tame; while he grew wild,
And quite regardless of my Smart,
Left me his Faun, but took his Heart.

    Thenceforth I set my self to play
My solitary time away,
With this: and very well content,
Could so mine idle Life have spent.
For it was full of sport; and light
Of foot, and heart; and did invite,
Me to its game: it seem'd to bless
Its self in me. How could I less
Than love it? O I cannot be
Unkind, t' a Beast that loveth me.

    Had it liv'd long, I do not know
Whether it too might have done so
As *Sylvio* did: his Gifts might be
Perhaps as false or more than he.
But I am sure, for ought that I
Could in so short a time espie,
Thy Love was far more better then
The love of false and cruel men.

    With sweetest milk, and sugar, first
I it at mine own fingers nurst.
And as it grew, so every day
It wax'd more white and sweet than they.
It had so sweet a Breath! And oft
I blusht to see its foot more soft,
And white, (shall I say then my hand?)
Nay any Ladies of the Land.

    It is a wond'rous thing, how fleet
'Twas on those little silver feet.
With what a pretty skipping grace,

It oft would challenge me the Race:
And when't had left me far away,
'Twoud stay, and run again, and stay.
For it was nimbler much than Hindes;
And trod, as on the four Winds.
  I have a Garden of my own,
But so with Roses over grown,
And Lillies, that you would it guess
To be a little Wilderness.
And all the Spring time of the year
It onely loved to be there.
Among the beds of Lillyes, I
Have sought it oft, where it should lye;
Yet could not, till it self would rise,
Find it, although before mine Eyes.
For, in the flaxen Lillies shade,
It like a bank of Lillies laid.
Upon the Roses it would feed,
Until its Lips ev'n seem'd to bleed:
And then to me 'twould boldly trip,
And print those Roses on my Lip.
But all its chief delight was still
On Roses thus its self to fill:
And its pure virgin Limbs to fold
In whitest sheets of Lillies cold.
Had it liv'd long, it would have been
Lillies without, Roses within.
  O help! O help! I see it faint:
And dye as calmely as a Saint.
See how it weeps. The Tears do come
Sad, slowly dropping like a Gumme.
So weeps the wounded Balsome: so
The holy Frankincense doth flow.
The brotherless *Heliades*
Melt in such Amber Tears as these.
  I in a golden Vial will
Keep these two crystal Tears; and fill
It till it do o'reflow with mine;
Then place it in *Diana's* Shrine.
  Now my sweet Faun is vanish'd to
Whether the Swans and Turtles go:
In fair *Elizium* to endure,
With milk-white Lambs, and Ermins pure.

O do not run too fast: for I
Will but bespeak thy Grave, and dye.
　First my unhappy Statue shall
Be cut in Marble; and withal,
Let it be weeping too: but there
Th' Engraver sure his Art may spare;
For I so truly thee bemoane,
That I shall weep though I be Stone:
Until my Tears, still dropping, wear
My breast, themselves engraving there.
There at my feet shalt thou be laid,
Of purest Alabaster made:
For I would have thine Image be
White as I can, though not as Thee.

HENRY VAUGHAN
(1622-1695)

The Bird

Hither thou com'st: the busy wind all night
Blew through thy lodging, where thy own warm wing
Thy pillow was. Many a sullen storm
(For which course man seems much the fitter born,)
　　Rained on thy bed
　　And harmless head.

And now as fresh and cheerful as the light
Thy little heart in early hymns doth sing
Unto that *Providence*, whose unseen arm
Curbed them, and clothed thee well and warm.
　　All things that be, praise him; and had
　　Their lesson taught them, when first made.

So hills and valleys into singing break,
And though poor stones have neither speech nor tongue,
While active winds and streams both run and speak,
Yet stones are deep in admiration.
Thus praise and prayer here beneath the sun
Make lesser mornings, when the great are done.

For each inclosèd spirit is a star
    Enlightening his own little sphere,
Whose light, though fetched and borrowèd from far,
    Both mornings makes, and evenings there.

But as these birds of light make a land glad,
Chirping their solemn Matins on each tree:
So in the shades of night some dark fowls be,
Whose heavy notes make all that hear them, sad.

    The turtle then in palm-trees mourns,
        While owls and satyrs howl;
    The pleasant land to brimstone turns
        And all her streams grow foul.

Brightness and mirth, and love and faith, all fly,
Till the Day-spring breaks forth again from high.

MARGARET LUCAS, DUCHESS OF NEWCASTLE
(1624?-1674)

The Hunting of the Hare

Betwixt two Ridges of Plowed-land sat Wat,
Whose body press'd to th'Earth, lay close and squat,
His Nose upon his two Fore-feet did lye,
With his gray Eyes he glared Obliquely;
His Head he always set against the Wind,
His Tail when turn'd, his Hair blew up behind,
And made him to get Cold; but being Wise,
Doth keep his Coat still down, so warm he lies:
Thus rests he all the Day, till th'Sun doth Set,
Then up he riseth his Relief to get,
And walks about, untill the Sun doth Rise,
Then coming back in's former Posture lies.
At last poor Wat was found, as he there lay,
By Huntsmen, which came with their Dogs that way,
Whom seeing, he got up, and fast did run,
Hoping some ways the Cruel Dogs to shun;
But they by Nature had so quick a Scent,
That by their Nose they Trac'd what way he went,

And with their deep wide Mouths set forth a Cry,
Which answer'd was by Echo in the Sky;
Then Wat was struck with Terrour and with Fear,
Seeing each Shadow thought the Dogs were there,
And running out some Distance from their Cry,
To hide himself, his Thoughts he did imploy;
Under a Clod of Earth in Sand-pit wide
Poor Wat sat close, hoping himself to hide,
There long he had not been, but strait in's Ears
The winding Horns and crying Dogs he hears;
Then starting up with fear, he Leap'd, and such
Swift speed he made, the Ground he scarce did touch;
Into a great thick Wood strait ways he got,
And underneath a broken Bough he sat,
Where every Leaf, that with the Wind did shake,
Brought him such Terrour, that his Heart did Ake;
That place he left, to Champain Plains he went,
Winding about, for to deceive their Scent,
And while they Snuffling were to find his Track,
Poor Wat being weary, his swift Pace did slack;
On his two hinder Legs for ease he Sat,
His Fore-feet rubb'd his Face from Dust and Sweat,
Licking his Feet, he wip'd his Ears so clean,
That none could tell that Wat had Hunted been;
But casting round about his fair gray Eyes,
The Hounds in full Career he near him 'Spies,
To Wat it was so Terrible a Sight,
Fear gave him Wings and made his Body light;
Though he was Tir'd before by Running long,
Yet now his Breath he never felt more Strong;
Like those that Dying are, think Health returns,
When 'tis but a faint Blast which Life out-burns;
For Spirits seek to Guard the Heart about,
Striving with Death, but Death doth quench them out.
The Hounds so fast came on, and with such Cry,
That he no hopes had left, nor help could 'spy;
With that the Winds did pitty poor Wat's Case,
And with their Breath the Scent blew from that place;
Then every Nose was busily imploy'd,
And every Nostril was set Open wide,
And every Head did seek a several way,
To find the Grass or Track where the Scent lay;

MARGARET LUCAS, DUCHESS OF NEWCASTLE

For *Witty Industry is never Slack,*
'Tis like to Witch-craft, and brings lost things back:
But though the Wind had tied the Scent up close,
A busie Dog thrust in his snuffling Nose
And drew it out, and that did fore-most run,
The Horns blew Loud, the rest to follow on;
The great slow Hounds their Throats did set a *Base,*
The Fleet, swift Hounds, as *Tenours* next in place,
The little Beagles did a *Treble* Sing,
And through the Air their Voices round did Ring,
Which made such Consort as they Ran along,
That, had they Spoken words, 't had been a Song;
And seem'd most Valiant, *poor Wat* to Destroy;
Spurring their Horses to a full Career,
Swom Rivers deep, Leap'd ditches without fear,
Indanger'd Life and Limbs, so fast they'ld Ride,
Only to see how patiently Wat Dy'd;
At last the Dogs so near his Heels did get,
That their sharp Teeth they in his Breech did set;
Then Tumbling down he fell, with weeping Eyes
Gave up his Ghost; and thus poor Wat he Dyes.
Men hooping Loud, such Acclamations made,
As if the Devil they Imprisoned had,
When they but did a shiftless Creature Kill;
To Hunt, their needs no Valiant Souldiers Skill:
But Men do think that Exercise and Toil,
To keep their Health, is best, which makes most Spoil,
Thinking that Food and Nourishment so good,
Which doth proceed from others Flesh and Blood.
When they do Lions, Wolves, Bears, Tigres see
Kill silly Sheep, they say, they Cruel be,
But for themselves all Creatures think too few,
For Luxury, wish God would make more New;
As if God did make Creatures for Mans meat,
And gave them Life and Sense for Man to Eat,
Or else for Sport or Recreations sake
For to Destroy those Lives that God did make,
Making their Stomacks Graves, which full they fill
With Murthered'd Bodies, which in Sport they Kill;
Yet Man doth think himself so Gentle and Mild,
When of all Creatures he's most Cruel, Wild,

Nay, so Proud, that he only thinks to Live,
That God a God-like Nature him did give,
And that all Creatures for his Sake alone
Were made, for him to Tyrannize upon.

(*Wat:* old name for a hare, short for "Walter".)

CHARLES COTTON
(1630-1687)

On My Pretty Marten

Come, my pretty little Muse,
Your assistence I must use,
And you must assist me too
Better than you used to do,
Or the Subject we disgrace
Has oblig'd us many ways.
Pretty *Matty* is our Theme,
Of all others the supreme;
Should we studdy for't a year,
Could we chuse a prettier?
Little *Mat*, whose pretty play
Does divert us ev'ry day,
Whose Caresses are so kind,
Sweet, and free, and undesign'd,
Meekness is not more disarming,
Youth and modesty more charming;
Nor from any ill intent
Nuns or Doves more innocent:
And for Beauty, Nature too
Here would shew what she could do;
Finer Creature ne'er was seen,
Half so pretty, half so clean.
Eyes as round and black as Sloe,
Teeth as white as morning Snow;
Breath as sweet as blowing Roses,
When the Morn their leaves discloses,
Or, what sweeter you'll allow,
Breath of Vestals when they vow,

David Koster

Or, that yet doth sweeter prove,
Sighs of Maids who die for Love.
Next his Feet my praise commands,
Which methinks we should call hands,
For so finely they are shap'd,
And for any use so apt,
Nothing can so dext'rous be,
Nor fine handed near as he.
These, without though black as Jet,
Within are soft and supple yet
As Virgins Palm, where Man's deceit
Seal of promise never set.
Back and Belly soft as Down,
Sleeps which peace of Conscience crown,
Or the whispers Love reveal,
Or the kisses Lovers steal:
And of such a rich perfume,
As, to say I dare presume,
Will out-ravish and out-wear
That of th'fulsome Milliner.
Tail so bushy and so long,
(Which t'omit would do him wrong)
As the proudest she of all
Proudly would be fann'd withall.

Having given thus the shape
Of this pretty little Ape,
To his Vertues next I come,
Which amount to such a summe,
As not only well may pass
Both my Poetry and Dress
To set forth as I should do't,
But Arithmetick to boot.

Valour is the ground of all
That we Mortals Vertues call;
And the little Cavalier
That I do present you here,
Has of that so great a share,
He might lead the World to war.
What the Beasts of greater size
Tremble at he does despise
And is so compos'd of heart,
Drums nor Guns can make him start:

Noises which make others quake,
Serve his Courage to awake.
Libyan Lyons make their Feasts
Of subdu'd *Plebean* Beasts,
And *Hyrcanian* Tigers prey
Still on Creatures less than they,
Or less arm'd; the *Russian* Bears
Of tamer Beasts make massacres.
Irish Wolves devour the Dams,
English Foxcs prey on Lambs.
These are all effects of course,
Not of Valour, but of Force;
But my *Matty* does not want
Heart t'attack an Elephant.
Yet his nature is so sweet,
Mice may nibble with his feet,
And may pass as if unseen,
If they spare his Magazine.
Constancy, a Vertue then
In this Age scarce known to men,
Or to Womankind at least,
In this pretty little Beast,
To the World might be restor'd,
And my *Matty* be ador'd.
Chaste he is as Turtle Doves,
That abhor adult'rate Loves;
True to Friendship, and to Love,
Nothing can his Vertue move,
But his Faith in either giv'n,
Seems as if 'twere seal'd in Heaven.
Of all Brutes to him alone
Justice is, and Favour known.
Nor is *Matty's* excellence
Mearly circumscrib'd by sense,
He for judgment what to do
Knows both good and evel too,
But is with such vertue bless'd,
That he chuses still the best,
And wants nothing of a Wit
But a Tongue to utter it:
Yet with that we may dispense,
For his Signs are Eloquence.

Then for Fashion, and for Mien,
Matty's fit to court a Queen;
All his motions graceful are,
And all Courts outshine as far
As our Courtiers peakish Clowns,
Or those peakrils Northern Loons,
Which should Ladies see, they sure
Other Beasts would ne'er endure;
Then no more they would make suit
For an ugly pissing-coat
Rammish Cat, nor make a pet
Of a bawdy Mamoset.
Nay, the Squerrel, though it is
Pretty'st Creature next to this,
Would henceforward be discarded,
And in Woods live unregarded.
Here sweet Beauty is a Creature
Purposely ordain'd by Nature,
Both for cleanness and for shape
Worthy a Fair Ladies lap;
Nor her Bosom would disgrace,
Nor a more beloved place.

Live long, my pretty little Boy,
Thy Master's Darling, Ladies Joy,
And when Fate will no more forbear
To lay his hands on him and her,
E'en then let Fate my *Matty* spare,
And when thou dy'st then turn a Star.

JOHN DRYDEN
(1631-1700)

From *Of the Pythagorean Philosophy* from *Ovid's Metamorphoses Book XV*

But this by sure Experiment we know,
That living Creatures from Corruption grow:
Hide in a hollow Pit a slaughter'd Steer,
Bees from his putrid Bowels will appear;
Who like their Parents haunt the Fields, and bring
They Hony-Harvest home, and hope another Spring.

The Warlike-Steed is multiply'd we find,
To Wasps and Hornets of the Warrior Kind.
Cut from a Crab his crooked Claws, and hide
The rest in Earth, a Scorpion thence will glide
And shoot his Sting, his Tail in Circles toss'd
Refers the Limbs his backward Father lost.
And Worms, that stretch on Leaves their filmy Loom,
Crawl from their Bags, and Butterflies become.
Ev'n Slime begets the Frog's loquacious Race:
Short of their Feet at first, in little space
With Arms and Legs endu'd, long leaps they take,
Rais'd on their hinder part, and swim the Lake,
And Waves repel: For Nature gives their Kind
To that intent, a length of Legs behind.
  The Cubs of Bears, a living lump appear,
When whelp'd, and no determin'd Figure wear.
Their Mother licks 'em into Shape, and gives
As much of Form, as she her self receives.
  The Grubs from their sexangular abode
Crawl out unfinish'd, like the Maggot's Brood:
Trunks without Limbs; till time at leisure brings
The Thighs they wanted, and their tardy Wings.
  The Bird who draws the Carr of *Juno*, vain
Of her crown'd Head, and of her Starry Train;
And he that bears th' Artillery of *Jove*,
The strong-pounc'd Eagle, and the billing Dove;
And all the feather'd Kind, who cou'd suppose
(But that from sight the surest Sense he knows)
They from th' included Yolk, not ambient White arose.
  There are who think the Marrow of a Man,
Which in the Spine, while he was living ran;
When dead, the Pith corrupted will become
A Snake, and hiss within the hollow Tomb.
  All these receive their Birth from other Things;
But from himself the *Phœnix* only springs:
Self-born, begotton by the Parent Flame
In which he burn'd, another and the same;
Who not by Corn or Herbs his Life sustains,
But the sweet Essence of *Amomum* drains:
And watches the rich Gums *Arabia* bears,
While yet in tender Dew they drop their Tears.
He, (his five Cent'ries of Life fulfill'd)
His Nest on Oaken Boughs begins to build,

Or trembling tops of Palm, and first he draws
The Plan with his broad Bill, and crooked Claws,
Nature's Artificers; on this the Pile
Is form'd, and rises round, then with the Spoil
Of *Casia, Cynamon*, and Stems of *Nard*,
(For softness strew'd beneath,) his Fun'ral Bed is rear'd:
Fun'ral and Bridal both; and all around
The Borders with corruptless Myrrh are crown'd,
On this incumbent; till ætherial Flame
First catches, then consumes the costly Frame:
Consumes him too, as on the Pile he lies;
He liv'd on Odours, and in Odours dies.

An Infant-*Phœnix* from the former springs
His Father's Heir, and from his Tender Wings
Shakes off his Parent Dust, his Method he pursues,
And the same Lease of Life on the same Terms renews.
When grown to Manhood he begins his reign,
And with stiff Pinions can his Flight sustain,
He lightens of its Load, the Tree that bore
His Father's Royal Sepulcher before,
And his own Cradle: (This with pious Care
Plac'd on his Back) he cuts the buxome Air,
Seeks the Sun's City, and his sacred Church,
And decently lays down his Burden in the Porch.

A Wonder more amazing wou'd we find?
Th' *Hyæna* shows it, of a double kind,
Varying the Sexes in alternate Years,
In one begets, and in another bears.
The thin *Camelion* fed with Air, receives
The colour of the Thing to which he cleaves.

India when conquer'd, on the conqu'ring God
For planted Vines the sharp-ey'd *Lynx* bestow'd,
Whose Urine shed, before it touches Earth,
Congeals in Air, and gives to Gems their Birth.
So *Coral* soft, and white in Oceans Bed,
Comes harden'd up in Air, and glows with Red.

THOMAS HEYRICK
(1649-1694)

On the Death of a Monkey

Here *Busy* and yet *Innocent* lyes Dead,
    Two things, that seldom meet:
No Plots nor Stratagems disturb'd his head,
    Or's his merry Soul did fret:
He shew'd like Superannuated *Peer*,
Grave was his look, and *Politick* his Air;
And he for *Nothing* too spent all his care.

But that he died of Discontent, 'tis fear'd,
    Head of the *Monkey* Rout;
To see so many Brother *Apes* preferr'd,
    And he himself left out:
On all below he did his Anger show'r,
Fit for a Court did all above adore,
H'had *Shows* of Reason, and few *Men* have more.

On an Indian Tomineois,
The Least of Birds

I'me made in sport by Nature, when
    Shee's tir'd with the stupendious weight
Of forming Elephants and Beasts of State;
Rhinoceros, that love the Fen;
    The Elkes, that scale the hills of Snow,
And Lions couching in their awfull Den:
    These do work Nature hard, and then,
    Her wearied Hand in Me doth show
What she can for her own Diversion doe.

    Man is a little World ('tis said),
    And I in Miniature am drawn,
A Perfect Creature, but in Short-hand shown.
    The Ruck, in Madagascar bred,
    (If new Discoveries Truth do speak)
Whom greatest Beasts and armed Horsemen dread,
    Both him and Me one Artist made:
    Nature in this Delight doth take,
That can so Great and Little Monsters make.

41

The Indians me a Sunbeam name,
  And I may be the Child of one:
So small I am, my Kind is hardly known.
  To some a sportive Bird I seem,
  And some believe me but a Fly;
Tho' me a Feather'd Fowl the Best esteem:
  What e're I am, I'me Nature's Gemm,
  And like a Sunbeam from the Sky,
I can't be follow'd by the quickest Eye.

I'me the true Bird of Paradise,
  And heavenly Dew's my only Meat:
My Mouth so small, 'twill nothing else admit.
  No Scales know how my weight to poise,
  So Light, I seem condensed Air;
And did at th'End of the Creation rise,
  When Nature wanted more Supplies,
  When she could little Matter spare,
But in Return did make the work more Rare.

(*Tomineois:* humming bird; *Ruck:* roc, mythical bird of enormou
size.)

On the Crocodile

  I am the Terrour of the Sea,
  Proud *Nile's* chief Glory and his Fear:
  From far I dart upon my Prey,
  Which to my watry Hold I bear.
  Dogs dare not drink for doubt of Me,
  Tho they 'gainst Bulls and Lyons dare.
  I am chief Instrument of Fate;
  Two Elements upon me wait;
Water and *Land* conspire to make me great.

  Of food I no Distinction make,
  But in my Cruelty am Just;
  Of Man and Beast alike I take,
  And eat them both with equal Gust.
  With Draughts of Gore my thirst I slake,
  And Flesh I down my throat do thrust.
  Fear gave rise to Divinity:
  And Gods have rose from Cruelty:
Wise *Ægypt* showd so; when she worship'd me.

The *Indians* kill me for their Food,
And say, I am Delicious meat:
They drink of their Relations Blood,
And eat, what did their Fathers eat.
In me they injure their own Brood,
Their Malice doth their Judgment cheat.
But I may yet a Question make,
Whether when Me they hunt and take,
They think their Hunger or Revenge to slake.

No Creature can my *Power* withstand:
Yet to that power *Deceit* I tie:
And by this Double *Gordian* band
Secure my hungry Tyranny;
The Terrour of the Sea and Land
In ambush on the Sands I lie.
What e're I take I do devour,
Yet o're the Head I tears do shower,
And weep and grieve, — because I have no more.

Men me Abhor, yet Imitate;
Like Falshood use without all Shame:
As Lawless Power, as deep Deceit
Doth *Christian* under *Christian* tame:
I live i'th' Actions of the Great;
What they're to Others, to them I am.
Would you then Power and Cunning see
Mixed with deep Hypocrisie?
They are conjoyn'd in *Man,* as well as *Me*!

ANNE, COUNTESS OF WINCHILSEA
(1661-1720)

Jealousie is the Rage of a Man

Whilst with his falling wings, the courtly Dove
Sweeps the low earth, and singles out his Love,
Now murmurs soft, then with a rowling note
Extends his crop, and fills his am'rous throate,
On ev'ry side accosts the charming Fair,
Turns round, and bows with an inticing ayre,

She, carelessly neglecting all his pain,
Or shifts her ground, or pecks the scatter'd grain.
But if he cease, and through the flight wou'd range,
(For though renown'd for truth, e'vn Doves will change)
The mildnesse of her nature laid aside,
The seeming coldnesse, and the carelesse pride,
On the next Rival, in a rage she flies;
Smooth, ev'ry clinging plume, with anger lies,
Employs in feeble fight her tender beck,
And shakes the Favrite's parti-colour'd neck.
Thus, jealousy, through ev'ry species moves;
And if so furious, in the gallesse Doves,
No wonder, that th' experienc'd Hebrew sage,
Of Man, pronounc'd it the extremest Rage.

WILLIAM KING
(1663-1712)

From *"Mully of Mountown"*

How fleet is air! how many things have breath
Which in a moment they resign to death,
Depriv'd of light and all their happiest state
Not by their fault but some o'erruling Fate!
Although fair flow'rs, that justly might invite,
Are cropt, nay, torn away, for man's delight,
Yet still those flow'rs, alas! can make no moan,
Nor has Narcissus now a pow'r to groan;
But all those things which breathe in diff'rent frame,
By tie of common breath, man's pity claim.
A gentle lamb has rhetoric to plead,
And when she sees the butcher's knife decreed,
Her voice entreats him not to make her bleed:
But, cruel gain and luxury of taste
With pride, still lays man's fellow-mortals waste.
What earth and waters breed, or air inspires,
Man, for his palate fits, by tort'ring fires.
Mully, a cow sprung from a beauteous race,
With spreading front did Mountown's pastures grace:
Gentle she was, and, with a gentle stream,
Each morn and night, gave milk that equall'd cream.

Offending none, of none she stood in dread,
Much less of persons which she daily fed;
"But innocence cannot itself defend
" 'Gainst treach'rous arts veil'd with the name of
    Friend."
  Robin, of Derbyshire, whose temper shocks
The constitution of his native rocks,
Born in a place* which, if it once be nam'd,
Would make a blushing modesty asham'd,
He with indulgence kindly, did appear
To make poor Mully his peculiar care;
But inwardly, this sullen churlish thief,
Had all his mind, plac'd upon Mully's beef:
His fancy fed on her; and thus he'd cry,
"Mully, as sure as I'm alive you die!
" 'Tis a brave cow! O, Sirs! when Christmas comes,
"These shins shall make the porridge grac'd with
    plums;
"Then, midst our cups, whilst we profusely *dine*,
"This blade shall enter deep in Mully's chine.
"What ribs, what rumps, what bak'd, boil'd, stew'd,
    and roast!
"There sha'nt one single tripe of her be lost!"
  When Peggy, nymph of Mountown, heard these
    sounds,
She griev'd to hear of Mully's future wounds.
"What crime," said she, "has gentle Mully done?
"Witness the rising and the setting sun,
'That knows, what milk she constantly would give!
"Let that, quench Robin's rage, and Mully live."
  Daniel, a sprightly swain, that us'd to flash
The vig'rous steeds that drew his lord's calash,
To Peggy's side inclin'd; for 'twas well known
How well he lov'd those cattle of his own.
  Then Terence spoke, oraculous and sly;
He'd neither grant the question, nor deny;
Pleading for milk, his thoughts were on mince pie:
But all his arguments so dubious were,
That Mully thence had neither hopes nor fear.
"You've spoke," says Robin; "but now let me tell ye

* The Devil's Arse of Peak, described by Hobbes in a poem *De
Mirabilibus Pecci*, the best of his poetical performances.

"Tis not fair spoken words, that fill the belly:
"Pudding and beef I love; and cannot stoop
"To recommend your bonny-clapper soup.
"You say she's innocent; but what of that?
"Tis more than crime sufficient that she's fat!
"And that which is prevailing in this case
"Is, there's another cow to fill her place:
"And, granting Mully to have milk in store,
"Yet still this other cow will give us more:
"She dies," — Stop here, my Muse! forbear the
    rest,
And veil that grief which cannot be exprest.

MATTHEW PRIOR
(1664-1721)

An Epitaph on True, Her Majesty's Dog

If Wit or Honesty cou'd save
Our mouldring Ashes from the Grave,
This Stone had yet remain'd unmark'd,
I still wrote Prose, and *True* still bark'd:
But envious Fate has claim'd its due,
Here lies the mortal Part of *True*;
His deathless Virtues must survive,
To better us that are alive.
His Prudence and his Wit were seen,
In that, from *Mary's* Grace and Meen,
He own'd the Pow'r, and lov'd the Queen.
By long Obedience he confest,
That serving her was to be blest.
Ye Murmurers, let *True* evince,
That Men are Beasts, and Dogs have Sence.
His Faith and Truth all White-hall knows,
He ne're could fawn, or flatter those
Whom he believ'd were *Mary's* Foes.
Ne're skulk'd from whence his Soveraign led him,
Nor snarl'd against the Hand that fed him.

Read this ye Statesmen now in Favour,
And mend your own, by *True's* Behaviour.

(*Her Majesty:* Mary II (William and Mary).)

46

MATHEW PRIOR

From *Solomon on the Vanity of the World*

Fix thy corporeal, and internal Eye
On the Young *Gnat*, or new-engender'd *Fly*;
On the vile *Worm*, that Yesterday began
To crawl; Thy Fellow-Creatures, abject Man!
Like Thee they breath, they move, they tast, they see,
They show their Passions by their Acts like Thee:
Darting their Stings, they previously declare
Design'd Revenge, and fierce intent of War:
Laying their Eggs, they evidently prove
The Genial Pow'r, and full Effect of Love.
Each then has Organs to digest his Food,
One to beget, and one receive the Brood:
Has Limbs and Sinews, Blood and Heart, and Brain,
Life, and her proper Functions to sustain;
Tho' the whole Fabric smaller than a Grain.
What more can our penurious Reason grant
To the large *Whale*, or Castled *Elephant*,
To those enormous Terrors of the NILE,
The crested *Snake*, and long-tail'd *Crocodile*,
Than that all differ but in Shape and Name,
Each destin'd to a less, or larger Frame?

For potent Nature loves a various Act,
Prone to enlarge, or studious to contract:
Now forms her Work too small, now too immense,
And scorns the Measures of our feeble Sense.
The Object spread too far, or rais'd too high,
Denies it's real Image to the Eye:
Too little, it eludes the dazl'd Sight;
Becomes mixt Blackness, or unparted Light.
Water and Air the varied Form confound;
The Strait looks crooked, and the Square grows round.

Thus while with fruitless Hope, and weary Pain,
We seek great Nature's Pow'r, but seek in vain;
Safe sits the Goddess in her dark Retreat;
Around Her, Myriads of *Ideas* wait,
And endless Shapes, which the Mysterious Queen
Can take or quit, can alter or retain:
As from our lost Pursuit She wills to hide
Her close Decrees, and chasten human Pride.

Untam'd and fierce the *Tiger* still remains:
He tires his Life in biting on his Chains:
For the kind Gifts of Water, and of Food,
Ungrateful, and returning Ill for Good,
He seeks his Keeper's Flesh, and thirsts his Blood:
While the strong *Camel*, and the gen'rous *Horse*,
Restrain'd and aw'd by Man's inferior Force,
Do to the Rider's Will their Rage submit,
And answer to the Spur, and own the Bit;
Stretch their glad Mouths to meet the Feeder's Hand,
Pleas'd with his Weight, and proud of his Command.

Again: the lonely *Fox* roams far abroad,
On secret Rapin bent, and Midnight Fraud;
Now haunts the Cliff, now traverses the Lawn;
And flies the hated Neighborhood of Man:
While the kind *Spaniel*, and the faithful *Hound*,
Likest that *Fox* in Shape and Species found,
Refuses thro' these Cliffs and Lawns to roam;
Pursues the noted Path, and covets home;
Does with kind Joy Domestic Faces meet;
Takes what the glutted Child denies to eat;
And dying, licks his long-lov'd Master's Feet.

By what immediate Cause They are inclin'd,
In many Acts, 'tis hard, I own, to find.
I see in others, or I think I see,
That strict their Principles, and our's agree.
Evil like Us they shun, and covet Good;
Abhor the Poison, and receive the Food.
Like Us they love or hate: like Us they know,
To joy the Friend, or grapple with the Foe.
With seeming Thought their Action they intend,
And use the Means proportion'd to the End.
Then vainly the Philosopher avers,
That Reason guides our Deed, and Instinct their's.
How can We justly diff'rent Causes frame,
When the Effects entirely are the same?
Instinct and Reason how can we divide?
'Tis the Fool's Ign'rance, and the Pedant's Pride.

With the same Folly sure, Man vaunts his Sway;
If the brute Beast refuses to Obey.
For tell me, when the empty Boaster's Word

Proclaims himself the Universal Lord;
Does He not tremble, lest the *Lion's* Paw
Should join his Plea against the fancy'd Law?
Would not the Learned Coward leave the Chair;
If in the Schools or Porches should appear
The fierce *Hyaena*, or the foaming *Bear*?

JONATHAN SWIFT
(1667-1745)

On the Collar of Mrs Dingley's Lap-Dog

Pray steal me not, I'm Mrs *Dingley's*
Whose Heart in this Four-footed Thing lies.

(*Mrs Dingley:* life-long companion of "Stella", subject of Swift's
romantic friendship.)

WILLIAM SOMERVILLE
(1675-1742)

From *Field Sports*

When Autumn smiles, all beauteous in decay,
And paints each chequer'd grove with various hues,
My setter ranges in the new-shorn fields,
His nose in air erect; from ridge to ridge
Panting he bounds, his quarter'd ground divides
In equal intervals, nor careless leaves
One inch untried. At length the tainted gales
His nostrils wide inhale; quick joy elates
His beating heart, which, awed by discipline
Severe, he dares not own, but cautious creeps
Low-cowering, step by step; at last attains
His proper distance; there he stops at once,
And points with his instructive nose upon
The trembling prey. On wings of wind upborne
The floating net unfolded flies, then drops,
And the poor fluttering captives rise in vain.

WILLIAM SOMERVILLE

The Wounded Man and the Swarm of Flies

E malis minimum

Squalid with wounds, and many a gaping sore,
    A wretched Lazar lay distrest,
A swarm of Flies his bleeding ulcers tore,
    And on his putrid carcass feast.

A courteous traveller, who pass'd that way,
    And saw the vile Harpeian brood,
Offer'd his help the monstrous crew to slay,
    That rioted on human blood.

"Ah! gentle Sir," the' unhappy wretch replied,
    "Your well-meant charity refrain;
The angry gods have that redress denied,
    Your goodness would increase my pain.

Fat, and full-fed, and with abundance cloy'd,
    But now and then these tyrants feed;
But were, alas! this pamper'd brood destroy'd,
    The lean and hungry would succeed."

MORAL

The body politic must soon decay,
When swarms of insects on its vitals prey;
When bloodsuckers of a state, a greedy brood,
Feast on our wounds, and fatten with our blood.
What must we do in this severe distress?
Come, doctor, give the patient some redress:
The quacks in politics a change advise,
But cooler counsels should direct the wise.
'Tis hard indeed; but better this than worse;
Mistaken blessings prove the greatest curse.
Alas! what would our bleeding country gain,
If, when this viperous brood at last is slain,
The teeming Hydra pullulates again,
Seizes the prey with more voracious bite,
To satisfy his hungry appetite?

WILLIAM DIAPER
(1685-1717)

From *Oppian's Halieuticks*

The Shelly Crawlers each returning Year,
Cast off their Coat, and new-made Armour wear.
Self-taught, when first the *Velvet-Crabs* perceive
Their loos'ning Shell will soon the Body leave,
They cram their Paunch, and bloated strive to thrust
From off their rising Back the tott'ring Crust.
But when their naked Bodies lie expos'd,
No longer with the shelly Fence enclos'd,
They senseless seem, stretcht on the sandy Bed
All pensive lie, and deem themselves as dead;
Nor cautious eat, lest gorging Food should swell
The tender Flesh, and stop the growing Shell.
But when slow Nature moulds the viscous Mass,
And Time begins to fix the hard'ning Case
The rising Crust half-form'd they joyous feel,
And suck the Sands, yet dread the hearty Meal;
Till the firm finisht Work can safe endure
The rudest Shock, and ev'ry Part secure.

JOHN GAY
(1685-1732)

From *Rural Sports (Canto I)*

When a brisk gale against the current blows,
And all the watry plain in wrinkles flows,
Then let the fisherman his art repeat,
Where bubbling eddys favour the deceit.
If an enormous salmon chance to spy
The wanton errors of the floating fly,
He lifts his silver gills above the flood,
And greedily sucks in th' unfaithful food;
Then downward plunges with the fraudful prey,
And bears with joy the little spoil away.
Soon in smart pain he feels the dire mistake,
Lashes the wave, and beats the foamy lake,

With sudden rage he now aloft appears,
And in his eye convulsive anguish bears;
And now again, impatient of the wound,
He rolls and wreaths his shining body round;
Then headlong shoots beneath the dashing tide,
The trembling fins the boiling wave divide;
Now hope exalts the fisher's beating heart,
Now he turns pale, and fears his dubious art;
He views the tumbling fish with longing eyes,
While the line stretches with th' unwieldy prize;
Each motion humours with his steady hands,
And one slight hair the mighty bulk commands:
'Til tir'd at last, despoil'd of all his strength,
The game athwart the stream unfolds his length.
He now, with pleasure, views the gasping prize
Gnash his sharp teeth, and roll his blood-shot eyes;
Then draws him to the shore, with artful care,
And lifts his nostrils in the sick'ning air;
Upon the burthen'd stream he floating lies,
Stretches his quivering fins, and gasping dies.

The Butterfly and the Snail

(Fable XXIV, First Series)

All upstarts, insolent in place,
Remind us of their vulgar race.

As, in the sun-shine of the morn,
A Butterfly (but newly born)
Sate proudly perking on a rose;
With pert conceit his bosom glows,
His wings (all glorious to behold)
Bedropt with azure, jet and gold,
Wide he displays; the spangled dew
Reflects his eyes and various hue.
His now forgotten friend, a Snail,
Beneath his house, with slimy trail
Crawles o'er the grass; whom when he spys,
In wrath he to the gard'ner crys:

JOHN GAY

What means yon peasant's daily toil,
From choaking weeds to rid the soil?
Why wake you to the morning's care?
Why with new arts correct the year?
Why glows the peach with crimsom hue?
And why the plum's inviting blue?
Were they to feast his taste design'd,
That vermine of voracious kind?
Crush then the slow, the pilfring race,
So purge thy garden from disgrace.

   What arrogance! the Snail reply'd;
How insolent is upstart pride!
Hadst thou not thus, with insult vain,
Provok'd my patience to complain;

I had conceal'd thy meaner birth,
Nor trac'd thee to the scum of earth.
For scarce nine suns have wak'd the hours,
To swell the fruit and paint the flowers,
Since I thy humbler life survey'd,
In base, in sordid guise array'd;
A hideous insect, vile, unclean,
You dragg'd a slow and noisome train,
And from your spider bowels drew
Foul film, and spun the dirty clue.
I own my humble life, good friend;
Snail was I born, and snail shall end.
And what's a butterfly? At best,
He's but a caterpillar, drest:
And all thy race (a num'rous seed)
Shall prove of caterpillar breed.

The Wild Boar and the Ram

(Fable V, First Series)

Against an elm a sheep was ty'd;
The butcher's knife in blood was dy'd;
The patient flock, in silent fright,
From far beheld the horrid sight;
A savage Boar, who near them stood,
Thus mock'd to scorn the fleecy brood.
  All cowards should be serv'd like you.
See, see, your murd'rer is in view;
With purple hands and reeking knife
He strips the skin yet warm with life:
Your quarter'd sires, your bleeding dams,
The dying bleat of harmless lambs
Call for revenge. O stupid race!
The heart that wants revenge is base.
  I grant, an ancient Ram replys,
We bear no terror in our eyes,
Yet think us not of soul so tame,
Which no repeated wrongs inflame;
Insensible of ev'ry ill,
Because we want thy tusks to kill.
Know, Those who violence pursue
Give to themselves the vengeance due,

For in these massacres they find
The two chief plagues that waste mankind.
Our skin supplys the wrangling bar,
It wakes their slumbring sons to war,
And well revenge may rest contented,
Since drums and parchment were invented.

ALEXANDER POPE
(1688-1744)

From *Windsor-Forest*

See! from the Brake the whirring Pheasant springs,
And mounts exulting on triumphant Wings;
Short is his Joy! he feels the fiery Wound,
Flutters in Blood, and panting beats the Ground.
Ah! what avail his glossie, varying Dyes,
His Purple Crest, and Scarlet-circled Eyes,
The vivid Green his shining Plumes unfold;
His painted Wings, and Breast that flames with Gold?
Nor yet, when moist *Arcturus* clouds the Sky,
The Woods and Fields their pleasing Toils deny.

To Plains with well-breath'd Beagles we repair,
And trace the Mazes of the circling Hare.
(Beasts, urg'd by us, their Fellow Beasts pursue,
And learn of Man each other to undo.)
With slaught'ring Guns th'unweary'd Fowler roves,
When Frosts have whiten'd all the naked Groves;
Where Doves in Flocks the leafless Trees o'ershade,
And lonely Woodcocks haunt the watry Glade.
He lifts the Tube, and levels with his Eye;
Strait a short Thunder breaks the frozen Sky.
Oft, as in Airy Rings they skim the Heath,
The clam'rous Lapwings feel the Leaden Death:
Oft as the mounting Larks their Notes prepare,
They fall, and leave their little Lives in Air.

In genial Spring, beneath the quiv'ring Shade
Where cooling Vapours breathe along the Mead,
The patient Fisher takes his silent Stand
Intent, his Angle trembling in his Hand;
With Looks unmov'd, he hopes the Scaly Breed,
And eyes the dancing Cork and bending Reed.
Our plenteous Streams a various Race supply;
The bright-ey'd Perch with Fins of *Tyrian* Dye,
The silver Eel, in shining Volumes roll'd,
The yellow Carp, in Scales bedrop'd with Gold,
Swift Trouts, diversify'd with Crimson Stains,
And Pykes, the Tyrants of the watry Plains.

From *An Essay on Man: Epistle 1*

Far as Creation's ample range extends,
The scale of sensual, mental pow'rs ascends:
Mark how it mounts, to Man's imperial race,
From the green myriads in the peopled grass:
What modes of sight betwixt each wide extreme,
The mole's dim curtain, and the lynx's beam:
Of smell, the headlong lioness between,
And hound sagacious on the tainted green:
Of hearing, from the life that fills the flood,
To that which warbles thro' the vernal wood:
The spider's touch, how exquisitely fine!
Feels at each thread, and lives along the line:

In the nice bee, what sense so subtly true
From pois'nous herbs extracts the healing dew:
How Instinct varies in the grov'ling swine,
Compar'd, half-reas'ning elephant, with thine:
'Twixt that, and Reason, what a nice barrier;
For ever sep'rate, yet for ever near!

Bounce to Fop

*An Heroick Epistle
from a Dog at Twickenham to
a Dog at Court*

To thee, sweet *Fop*, these Lines I send,
Who, tho' no Spaniel, am a Friend.
Tho, once my Tail in wanton play,
Now frisking this, and then that way,
Chanc'd, with a Touch of just the Tip,
To hurt your Lady-lap-dog-ship;
Yet thence to think I'd bite your Head off!
Sure *Bounce* is one you never read of.

FOP! you can dance, and make a Leg,
Can fetch and carry, cringe and beg,
And (what's the Top of all your Tricks)
Can stoop to pick up *Strings* and *Sticks*.
We Country Dogs love nobler Sport,
And scorn the Pranks of Dogs at Court.
Fye, naughty Fop! where e'er you come
To f—t and p—ss about the Room,
To lay your Head in every Lap,
And, when they think not of you—snap!
The worst that Envy, or that spite
E'er said of me, is, I can bite:
That sturdy Vagrants, Rogues in Rags,
Who poke at me, can make no Brags;
And that to towze such Things as *flutter*,
To honest *Bounce* is Bread and Butter.

While you, and every courtly Fop,
Fawn on the Devil for a Chop,
I've the Humanity to hate
A Butcher, tho' he brings me Meat;

And let me tell you, have a Nose,
(Whatever stinking Fops suppose)
That under Cloth of Gold or Tissue,
Can smell a Plaister, or an Issue.

Your pilf'ring Lord, with simple Pride,
May wear a Pick-lock at his Side;
My Master wants no Key of State,
For *Bounce* can keep his House and Gate.

When all such Dogs have had their Days,
As knavish *Pams*, and fawning *Trays*;
When pamper'd *Cupids*, bestly *Veni's*,
And motly, squinting *Harvequini's*,
Shall lick no more their Lady's Br—,
But die of Looseness, Claps, or Itch;
Fair *Thames* from either ecchoing Shoare
Shall hear, and dread my manly Roar.

See *Bounce*, like *Berecynthia*, crown'd
With thund'ring Offspring all around,
Beneath, beside me, and a top,
A hundred Sons! and not one *Fop*.

Before my Children set your Beef,
Not one true *Bounce* will be a Thief;
Not one without Permission feed,
(Tho' some of *J*—'s hungry Breed)
But whatso'er the Father's Race,
From me they suck a little Grace.
While your fine Whelps learn all to steal,
Bred up by Hand on Chick and Veal.

My Eldest-born resides not far,
Where shines great *Stafford's* glittering Star:
My second (Child of Fortune!) waits
At *Burlington's* Palladian Gates:
A third majestically stalks
(Happiest of Dogs!) in *Cobham's* Walks:
One ushers Friends to *Bathurst's* Door;
One fawns, at *Oxford's*, on the Poor.

Nobles, whom Arms or Arts adorn,
Wait for my Infants yet unborn.
None but a Peer of Wit and Grace,
Can hope a Puppy of my Race.

ALEXANDER POPE

And O! wou'd Fate the Bliss decree
To mine (a Bliss too great for me)
That two, my tallest Sons, might grace
Attending each with stately Pace,
Iülus' Side, as erst *Evander's,*
To keep off Flatt'rers, Spies, and Panders,
To let no noble Slave come near,
And scare Lord *Fannys* from his Ear:
Then might a Royal Youth, and true,
Enjoy at least a Friend—or two:
A Treasure, which, of Royal kind,
Few but Himself deserve to find.

Then *Bounce* ('tis all that *Bounce* can crave)
Shall wag her Tail within the Grave.

And tho' no Doctors, Whig, or Tory ones,
Except the Sect of *Pythagoreans,*
Have Immortality assign'd
To any Beast, but *Dryden's* Hind:
Yet Master *Pope*, whom Truth and Sense
Shall call their Friend some Ages hence,
Tho' now on loftier Themes he sings
Than to bestow a Word on *Kings,*
Has sworn by *Sticks* (the Poet's Oath,
And Dread of Dogs and Poets both)
Man and his Works he'll soon renounce,
And roar in Numbers worthy *Bounce.*

(*Bounce:* Pope's bitch (see "Lines on Bounce"); *Fop:* probably Lady
Suffolk's dog; the name "J—" remains to be supplied.)

Epigram. Engraved on the Collar of a Dog which I gave to His Royal Highness

I am his Highness' Dog at *Kew*;
Pray tell me, Sir, whose Dog are you?

(Pope's dog Bounce had, to the poet's sorrow, died while in the care
of Lord Orrery. The couplet that follows was written a few weeks
before Pope's death: it is a parody of a couplet about Arcite from
Chaucer's 'The Knight's Tale', probably recalling Dryden's translation.
The original runs:

"Why woldestow be deed," thise wommen crye,
"And haddest gold y-nough, and Emelye?")

Lines on Bounce

Ah Bounce! ah gentle Beast! why wouldst thou dye,
When thou had'st Meat enough, and Orrery?

MATTHEW GREEN
(1696-1737)

The Sparrow & Diamond
A Song

I lately saw, what now I sing,
    Fair Lucia's hand display'd;
This finger grac'd a diamond ring,
    On that a sparrow play'd.

The feather'd plaything she carest,
    She stroak'd its head and wings;
And while it nestled on her breast,
    She lisp'd the dearest things.

With chizzel bill a spark illset
    He loosen'd from the rest,
And swallow'd down to grind his meat,
    The easier to digest.

She seiz'd his bill with wild affright,
    Her diamond to discry:
'Twas gone! she sicken'd at the sight,
    Moaning her bird would die.

The tongue ty'd knocker none might use,
    The curtains none undraw,
The footmen went without their shoes,
    The street was laid with straw.

The doctor us'd his oily art
    Of strong emetick kind,
The apothecary play'd his part,
    And engineer'd behind.

When physick ceas'd to spend its store,
    To bring away the stone,
Dicky, like people given o'er,
    Picks up, when let alone.

His eyes dispelld their sickly dews,
   He peck'd behind his wing;
Lucia recov'ring at the news,
   Relapses for the ring.

Meanwhile within her beauteous breast
   Two different passions strove;
When av'rice ended the contest,
   And triumph'd over love.

Poor little, pretty, fluttering thing,
   Thy pains the sex display,
Who only to repair a ring,
   Could take thy life away!

Drive avarice from your breasts, ye fair,
   Monster of foulest mien,
Ye would not let it harbour there,
   Could but its form be seen.

It made a virgin put on guile,
   Truth's image break her word,
A Lucia's face forbear to smile,
   A Venus kill her bird.

JAMES THOMSON
(1700-1748)

From *The Seasons*

Spring

Should I my steps turn to the rural seat
Whose lofty elms and venerable oaks
Invite the rook, who high amid the boughs
In early Spring his airy city builds,
And ceaseless caws amusive; there, well-pleased,
I might the various polity survey
Of the mixed household-kind. The careful hen
Calls all her chirping family around,
Fed and defended by the fearless cock,
Whose breast with ardour flames, as on he walks
Graceful, and crows defiance. In the pond

The finely-chequered duck before her train
Rows garrulous. The stately-sailing swan
Gives out his snowy plumage to the gale,
And, arching proud his neck, with oary feet
Bears forward fierce, and guards his osier-isle,
Protective of his young. The turkey nigh,
Loud-threatening, reddens; while the peacock spreads
His every-coloured glory to the sun,
And swims in radiant majesty along.
O'er the whole homely scene the cooing dove
Flies thick in amorous chase, and wanton rolls
The glancing eye, and turns the changeful neck.
    While thus the gentle tenants of the shade
Indulge their purer loves, the rougher world
Of brutes below rush furious into flame
And fierce desire. Through all his lusty veins
The bull, deep-scorched, the raging passion feels.
Of pasture sick, and negligent of food,
Scarce seen he wades among the yellow broom,
While o'er his ample sides the rambling sprays
Luxuriant shoot; or through the mazy wood
Dejected wanders, nor the enticing bud
Crops, though it presses on his careless sense.
And oft, in jealous maddening fancy wrapt,
He seeks the fight; and idly-butting, feigns
His rival gored in every knotty trunk.
Him should he meet, the bellowing war begins:
Their eyes flash fury; to the hollowed earth,
Whence the sand flies, they mutter bloody deeds,
And, groaning deep, the impetuous battle mix:
While the fair heifer, balmy-breathing near,
Stands kindling up their rage. The trembling steed,
With this hot impulse seized in every nerve,
Nor heeds the rein, nor hears the sounding thong;
Blows are not felt; but, tossing high his head,
And by the well-known joy to distant plains
Attracted strong, all wild he bursts away;
O'er rocks, and woods, and craggy mountains flies;
And, neighing, on the aerial summit takes
The exciting gale; then, steep-descending, cleaves
The headlong torrents foaming down the hills,
Even where the madness of the straitened stream
Turns in black eddies round: such is the force
With which his frantic heart and sinews swell.

JAMES THOMSON

Summer

Home from his morning task the swain retreats,
His flock before him stepping to the fold;
While the full-uddered mother lows around
The cheerful cottage then expecting food,
The food of innocence and health! The daw,
The rook, and magpie, to the grey-grown oaks
(That the calm village in their verdant arms,
Sheltering, embrace) direct their lazy flight;
Where on the mingling boughs they sit embowered
All the hot noon, till cooler hours arise.
Faint underneath the household fowls convene;
And, in a corner of the buzzing shade,
The house-dog with the vacant greyhound lies
Out-stretched and sleepy. In his slumbers one
Attacks the nightly thief, and one exults
O'er hill and dale; till, wakened by the wasp,
They starting snap. Nor shall the muse disdain
To let the little noisy summer-race
Live in her lay and flutter through her song:
Not mean though simple—to the sun allied,
From him they draw their animating fire.
    Waked by his warmer ray, the reptile young
Come winged abroad, by the light air upborne,
Lighter, and full of soul. From every chink
And secret corner, where they slept away
The wintry storms, or rising from their tombs
To higher life, by myriads forth at once
Swarming they pour, of all the varied hues
Their beauty-beaming parent can disclose.
Ten thousand forms, ten thousand different tribes
People the blaze. To sunny waters some
By fatal instinct fly; where on the pool
They sportive wheel, or, sailing down the stream,
Are snatched immediate by the quick-eyed trout
Or darting salmon. Through the green-wood glade
Some love to stray; there lodged, amused, and fed
In the fresh leaf. Luxurious, others make
The meads their choice, and visit every flower
And every latent herb: for the sweet task
To propagate their kinds, and where to wrap
In what soft beds their young, yet undisclosed,
Employs their tender care. Some to the house,

The fold, and dairy hungry bend their flight;
Sip round the pail, or taste the curdling cheese:
Oft, inadvertent, from the milky stream
They meet their fate; or, weltering in the bowl,
With powerless wings around them wrapt, expire.
But chief to heedless flies the window proves
A constant death; where gloomily retired,
The villain spider lives, cunning and fierce,
Mixture abhorred! Amid a mangled heap
Of carcases in eager watch he sits,
O'erlooking all his waving snares around.
Near the dire cell the dreadless wanderer oft
Passes; as oft the ruffian shows his front.
The prey at last ensnared, he dreadful darts
With rapid glide along the leaning line;
And, fixing in the wretch his cruel fangs,
Strikes backward grimly pleased: the fluttering wing
And shriller sound declare extreme distress,
And ask the helping hospitable hand.

Autumn

Poor is the triumph o'er the timid hare!
Scared from the corn, and now to some lone seat
Retired—the rushy fen, the ragged furze
Stretched o'er the stony heath, the stubble chapped,
The thistly lawn, the thick entangled broom,
Of the same friendly hue the withered fern,
The fallow ground laid open to the sun
Concoctive, and the nodding sandy bank
Hung o'er the mazes of the mountain brook.
Vain is her best precaution; though she sits
Concealed with folded ears, unsleeping eyes
By Nature raised to take the horizon in,
And head couched close betwixt her hairy feet
In act to spring away. The scented dew
Betrays her early labyrinth; and deep,
In scattered sullen openings, far behind,
With every breeze she hears the coming storm;
But, nearer and more frequent as it loads
The sighing gale, she springs amazed, and all

The savage soul of game is up at once—
The pack full-opening various, the shrill horn
Resounded from the hills, the neighing steed
Wild for the chase, and the loud hunter's shout—
O'er a weak, harmless, flying creature, all
Mixed in mad tumult and discordant joy.

Winter

. . . Drooping, the labourer-ox
Stands covered o'er with snow, and then demands
The fruit of all his toil. The fowls of heaven,
Tamed by the cruel season, crowd around
The winnowing store, and claim the little boon
Which Providence assigns them. One alone,
The redbreast, sacred to the household gods,
Wisely regardful of the embroiling sky,
In joyless fields and thorny thickets leaves
His shivering mates, and pays to trusted man
His annual visit. Half afraid, he first
Against the window beats; then brisk alights
On the warm hearth; then, hopping o'er the floor,
Eyes all the smiling family askance,
And pecks, and starts, and wonders where he is—
Till, more familiar grown, the table-crumbs
Attract his slender feet. The foodless wilds
Pour forth their brown inhabitants. The hare,
Though timorous of heart, and hard beset
By death in various forms, dark snares, and dogs,
And more unpitying men, the garden seeks,
Urged on by fearless want. The bleating kind
Eye the bleak heaven, and next the glistening earth,
With looks of dumb despair; then, sad-dispersed,
Dig for the withered herb through heaps of snow.

STEPHEN DUCK
(1705-1756)

On Mites. To a Lady

'Tis but by way of Simile: Prior

Dear Madam, did you never gaze,
Thro' Optic-glass, on rotten Cheese?
There, Madam, did you ne'er perceive
A Crowd of Dwarfish Creatures live?
The little Things, elate with Pride,
Strut to and fro, from Side to Side:
In tiny Pomp, and pertly vain,
Lords of their pleasing Orb, they reign;
And, fill'd with harden'd Curds and Cream,
Think the whole Dairy made for *them*.

So Men, conceited Lords of all,
Walk proudly o'er this pendent Ball,
Fond of their little Spot below,
Nor greater Beings care to know;
But think, those *Worlds*, which deck the Skies,
Were only form'd to please *their* Eyes.

MR MEREDYTH?
(fl. 1757)

To Miss * * * * * on the Death of her Goldfish

Ah, dry those tears; they flow too fast—
His time has come! his Die was cast!
The shineing Fin, the golden scale
Alas you see could naught avail!
Nor Virtue's prayr, nor Beauty's pow'r,
Arrest his Fate, one single hour.
Fair Lady! moderate your grief
A Friend's advice may bring relief
Consider that we All must dye;
Your Fish—you Dog—your Cat—& I.

MR. MEREDYTH

You'll not attend to what I'v said—
Your Peace is gone—your Fish is dead!
And shoud your Lover now draw near
And sigh, & call you all that's dear
To tenderest sighs you'd answer—Pish
I hate mankind—I've lost my *Fish*.
I grant he was a Fish of merit
A Fish of Parts—a Fish of Spirit
But sure *no* Fish should have the art
To captivate a Lady's heart.
Allow him every perfection
Yet still deny him your affection
Your Father'd swear you was undone—
He'd never bear a scaly Son
I'm very sure he ne'er would wish
To see his daughter suckle Fish
And well indeed might tak't in dudgeon
To be a Grandsire to a Gudgeon.
Your Sister too would make a Pother—
She'd never brook to call him Brother
Tis better far your Fish is dead
Than you should take him to your Bed
Your Mother never would abide
To see you lying side by side
Even you your self would think it odd
Should * * * stoop to kiss a Cod
Or asked her Fishmonger about
Some lovely, darling, amorous Trowt.
And swore no joy could eer be felt
While panting for her absent Smelt
Twou'd be most strange with streaming eye
To hear some tender Mother cry
Alas, my Child! poor thoughtless wench
Seduc'd, & Ruin'd by—a Tench!
And now he swears he'll never marry
The Fright has made my girl miscarry
Cruel the Pangs we mothers feel
My Childs miscarried of an Eel
A Bird, a Beast, the mighty Jove
Became to gratify his Love
But you, O wonderful declare
A Fish is form'd to please the Fair

THOMAS GRAY

O could I but thy Favour win
Transform'd to Fish with golden Fin
I'd gladly swim the Little Lake
Confind in Bason for thy sake
Of to the surface raise my head
And from thy fingers nibble bread
In China or in earthen dish
I'd live & dye your faithful Fish
But since I've got no golden scale
No shining Fin, no forky Tail
But arms & Legs, can speak & hear
I'm doom'd to languish & despair
With skin strippd off, no wriggling Eel
Expresses half the Pangs I feel.

(This poem comes from a manuscript collection of poems made by
William Shenstone, first published by the Oxford University Press in
1952 (edited by Ian A. Gordon) under the title *Shenstone's Miscellany
1759-1763*. Shenstone's note shows him as not quite certain of the
authorship. The poet has been assigned an arbitrary birth-year corres-
ponding to Shenstone's (1714) for the purpose of this anthology.

THOMAS GRAY
(1716-1771)

Fragment: *"There pipes the wood-lark,
and the song thrush there"*

There pipes the wood-lark, and the song thrush there
Scatters his loose notes in the waste of air.

Ode On the Death of a Favourite Cat,
Drowned in a Tub of Gold Fishes

'Twas on a lofty vase's side,
Where China's gayest art had dy'd
  The azure flowers, that blow;
Demurest of the tabby kind,
The pensive Selima reclin'd,
  Gazed on the lake below.

Her conscious tail her joy declar'd;
The fair round face, the snowy beard,
   The velvet of her paws,
Her coat, that with the tortoise vies,
Her ears of jet, and emerald eyes,
   She saw; and purr'd applause.

Still had she gaz'd; but 'midst the tide
Two angel forms were seen to glide,
   The Genii of the stream:
Their scaly armour's Tyrian hue
Thro' richest purple to the view
   Betray'd a golden gleam.

The hapless Nymph with wonder saw:
A whisker first and then a claw,
   With many an ardent wish,
She stretch'd in vain to reach the prize.
What female heart can gold despise?
   What Cat's averse to fish?

Presumptuous Maid! with looks intent
Again she stretch'd, again she bent,
   Nor knew the gulf between.
(Malignant Fate sat by, and smil'd)
The slipp'ry verge her feet beguil'd,
   She tumbled headlong in.

Eight times emerging from the flood
She mew'd to ev'ry watery God,
   Some speedy aid to send.
No Dolphin came, no Nereid stirr'd:
Nor cruel *Tom*, nor *Susan* heard.
   A Fav'rite has no friend!

From hence, ye Beauties, undeceiv'd,
Know, one false step is ne'er retriev'd,
   And be with caution bold.
Not all that tempts your wand'ring eyes
And heedless hearts, is lawful prize;
   Nor all, that glisters, gold.

WILLIAM HAWKINS
(1722-1801)

To a worm
which the author accidentally trode upon

Methinks thou writhest as in rage;—
    But, dying reptile, know,
Thou ow'st to chance thy death! — I scorn
    To crush my meanest foe.

Anger, 'tis true, and justice stern
    Might fairly here have place. —
Are not thy subterraneous tribes
    Devourers of our race?

On princes they have richly fed,
    When their vast work was done;
And monarchs have regal'd vile worms,
    Who first the world had won.

Let vengeance then thine exit cheer,
    Nor at thy fate repine:
Legions of worms (who knows how soon?)
    Shall feast on me, and mine.

CHRISTOPHER SMART
(1722-1771)

From *Jubilate Agno*

For I will consider my Cat Jeoffry.

For he is the servant of the Living God duly and daily
serving him.

For at the first glance of the glory of God in the East
he worships in his way.

For is this done by wreathing his body seven times
round with elegant quickness.

For then he leaps up to catch the musk, wch is the
blessing of God upon his prayer.

For he rolls upon prank to work it in.

For having done duty and received blessing he begins to consider himself.

For this he performs in ten degrees.

For first he looks upon his fore-paws to see if they are clean.

For secondly he kicks up behind to clear away there.

For thirdly he works it upon stretch with the fore paws extended.

For fourthly he sharpens his paws by wood.

For fifthly he washes himself.

For sixthly he rolls upon wash.

For seventhly he fleas himself, that he may not be interrupted upon the beat.

For eighthly he rubs himself against a post.

For ninthly he looks up for his instructions.

For tenthly he goes in quest of food.

For having consider'd God and himself he will consider his neighbour.

For if he meets another cat he will kiss her in kindness.

For when he takes his prey he plays with it to give it a chance.

For one mouse in seven escapes by his dallying.

For when his day's work is done his business more properly begins.

For he keeps the Lord's watch in the night against the adversary.

For he counteracts the powers of darkness by his electrical skin & glaring eyes.

For he counteracts the Devil, who is death, by brisking about the life.

For in his morning orisons he loves the sun and the
sun loves him.

For he is of the tribe of Tiger.

For the Cherub Cat is a term of the Angel Tiger.

For he has the subtlety and hissing of a serpent,
which in goodness he suppresses.

For he will not do destruction if he is well-fed,
neither will he spit without provocation.

For he purrs in thankfulness, when God tells him he's
a good Cat.

For he is an instrument for the children to learn
bencvolence upon.

For every house is incompleat without him & a
blessing is lacking in the spirit.

For the Lord commanded Moses concerning the cats
at the departure of the Children of Israel from Egypt.

For every family had one cat at least in the bag.

For the English Cats are the best in Europe.

For he is the cleanest in the use of his fore-paws of
any quadrupede.

For dexterity of his defence is an instance of the love
of God to him exceedingly.

For he is the quickest to his mark of any creature.

For he is tenacious of his point.

For he is a mixture of gravity and waggery.

For he knows that God is his Saviour.

For there is nothing sweeter than his peace when at
rest.

For there is nothing brisker than his life when in
motion.

For he is of the Lord's poor and so indeed is he called
by benevolence perpetually—Poor Jeoffry! poor
Jeoffry! the rat has bit thy throat.

For I bless the name of the Lord Jesus that Jeoffry is better.

For the divine spirit comes about his body to sustain it in compleat cat.

For his tongue is exceeding pure so that it has in purity what it wants in musick.

For he is docile and can learn certain things.

For he can set up with gravity which is patience upon approbation.

For he can fetch and carry, which is patience in employment.

For he can jump over a stick which is patience upon proof positive.

For he can spraggle upon waggle at the word of command.

For he can jump from an eminence into his master's bosom.

For he can catch the cork and toss it again.

For he is hated by the hypocrite and miser.

For the former is affraid of detection.

For the latter refuses the charge.

For he camels his back to bear the first notion of business.

For he is good to think on, if a man would express himself neatly.

For he made a great figure in Egypt for his signal services.

For he killed the Icneumon-rat very pernicious by land.

For his ears are so acute that they sting again.

For from this proceeds the passing quickness of his attention.

For by stroaking of him I have found out electricity.

For I perceived God's light about him both wax and
   fire.

For the Electrical fire is the spiritual substance, which
   God sends from heaven to sustain the bodies both
   of man and beast.

For God has blessed him in the variety of his
   movements.

For, tho he cannot fly, he is an excellent clamberer.

For his motions upon the face of the earth are more
   than any other quadrupede.

For he can tread to all the measures upon the musick.

For he can swim for life.

For he can creep.

WILLIAM COWPER
(1731-1800)

The Faithful Friend

The green-house is my summer seat;
My shrubs displac'd from that retreat
   Enjoy'd the open air;
Two goldfinches, whose sprightly song
Had been their mutual solace long,
   Liv'd happy pris'ners there.

They sang, as blithe as finches sing
That flutter loose on golden wing,
   And frolic where they list;
Strangers to liberty, 'tis true,
But that delight they never knew,
   And, therefore, never miss'd.

But nature works in ev'ry breast;
Instinct is never quite suppress'd;
   And Dick felt some desires,
Which, after many an effort vain,
Instructed him at length to gain
   A pass between his wires.

The open windows seem'd to invite
The freeman to a farewell flight;
   But Tom was still confin'd;
And Dick, although his way was clear,
Was much too gen'rous and sincere
   To leave his friend behind.

For, settling on his grated roof,
He chirp'd and kiss'd him, giving proof
   That he desir'd no more;
Nor would forsake his cage at last,
Till gently seiz'd I shut him fast,
   A pris'ner as before.

Oh ye, who never knew the joys
Of Friendship, satisfied with noise,
   Fandango, ball and rout!
Blush, when I tell you how a bird,
A prison, with a friend, preferr'd
   To liberty without.

Epitaph on a Hare

Here lies, whom hound did ne'er pursue,
　　Nor swifter greyhound follow,
Whose foot ne'er tainted morning dew,
　　Nor ear heard huntsman's halloo,

Old Tiney, surliest of his kind,
　　Who, nurs'd with tender care,
And to domestic bounds confin'd,
　　Was still a wild Jack-hare.

Though duly from my hand he took
　　His pittance ev'ry night,
He did it with a jealous look,
　　And, when he could, would bite.

His diet was of wheaten bread,
　　And milk, and oats, and straw;
Thistles, or lettuces instead,
　　With sand to scour his maw.

On twigs of hawthorn he regal'd,
　　On pippins' russet peel,
And, when his juicy salads fail'd,
　　Slic'd carrot pleas'd him well.

A Turkey carpet was his lawn,
　　Whereon he lov'd to bound,
To skip and gambol like a fawn,
　　And swing his rump around.

His frisking was at ev'ning hours,
　　For then he lost his fear,
But most before approaching show'rs,
　　Or when a storm drew near.

Eight years and five round-rolling moons
　　He thus saw steal away,
Dozing out all his idle noons,
　　And ev'ry night at play.

I kept him for his humour's sake,
　　For he would oft beguile
My heart of thoughts, that made it ache,
　　And force me to a smile.

But now beneath his walnut shade
   He finds his long last home,
And waits in snug concealment laid,
   Till gentler Puss shall come.

He still more aged feels the shocks,
   From which no care can save,
And, partner once of Tiney's box,
   Must soon partake his grave.

The Retired Cat

A poet's cat, sedate and grave,
As poet well could wish to have,
Was much addicted to inquire
For nooks, to which she might retire,
And where, secure as mouse in chink,
She might repose, or sit and think.
I know not where she caught the trick—
Nature perhaps herself had cast her
In such a mould PHILOSOPHIQUE,
Or else she learn'd it of her master.
Sometimes ascending, debonair,
An apple-tree or lofty pear,
Lodg'd with convenience in the fork,
She watched the gard'ner at his work;
Sometimes her ease and solace sought
In an old empty wat'ring pot,
There wanting nothing, save a fan,
To seem some nymph in her sedan,
Apparell'd in exactest sort,
And ready to be borne to court.
   But love of change it seems has place
Not only in our wiser race;
Cats also feel as well as we
That passion's force, and so did she.
Her climbing, she began to find,
Expos'd her too much to the wind,
And the old utensil of tin
Was cold and comfortless within:

She therefore wish'd instead of those,
Some place of more serene repose,
Where neither cold might come, nor air
Too rudely wanton with her hair,
And sought it in the likeliest mode
Within her master's snug abode.
   A draw'r,—it chanc'd, at bottom lin'd
With linen of the softest kind,
With such as merchants introduce
From India, for the ladies' use,—
A draw'r impending o'er the rest,
Half open in the topmost chest,
Of depth enough, and none to spare,
Invited her to slumber there.
Puss with delight beyond expression,
Survey'd the scene and took possession.
Recumbent at her ease ere long,
And lull'd by her own hum-drum song,
She left the cares of life behind,
And slept as she would sleep her last,
When in came, housewifely inclin'd,
The chambermaid, and shut it fast,
By no malignity impell'd,
But all unconscious whom it held.
   Awaken'd by the shock (cried puss)
Was ever cat attended thus!
The open draw'r was left, I see,
Merely to prove a nest for me,
For soon as I was well compos'd,
Then came the maid, and it was closed:
How smooth these 'kerchiefs, and how sweet,
O what a delicate retreat!
I will resign myself to rest
Till Sol, declining in the west,
Shall call to supper; when, no doubt,
Susan will come and let me out.
   The evening came, the sun descended,
And puss remain'd still unattended.
The night roll'd tardily away,
(With her indeed 'twas never day)
The sprightly morn her course renew'd,
The evening gray again ensued,

And puss came into mind no more
Than if entomb'd the day before.
With hunger pinch'd, and pinch'd for room,
She now presag'd approaching doom,
Not slept a single wink, or purr'd,
Conscious of jeopardy incurr'd.
  That night, by chance, the poet watching,
Heard an inexplicable scratching,
His noble heart went pit-a-pat,
And to himself he said—what's that?
He drew the curtain at his side,
And forth he peep'd, but nothing spied.
Yet, by his ear directed, guess'd
Something imprison'd in the chest,
And doubtful what, with prudent care,
Resolv'd it should continue there.
At length a voice, which well he knew,
A long and melancholy mew,
Saluting his poetic ears,
Consol'd him, and dispell'd his fears;
He left his bed, he trod the floor,
He 'gan in haste the draw'rs explore,
The lowest first, and without stop,
The rest in order to the top.
For 'tis a truth well known to most,
That whatsoever thing is lost,
We seek it, ere it come to light,
In ev'ry cranny but the right.
Forth skipp'd the cat; not now replete
As erst with airy self-conceit,
Nor in her own fond apprehension,
A theme for all the world's attention,
But modest, sober, cur'd of all
Her notions hyberbolical,
And wishing for a place of rest
Any thing rather than a chest:
Then stept the poet into bed,
With this reflexion in his head:

MORAL

Beware of too sublime a sense
Of your own worth and consequence!

The man who dreams himself so great,
And his importance of such weight,
That all around, in all that's done,
Must move and act for him alone,
Will learn, in school of tribulation,
The folly of his expectation.

ERASMUS DARWIN
(1731-1802)

From *The Temple of Nature; or the Origin of Society. Canto IV: Of Good and Evil*

(The footnotes are extracts from Darwin's own.)

"How few," the Muse in plaintive accents cries,
And mingles with her words pathetic sighs.—
"How few, alas! in Nature's wide domains
The sacred charm of Sympathy restrains!
Uncheck'd desires from appetite commence,
And pure reflection yields to selfish sense!
—Blest is the Sage, who learned in Nature's laws
With nice distinction marks effect and cause;
Who views the insatiate Grave with eye sedate,
Nor fears thy voice, inexorable Fate!

"When war, the Demon, lifts his banner high,
And loud artillery rends the affrighted sky;
Swords clash with swords, on horses horses rush,
Man tramples man, and nations nations crush;
Death his vast sithe with sweep enormous wields,
And shuddering Pity quits the sanguine fields.

"The wolf, escorted by his milk-drawn dam,
Unknown to mercy, tears the guiltless lamb;
The towering eagle, darting from above,
Unfeeling rends the inoffensive dove;
The lamb and dove on living nature feed,
Crop the young herb, or crush the embryon seed.
Nor spares the loud owl in her dusky flight,
Smit with sweet notes, the minstrel of the night;

Nor spares, enamour'd of his radiant form,
The hungry nightingale the glowing worm;
Who with bright lamp alarms the midnight hour,
Climbs the green stem, and slays the sleeping flower.

"Fell Œstrus buries in her rapid course
Her countless brood in stag, or bull, or horse;
Whose hungry larva eats its living way,
Hatch'd by the warmth, and issues into day.
The wing'd Ichneumon for her embryon young
Gores with sharp horn the caterpillar throng.
The cruel larva mines its silky course,
And tears the vitals of its fostering nurse.
While fierce Libellula with jaws of steel
Ingulfs an insect-province at a meal;
Contending bee-swarms rise on rustling wings,
And slay their thousands with envenom'd stings.

"Yes! smiling Flora drives her armed car
Through the thick ranks of vegetable war;
Herb, shrub, and tree, with strong emotions rise
For light and air, and battle in the skies;
Whose roots diverging with opposing toil
Contend below for moisture and for soil;
Round the tall Elm the flattering Ivies bend,
And strangle, as they clasp, their struggling friend;
Envenom'd dews from Mancinella flow,
And scald with caustic touch the tribes below;
Dense shadowy leaves on stems aspiring borne
With blight and mildew thin the realms of corn;
And insect hordes with restless tooth devour
The unfolded bud, and pierce the ravell'd flower.

"In ocean's pearly haunts, the waves beneath
Sits the grim monarch of insatiate Death;
The shark rapacious with descending blow
Darts on the scaly brood, that swims below;
The crawling crocodiles, beneath that move,
Arrest with rising jaw the tribes above;
With monstrous gape sepulchral whales devour
Shoals at a gulp, a million in an hour.
—Air, earth and ocean, to astonish'd day
One scene of blood, one mighty tomb display!
From Hunger's arms the shafts of Death are hurl'd,
And one great Slaughter-house the warring world!

81

Line 29, *Fell Œstrus buries*. The gadfly, botfly, or sheep-fly: the larva lives in the bodies of cattle throughout the whole winter; it is extracted from their backs by an African bird called Buphaga. Adhering to the anus it artfully introduces itself into the intestines of horses, and becomes so numerous in their stomachs, as sometimes to destroy them.

Line 33, *The wing'd Ichneumon*. Linneus describes seventy-seven species of the ichneumon fly, some of which have a sting as long, and some twice as long as their bodies. Many of them insert their eggs into various caterpillars, which when they are hatched seem for a time to prey on the reservoir of silk in the backs of those animals designed for their own use to spin a cord to support them, or a bag to contain them, while they change from their larva form to a butterfly; as I have seen in above fifty cabbage caterpillars. The ichneumon larva then makes its way out of the caterpillar, and spins itself a small cocoon like a silk worm; these cocoons are about the size of a small pin's head, and I have seen about ten of them on each cabbage caterpillar, which soon dies after their exclusion.

Line 37, *While fierce Libellula*. The Libellula or Dragon-fly is said to be a most voracious animal; Linneus says in their perfect state they are the hawks to naked winged flies; in their larva state they run beneath the water, and are the cruel crocodiles of aquatic insects.

Line 39, *Contending bee-swarms*. Stronger bee-swarms frequently attack weak hives, and in two or three days destroy them and carry away their honey; this I once prevented by removing the attacked hive after the first day's battle to a distinct part of the garden.

Line 57, *The shark rapacious*. The shark has three rows of sharp teeth within each other, which he can bend downwards internally to admit larger prey, and raise to prevent its return; his snout hangs so far over his mouth, that he is necessitated to turn upon his back, when he takes fish that swim over him, and hence seems peculiarly formed to catch those that swim under him.

Line 59, *The crawling crocodiles*. As this animal lives chiefly at the bottom of the rivers, which he frequents, he has the power of opening the upper jaw as well as the under one, and thus with greater facility catches the fish or water-fowl which swim over him.

Line 66, *One great slaughter-house*. As vegetables are an inferior order of animals fixed to the soil; and as the locomotive animals prey upon them, or upon each other; the world may indeed be said to be one great slaughter-house. As the digested food of vegetables consists principally of sugar, and from this is produced again their mucilage, starch and oil, and since animals are sustained by these vegetable-productions, it would seem that the sugar-making process carried on in vegetable vessels was the great source of life to all organized beings. And that if our improved chemistry should ever discover the art of making sugar from fossile or aerial matter without the assistance of vegetation, food for animals would then become as plentiful as water, and they might live upon the earth without preying on each other, as thick as blades of grass, with no restraint to their numbers but the want of local room.

ANNA LETITIA BARBAULD
(1743-1825)

The Mouse's Petition*

O hear a pensive prisoner's prayer,
    For liberty that sighs;
And never let thine heart be shut
    Against the wretch's cries!

For here forlorn and sad I sit,
    Within the wiry grate;
And tremble at the' approaching morn,
    Which brings impending fate.

If e'er thy breast with freedom glowed,
    And spurned a tyrant's chain,
Let not thy strong oppressive force
    A free-born mouse detain!

O do not stain with guiltless blood
    Thy hospitable hearth!
Nor triumph that thy wiles betrayed
    A prize so little worth.

The scattered gleanings of a feast
    My frugal meals supply;
But if thine unrelenting heart
    That slender boon deny,—

The cheerful light, the vital air,
    Are blessings widely given;
Let Nature's commoners enjoy
    The common gifts of Heaven.

The well-taught philosophic mind
    To all compassion gives;
Casts round the world an equal eye,
    And feels for all that lives.

*Found in the trap where he had been confined all night by Dr. Priestley, for the sake of making experiments with different kinds of air.

If mind,—as ancient sages taught,—
  A never dying flame,
Still shifts through matter's varying forms,
  In every form the same;

Beware, lest in the worm you crush,
  A brother's soul you find;
And tremble lest thy luckless hand
  Dislodge a kindred mind.

Or, if this transient gleam of day
  Be *all* of life we share,
Let pity plead within thy breast
  That little *all* to spare.

So may thy hospitable board
  With health and peace be crowned;
And every charm of heartfelt ease
  Beneath thy roof be found.

So when destruction lurks unseen,
  Which men, like mice, may share,
May some kind angel clear thy path,
  And break the hidden snare.

ANNA SEWARD
(1747-1809)

A Favourite Cat's Dying Soliloquy,
Addressed to

Mrs Patton of Lichfield

Long years beheld me PATTON'S mansion grace,
The gentlest, fondest of the feline race;
Before her frisking thro' the garden glade,
Or at her feet, in quiet slumber, laid;
Prais'd for my glossy back, of tortoise streak,
And the warm smoothness of my snowy neck;
Soft paws, that sheath'd for her the clawing nail;
The shining whisker, and meand'ring tail.
Now feeble age each glazing eye-ball dims;
And pain has stiffen'd these once supple limbs;
Fate of eight lives the forfeit gasp obtains,
And e'en the ninth creeps languid thro' my veins.

ANNA SEWARD

Much, sure, of good the future has in store,
When Lucy basks on PATTON's hearth no more,
In those blest climes where fishes oft forsake
The winding river and the glassy lake;
There as our silent-footed race behold
The spots of crimson and the fins of gold,
Venturing beyond the shielding waves to stray,
They gasp on shelving banks, our easy prey;
While birds unwing'd hop careless o'er the ground,
And the plump mouse incessant trots around,
Near wells of cream, which mortals never skim,
Warm marum creeping round their shallow brim;
Where green valerian tufts, luxuriant spread,
Cleanse the sleek hide, and form the fragrant bed.

Yet, stern dispenser of the final blow,
Before thou lay'st an aged Grimalkin low,
Bend to her last request a gracious ear,
Some days, some few short days to linger here!
So, to the guardian of her earthly weal
Shall softest purs these tender truths reveal:
Ne'er shall thy now expiring Puss forget
To thy kind cares her long-enduring debt;
Nor shall the joys that painless realms decree,
Efface the comforts once bestow'd by thee;
To countless mice thy chicken bones preferr'd,
Thy toast to golden fish and wingless bird:
O'er marum border and valerian bed
Thy Lucy shall decline her moping head;
Sigh that she climbs no more, with grateful glee,
Thy downy sofa and thy cradling knee;
Nay, e'en by wells of cream shall sullen swear,
Since PATTON, her lov'd mistress, is not there.

(*Warm marum:* The affection of cats for marum and valerian is well known. They will beat down the stems, mat them with their feet, and roll upon them. (Note from Sir Walter Scott's edition of 1810).)

CHARLOTTE SMITH
(1749-1806)

The Glow-worm

When on some balmy-breathing night of Spring
 The happy child, to whom the world is new,
Pursues the evening moth, of mealy wing,
 Of from the heath-bell beats the sparkling dew;
He sees before his inexperienced eyes
 The brilliant Glow-worm, like a meteor, shine
On the turf-bank; — amazed, and pleased, he cries,
 "Star of the dewy grass! — I make thee mine!" —
Then, ere he sleep, collects the moisten'd flower,
 And bids soft leaves his glittering prize enfold,
And dreams that Fairy-lamps illume his bower:
 Yet with the morning shudders to behold
His lucid treasure, rayless as the dust!
— So turn the World's bright joys to cold and blank disgust.

GEORGE CRABBE
(1754-1832)

From *The Borough, Letter IX*

(Crabbe's own notes are printed at the end of the extract)

 Now is it pleasant in the summer-eve,
When a broad shore retiring waters leave,
Awhile to wait upon the firm fair sand,
When all is calm at sea, all still at land;
And there the ocean's produce to explore,
As floating by, or rolling on the shore;
Those living jellies[1] which the flesh inflame,
Fierce as a nettle, and from that its name;
Some in huge masses, some that you may bring
In the small compass of a lady's ring;
Figured by hand divine—there's not a gem
Wrought by man's art to be compared to them;
Soft, brilliant, tender, through the wave they glow,
And make the moonbeam brighter where they flow.

Involved in sea-wrack, here you find a race,
Which science doubting, knows not where to place;
On shell or stone is dropp'd the embryo-seed,
And quickly vegetates a vital breed.[2]
  While thus with pleasing wonder you inspect
Treasures the vulgar in their scorn reject,
See as they float along th' entangled weeds
Slowly approach, upborne on bladdery beads;
Wait till they land, and you shall then behold
The fiery sparks those tangled frons' infold,
Myriads of living points[3] ; th' unaided eye
Can but the fire and not the form descry.
And now your view upon the ocean turn,
And there the splendour of the waves discern,
Cast but a stone, or strike them with an oar,
And you shall flames within the deep explore,
Or scoop the stream phosphoric as you stand,
And the cold flames shall flash along your hand;
When, lost in wonder, you shall walk and gaze
On weeds that sparkle, and on waves that blaze.[4]

WILLIAM BLAKE

1. Some of the smaller species of the *Medusa* (sea-nettle) are exquisitely beautiful: their form is nearly oval, varied with serrated longitudinal lines; they are extremely tender, and by no means which I am acquainted with can be preserved, for they soon dissolve in either spirit of wine or water, and lose every vestige of their shape, and indeed of their substance: the larger species are found in mis-shapen masses of many pounds weight; these, when handled, have the effect of the nettle, and the stinging is often accompanied or succeeded by the more unpleasant feeling perhaps in a slight degree resembling that caused by the torpedo.

2. Various tribes and species of marine *vermes* are here meant: that which so nearly resembles a vegetable in its form, and perhaps, in some degree, manner of growth, is the coralline called by naturalists *Sertularia*, of which there are many species in almost every part of the coast. The animal protrudes its many claws (apparently in search of prey) from certain pellucid vesicles which proceed from a horny, tenacious, branchy stem.

3. These are said to be a minute kind of animal of the same class; when it does not shine, it is invisible to the naked eye.

4. For the cause or causes of this phenomenon, which is sometimes, though rarely, observed on our coasts, I must refer the reader to the writers on natural philosophy and natural history.

WILLIAM BLAKE
(1757-1827)

The Fly

Little Fly
Thy summers play,
My thoughtless hand
Has brush'd away.

Am not I
A fly like thee?
Or art not thou
A man like me?

For I dance
And drink & sing;
Till some blind hand
Shall brush my wing.

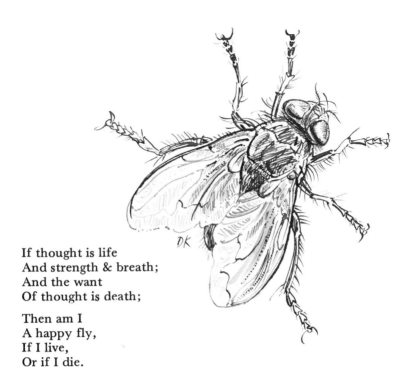

If thought is life
And strength & breath;
And the want
Of thought is death;

Then am I
A happy fly,
If I live,
Or if I die.

The Tyger

Tyger Tyger, burning bright,
In the forests of the night:
What immortal hand or eye,
Could frame thy fearful symmetry?

In what distant deeps or skies
Burnt the fire of thine eyes!
On what wings dare he aspire?
What the hand, dare sieze the fire?

And what shoulder, & what art,
Could twist the sinews of thy heart?
And when thy heart began to beat,
What dread hand? & what dread feet?

What the hammer? what the chain,
In what furnace was thy brain?
What the anvil? what dread grasp,
Dare its deadly terrors clasp?

When the stars threw down their spears
And water'd heaven with their tears:
Did he smile his work to see?
Did he who made the Lamb make thee?

Tyger, Tyger burning bright,
In the forests of the night:
What immortal hand or eye,
Dare frame thy fearful symmetry?

Auguries of Innocence

To see a World in a Grain of Sand
And a Heaven in a Wild Flower
Hold Infinity in the palm of your hand
And Eternity in an hour
A Robin Red breast in a Cage
Puts all Heaven in a Rage
A dove house filld with doves & Pigeons
Shudders Hell thro all its regions
A dog starvd at his Masters Gate
Predicts the ruin of the State
A Horse misusd upon the Road
Calls to Heaven for Human blood
Each outcry of the hunted Hare
A fibre from the Brain does tear
A Skylark wounded in the wing
A Cherubim does cease to sing
The Game Cock clipd & armd for fight
Does the Rising Sun affright
Every Wolfs & Lions howl
Raises from Hell a Human Soul
The wild deer wandring here & there
Keeps the Human Soul from Care
The Lamb misusd breeds Public strife
And yet forgives the Butchers Knife
The Bat that flits at close of Eve
Has left the Brain that wont Believe
The Owl that calls upon the Night
Speaks the Unbelievers fright
He who shall hurt the little Wren
Shall never be belovd by Men

WILLIAM BLAKE

He who the Ox to wrath has moved
Shall never be by Woman lovd
The wanton Boy that kills the Fly
Shall feel the Spiders enmity
He who torments the Chafers sprite
Weaves a Bower in endless Night
The Catterpiller on the Leaf
Repeats to thee thy Mothers grief
Kill not the Moth nor Butterfly
For the Last Judgment draweth nigh
He who shall train the Horse to War
Shall never pass the Polar Bar
The Beggers Dog & Widows Cat
Feed them & thou wilt grow fat
The Gnat that sings his Summers song
Poison gets from Slanders tongue
The poison of the Snake & Newt
Is the sweat of Envys Foot
The Poison of the Honey Bee
Is the Artists Jealousy
The Princes Robes & Beggars Rags
Are Toadstools on the Misers Bags
A truth thats told with bad intent
Beats all the Lies you can invent
It is right it should be so
Man was made for Joy & Woe
And when this we rightly know
Thro the World we safely go
Joy & Woe are woven fine
A Clothing for the Soul divine
Under every grief & pine
Runs a joy with silken twine
The Babe is more than swadling Bands
Throughout all these Human Lands
Tools were made & Born were hands
Every Farmer Understands
Every Tear from Every Eye
Becomes a Babe in Eternity
This is caught by Females bright
And returned to its own delight
The Bleat the Bark Bellow & Roar
Are Waves that Beat on Heavens Shore

The Babe that weeps the Rod beneath
Writes Revenge in realms of death
The Beggars Rags fluttering in Air
Does to Rags the Heavens tear
The Soldier armd with Sword & Gun
Palsied strikes the Summers Sun
The poor Mans Farthing is worth more
Than all the Gold on Africs Shore
One Mite wrung from the Labrers hands
Shall buy & sell the Misers Lands
Or if protected from on high
Does that whole Nation sell & buy
He who mocks the Infants Faith
Shall be mock'd in Age & Death
He who shall teach the Child to Doubt
The rotting Grave shall neer get out
He who respects the Infants faith
Triumphs over Hell & Death
The Childs Toys & the Old Mans Reasons
Are the Fruits of the Two seasons
The Questioner who sits so sly
Shall never know how to Reply
He who replies to words of Doubt
Doth put the Light of Knowledge out
The Strongest Poison ever known
Came from Caesars Laurel Crown
Nought can deform the Human Race
Like to the Armours iron brace
When Gold & Gems adorn the Plow
To peaceful Arts shall Envy Bow
A Riddle or the Crickets Cry
Is to Doubt a fit Reply
The Emmets Inch & Eagles Mile
Make Lame Philosophy to smile
He who Doubts from what he sees
Will neer Believe do what you Please
If the Sun & Moon should doubt
Theyd immediately Go out
To be in a Passion you Good may do
But no Good if a Passion is in you
The Whore & Gambler by the State
Licencd build that Nations Fate

The Harlots cry from Street to Street
Shall weave Old Englands winding Sheet
The Winners Shout the Losers Curse
Dance before dead Englands Hearse
Every Night & every Morn
Some to Misery are Born
Every Morn & every Night
Some are Born to sweet delight
Some are Born to sweet delight
Some are Born to Endless Night
We are led to Believe a Lie
When we see [*with*] not Thro the Eye
Which was Born in a Night to perish in a Night
When the Soul Slept in Beams of Light
God Appears & God is Light
To those poor Souls who dwell in Night
But does a Human Form Display
To those who Dwell in Realms of day

ROBERT BURNS
(1759-1796)

Poor Mailie's Elegy

Lament in rhyme, lament in prose,
Wi' saut tears trickling down your nose;
Our *Bardie*'s fate is at a close,
         Past a' remead!
The last, sad cape-stane of his woes;
         Poor Mailie's dead!

It's no the loss o' warl's gear,
That could sae bitter draw the tear,
Or make our *Bardie*, dowie, wear
         The mourning weed:
He's lost a friend and neebor dear,
         In *Mailie* dead.

Thro' a' the town she trotted by him;
A lang half-mile she could descry him;
Wi' kindly bleat, when she did spy him,
         She ran wi' speed:
A friend mair faithfu' ne'er came nigh him,
         Than *Mailie* dead.

I wat she was a *sheep* o' sense,
An' could behave hersel wi' mense:
I'll say't, she never brak a fence,
　　Thro' thievish greed.
Our *Bardie*, lanely, keeps the spence
　　Sin' *Mailie*'s dead.

Or, if he wanders up the howe,
Her living image in *her yowe*,
Comes bleating to him, owre the knowe,
　　For bits o' bread;
An' down the briny pearls rowe
　　For *Mailie* dead.

She was nae get o' moorlan tips,
Wi' tauted ket, an' hairy hips;
For her forbears were brought in ships,
　　Frae 'yont the TWEED:
A bonier *fleesh* ne'er cross'd the clips
　　Than *Mailie*'s dead.

Wae worth that man wha first did shape,
That vile, wanchancie thing—*a raep!*
It maks guid fellows girn an' gape,
　　Wi' chokin dread;
An' *Robin*'s bonnet wave wi' crape
　　For *Mailie* dead.

O, a' ye *Bards* on bonie DOON!
An' wha on AIRE your chanters tune!
Come, join the melancholious croon
　　O' *Robin*'s reed!
His heart will never get aboon!
　　His *Mailie*' s dead!

(*Mailie:* the poet's pet sheep; *dowie:* sad; *mense:* decorum; *spence:*
parlour; *howe:* valley; *tips:* rams; *tauted ket:* matted fleece; *wae
worth:* cursed be; *wanchancie:* dangerous; *raep:* rope; *get aboon:*
rejoice.)

ROBERT BURNS

To a Mouse, on turning her up in her Nest, with the Plough, November, 1785

Wee, sleeket, cowran, tim'rous *beastie,*
O, what a panic's in thy breastie!
Thou need na start awa sae hasty,
   Wi' bickering brattle!
I wad be laith to rin an' chase thee,
   Wi' murd'ring *pattle!*

I'm truly sorry Man's dominion
Has broken Nature's social union,
An' justifies that ill opinion,
   Which makes thee startle,
At me, thy poor, earth-born companion,
   An' *fellow-mortal!*

I doubt na, whyles, but thou may *thieve*;
What then? poor beastie, thou maun live!
A *daimen-icker* in a *thrave*
   'S a sma' request:
I'll get a blessin wi' the lave,
   An' never miss 't!

Thy wee-bit *housie*, too, in ruin!
It's silly wa's the win's are strewin!
An' naething, now, to big a new ane,
   O' foggage green!
An' bleak *December's winds* ensuin,
   Baith snell an' keen!

Thou saw the fields laid bare an' wast,
An' weary *Winter* comin fast,
An' cozie here, beneath the blast,
Thou thought to dwell,
Till crash! the cruel *coulter* past
Out thro' thy cell.

That wee-bit heap o' leaves an' stibble,
Has cost thee monie a weary nibble!
Now thou's turn'd out, for a' thy trouble,
But house or hald,
To thole the Winter's *sleety dribble*,
An' *cranreuch* cauld!

But Mousie, thou art no thy-lane,
In proving *foresight* may be vain:
The best laid schemes o' *Mice* an' *Men*,
Gang aft agley,
An' lea'e us nought but grief an' pain,
For promis'd joy!

Still, thou art blest, compar'd wi' *me*!
The *present* only toucheth thee:
But Och! I *backward* cast my e'e,
On prospects drear!
An' *forward*, tho' I canna *see*,
I *guess* an' *fear*!

(*brattle:* hurry; *pattle:* long-handled spade; *daimen-icker:* occasional
ear of corn; *thrave:* two corn-stooks; *lave:* remainder; *foggage:* rank
grass; *snell:* severe; *coulter:* plough-blade; *cranreuch:* hoar-frost; *thy-
lane:* by yourself; *agley:* wrong.)

SAMUEL ROGERS
(1763-1855)

An Epitaph* on a Robin Redbreast

Tread lightly here, for here, 'tis said,
When piping winds are hush'd around,
A small note wakes from underground,
Where now his tiny bones are laid.

*Inscribed on an urn in the flower-garden at Hafod.

No more in lone and leafless groves,
With ruffled wing and faded breast,
His friendless, homeless spirit roves;
—Gone to the world where birds are blest!
Where never cat glides o'er the green,
Or school-boy's giant form is seen;
But Love, and Joy, and smiling Spring
Inspire their little souls to sing!

WILLIAM WORDSWORTH
(1770-1850)

To a Butterfly

I've watched you now a full half-hour,
Self-poised upon that yellow flower;
And, little Butterfly! indeed
I know not if you sleep or feed.
How motionless! — not frozen seas
More motionless! and then
What joy awaits you, when the breeze
Hath found you out among the trees,
And calls you forth again!

This plot of orchard-ground is ours;
My trees they are, my Sister's flowers;
Here rest your wings when they are weary;
Here lodge as in a sanctuary!
Come often to us, fear no wrong;
Sit near us on the bough!
We'll talk of sunshine and of song,
And summer days, when we were young;
Sweet childish days, that were as long
As twenty days are now.

Fidelity

A barking sound the Shepherd hears,
A cry as of a dog or fox;
He halts — and searches with his eyes

Among the scattered rocks:
And now at distance can discern
A stirring in a brake of fern;
And instantly a dog is seen,
Glancing through that covert green.

The Dog is not of mountain breed;
Its motions, too, are wild and shy;
With something, as the Shepherd thinks,
Unusual in its cry:
Nor is there anyone in sight
All round, in hollow or on height;
Nor shout, nor whistle strikes his ear;
What is the creature doing here?

It was a cove, a huge recess,
That keeps, till June, December's snow;
A lofty precipice in front,
A silent tarn below!
Far in the bosom of Helvellyn,
Remote from public road or dwelling,
Pathway, or cultivated land;
From trace of human foot or hand.

There sometimes doth a leaping fish
Send through the tarn a lonely cheer;
The crags repeat the raven's croak,
In symphony austere;
Thither the rainbow comes — the cloud —
And mists that spread the flying shroud;
And sunbeams; and the sounding blast,
That, if it could, would hurry past;
But that enormous barrier holds it fast.

Not free from boding thoughts, a while
The Shepherd stood; then makes his way
O'er rocks and stones, following the Dog
As quickly as he may;
Nor far had gone before he found
A human skeleton on the ground;
The appalled Discoverer with a sigh
Looks round, to learn the history.

From those abrupt and perilous rocks
The Man had fallen, that place of fear!
At length upon the Shepherd's mind
It breaks, and all is clear:
He instantly recalled the name,
And who he was, and whence he came;
Remembered, too, the very day
On which the Traveller passed this way.

But hear a wonder, for whose sake
This lamentable tale I tell!
A lasting monument of words
This wonder merits well.
The Dog, which still was hovering nigh,
Repeating the same timid cry,
This Dog, had been through three months' space
A dweller in that savage place.

Yes, proof was plain that, since the day
When this ill-fated Traveller died,
The Dog had watched about the spot,
Or by his master's side:
How nourished here through such long time
He knows, Who gave that love sublime;
And gave that strength of feeling, great
Above all human estimate!

Incident Characteristic of a Favourite Dog

On his morning rounds the Master
Goes to learn how all things fare;
Searches pasture after pasture,
Sheep and cattle eyes with care;
And, for silence or for talk,
He hath comrades in his walk;
Four dogs, each pair of different breed,
Distinguished two for scent, and two for speed.

See, a hare before him started!
— Off they fly in earnest chase;
Every dog is eager-hearted,
All the four are in the race:
And the hare whom they pursue,
Knows from instinct what to do;
Her hope is near: no turn she makes;
But, like an arrow, to the river takes.

Deep the river was, and crusted
Thinly by a one night's frost;
But the nimble Hare hath trusted
To the ice, and safely crost;
She hath crost, and without heed
All are following at full speed,
When, lo! the ice, so thinly spread,
Breaks — and the greyhound, DART, is over-head!

Better fate have PRINCE and SWALLOW —
See them cleaving to the sport!
MUSIC has no heart to follow,
Little MUSIC, she stops short.
She hath neither wish nor heart,
Hers is now another part:
A loving creature she, and brave!
And fondly strives her struggling friend to save.

From the brink her paws she stretches,
Very hands as you would say!
And afflicting moans she fetches,
As he breaks the ice away.
For herself she hath no fears, —
Him alone she sees and hears, —
Makes efforts with complainings; nor gives o'er
Until her fellow sinks to re-appear no more.

WILLIAM WORDSWORTH

Tribute to the Memory of the Same Dog

Lie here, without a record of thy worth,
Beneath a covering of the common earth!
It is not from unwillingness to praise,
Or want of love, that here no Stone we raise;
More thou deserv'st; but *this* man gives to man,
Brother to brother, *this* is all we can.
Yet they to whom thy virtues made thee dear
Shall find thee through all changes of the year:
This Oak points out thy grave; the silent tree
Will gladly stand a monument of thee.

We grieved for thee, and wished thy end were past;
And willingly have laid thee here at last:
For thou hadst lived till everything that cheers
In thee had yielded to the weight of years;
Extreme old age had wasted thee away,
And left thee but a glimmering of the day;
Thy ears were deaf, and feeble were thy knees, —
I saw thee stagger in the summer breeze,
Too weak to stand against its sportive breath,
And ready for the gentlest stroke of death.

It came, and we were glad; yet tears were shed;
Both man and woman wept when thou wert dead;
Not only for a thousand thoughts that were,
Old household thoughts, in which thou hadst thy share;
But for some precious boons vouchsafed to thee,
Found scarcely anywhere in like degree!
For love, that comes wherever life and sense
Are given by God, in thee was most intense;
A chain of heart, a feeling of the mind,
A tender sympathy, which did thee bind
Not only to us Men, but to thy Kind:
Yea, for thy fellow-brutes in thee we saw
A soul of love, love's intellectual law:-
Hence, if we wept, it was not done in shame;
Our tears from passion and from reason came,
And, therefore, shalt thou be an honoured name!

WILLIAM WORDSWORTH

Water Fowl

"Let me be allowed the aid of verse to describe the evolutions which these
visitants sometimes perform, on a fine day towards the close of winter." —
Extract from the Author's Book on the Lakes.

Mark how the feathered tenants of the flood,
With grace of motion that might scarcely seem
Inferior to angelical, prolong
Their curious pastime! shaping in mid air
(And sometimes with ambitious wing that soars
High as the level of the mountain-tops)
A circuit ampler than the lake beneath —
Their own domain; but ever, while intent
On tracing and retracing that large round,
Their jubilant activity evolves
Hundreds of curves and circlets, to and fro,
Upward and downward, progress intricate
Yet unperplexed, as if one spirit swayed
Their indefatigable flight. 'Tis done —
Ten times, or more, I fancied it had ceased;
But lo! the vanished company again
Ascending; they approach — I hear their wings,
Faint, faint at first; and then an eager sound,
Past in a moment — and as faint again!
They tempt the sun to sport amid their plumes;
They tempt the water, or the gleaming ice,
To show them a fair image; 'tis themselves,
Their own fair forms, upon the glimmering plain,
Painted more soft and fair as they descend
Almost to touch; — then up again aloft,
Up with a sally and a flash of speed,
As if they scorned both resting-place and rest!

The Wild Duck's Nest

The imperial Consort of the Fairy-king
Owns not a sylvan bower; or gorgeous cell
With emerald floored, and with purpureal shell
Ceilinged and roofed; that is so fair a thing
As this low structure, for the tasks of Spring,

Prepared by one who loves the buoyant swell
Of the brisk waves, yet here consents to dwell;
And spreads in stedfast peace her brooding wing.
Words cannot paint the o'ershadowing yew-tree bough
And dimly-gleaming Nest, — a hollow crown
Of golden leaves inlaid with silver down,
Fine as the mother's softest plumes allow;
I gazed — and, self-accused while gazing, sighed
For human-kind, weak slaves of cumbrous pride!

The Contrast
The Parrot and the Wren

I

Within her gilded cage confined,
I saw a dazzling Belle,
A Parrot of that famous kind
Whose name is NON-PAREIL.

Like beads of glossy jet her eyes;
And, smoothed by Nature's skill,
With pearl or gleaming agate vies
Her finely-curvèd bill.

Her plumy mantle's living hues
In mass opposed to mass,
Outshine the splendour that imbues
The robes of pictured glass.

And, sooth to say, an apter Mate
Did never tempt the choice
Of feathered Thing most delicate
In figure and in voice.

But, exiled from Australian bowers,
And singleness her lot,
She trills her song with tutored powers,
Or mocks each casual note.

No more of pity for regrets
With which she may have striven!
Now but in wantonness she frets,
Or spite, if cause be given;

Arch, volatile, a sportive bird
By social glee inspired;
Ambitious to be seen or heard,
And pleased to be admired!

II
This moss-lined shed, green, soft, and dry,
Harbours a self-contented Wren,
Not shunning man's abode, though shy,
Almost as thought itself, of human ken.

Strange places, coverts unendeared,
She never tried; the very nest
In which this Child of Spring was reared
Is warmed, through winter, by her feathery breast.

To the bleak winds she sometimes gives
A slender unexpected strain;
Proof that the hermitess still lives,
Though she appear not, and be sought in vain.

Say, Dora! tell me, by yon placid moon,
If called to choose between the favoured pair,
Which you would be, — the bird of the saloon,
By lady-fingers tended with nice care,
Caressed, applauded, upon dainties fed,
Or Nature's DARKLING of this mossy shed?

"The leaves that rustled on this oak-crowned hill"

The leaves that rustled on this oak-crowned hill,
And sky that danced among those leaves, are still;
Rest smooths the way for sleep; in field and bower
Soft shades and dews have shed their blended power
On drooping eyelid and the closing flower;
Sound is there none at which the faintest heart
Might leap, the weakest nerve of superstition start;
Save when the Owlet's unexpected scream
Pierces the ethereal vault; and ('mid the gleam
Of unsubstantial imagery, the dream,
From the hushed vale's realities, transferred
To the still lake) the imaginative Bird
Seems, 'mid inverted mountains, not unheard.

Grave Creature! — whether, while the moon shines bright
On thy wings opened wide for smoothest flight,
Thou art discovered in a roofless tower,
Rising from what may once have been a lady's bower;
Or spied where thou sitt'st moping in thy mew
At the dim centre of a churchyard yew;
Or, from a rifted crag or ivy tod
Deep in a forest, thy secure abode,
Thou giv'st, for pastime's sake, by shriek or shout,
A puzzling notice of thy whereabout —
May the night never come, nor day be seen,
When I shall scorn thy voice or mock thy mien!

In classic ages men perceived a soul
Of sapience in thy aspect, headless Owl!
The Athens reverenced in the studious grove;
And, near the golden sceptre grasped by Jove,
His Eagle's favourite perch, while round him sate
The Gods revolving the decrees of Fate,
Thou, too, wert present at Minerva's side:
Hark to that second larum! — far and wide
The elements have heard, and rock and cave replied.

WALTER SCOTT
(1771-1832)

Hellvellyn
(1805)

I climb'd the dark brow of the mighty Hellvellyn,
    Lakes and mountains beneath me gleam'd misty
        and wide;
All was still, save by fits, when the eagle was yelling,
    And starting around me the echoes replied.
On the right, Striden-edge round the Red-tarn was
        bending,
And Catchedicam its left verge was defending,
One huge nameless rock in the front was ascending,
    When I mark'd the sad spot where the wanderer
        had died.

Dark green was that spot 'mid the brown mountain-
    heather,
  Where the Pilgrim of Nature lay stretch'd in decay.
Like the corpse of an outcast abandon'd to weather,
  Till the mountain winds wasted the tenantless clay.
Nor yet quite deserted, though lonely extended,
For, faithful in death, his mute favourite attended,
The much-loved remains of her master defended,
  And chased the hill-fox and the raven away.

How long didst thou think that his silence was slumber?
  When the wind waved his garment, how oft didst
    thou start?
How many long days and long weeks didst thou
    number,
  Ere he faded before thee, the friend of thy heart?
And, oh, was it meet, that—no requiem read o'er him—
No mother to weep, and no friend to deplore him,
And thou, little guardian, alone stretched before him—
  Unhonour'd the Pilgrim from life should depart?

When a Prince to the fate of the Peasant has yielded,
  The tapestry waves dark round the dim-lighted hall;
With scutcheons of silver the coffin is shielded,
  And pages stand mute by the canopied pall:
Through the courts, at deep midnight, the torches are
    gleaming;
In the proudly-arch'd chapel the banners are beaming,
Far down the long aisle sacred music is streaming,
  Lamenting a Chief of the people should fall.

But meeter for thee, gentle lover of nature,
  To lay down thy head like the meek mountain lamb,
When, wilder'd, he drops from some cliff huge in
    stature,
  And draws his last sob by the side of his dam.
And more stately thy couch by this desert lake lying,
Thy obsequies sung by the grey plover flying,
With one faithful friend but to witness thy dying,
  In the arms of Hellvellyn and Catchedicam.

SAMUEL TAYLOR COLERIDGE
(1772-1834)

The Nightingale
A Conversation Poem, April, 1798

No cloud, no relique of the sunken day
Distinguishes the West, no long thin slip
Of sullen light, no obscure trembling hues.
Come, we will rest on this old mossy bridge!
You see the glimmer of the stream beneath,
But hear no murmuring: it flows silently,
O'er its soft bed of verdure. All is still,
A balmy night! and though the stars be dim,
Yet let us think upon the vernal showers
That gladden the green earth, and we shall find
A pleasure in the dimness of the stars.
And hark! the Nightingale begins its song,
'Most musical, most melancholy' bird!*
A melancholy bird? Oh! idle thought!
In Nature there is nothing melancholy.
But some night-wandering man whose heart was pierced
With the remembrance of a grievous wrong.
Or slow distemper, or neglected love,
(And so, poor wretch! filled all things with himself,
And made all gentle sounds tell back the tale
Of his own sorrow) he, and such as he,
First named these notes a melancholy strain.
And many a poet echoes the conceit;
Poet who hath been building up the rhyme
When he had better far have stretched his limbs
Beside a brook in mossy forest-dell,
By sun or moon-light, to the influxes
Of shapes and sounds and shifting elements

Most musical, most melancholy. This passage in Milton possesses an excellence
ᵣr superior to that of mere description; it is spoken in the character of the
ᵣelancholy Man, and has therefore a *dramatic* propriety. The Author makes
ᵣis remark, to rescue himself from the charge of having alluded with levity to
 line in Milton; a charge than which none could be more painful to him,
ᵪcept perhaps that of having ridiculed his Bible.

Surrendering his whole spirit, of his song
And of his fame forgetful! so his fame
Should share in Nature's immortality,
A venerable thing! and so his song
Should make all Nature lovelier, and itself
Be loved like Nature! But 'twill not be so;
And youths and maidens most poetical,
Who lose the deepening twilights of the spring
In ball-rooms and hot theatres, they still
Full of meek sympathy must heave their sighs
O'er Philomela's pity-pleading strains.
My Friend, and thou, our Sister! we have learnt
A different lore: we may not thus profane
Nature's sweet voices, always full of love
And joyance! 'Tis the merry Nightingale
That crowds, and hurries, and precipitates
With fast thick warble his delicious notes,
As he were fearful that an April night
Would be too short for him to utter forth
His love-chant, and disburthen his full soul
Of all its music!

           And I know a grove
Of large extent, hard by a castle huge,
Which the great lord inhabits not; and so
This grove is wild with tangling underwood,
And the trim walks are broken up, and grass,
Thin grass and king-cups grow within the paths.
But never elsewhere in one place I knew
So many nightingales; and far and near,
In wood and thicket, over the wide grove,
They answer and provoke each other's song.
With skirmish and capricious passagings,
And murmurs musical and swift jug jug,
And one low piping sound more sweet than all—
Stirring the air with such a harmony.
That should you close your eyes, you might almost
Forget it was not day! On moonlight bushes,
Whose dewy leaflets are but half-disclosed,
You may perchance behold them on the twigs,
Their bright, bright eyes, their eyes both bright and full,
Glistening, while many a glow-worm in the shade
Lights up her love-torch.

                    A most gentle Maid,
Who dwelleth in her hospitable home
Hard by the castle, and at latest eve
(Even like a Lady vowed and dedicate
To something more than Nature in the grove)
Glides through the pathways; she knows all their notes,
That gentle Maid! and oft, a moment's space,
What time the moon was lost behind a cloud,
Hath heard a pause of silence; till the moon
Emerging, hath awakened earth and sky
With one sensation, and those wakeful birds
Have all burst forth in choral minstrelsy,
As if some sudden gale had swept at once
A hundred airy harps! And she hath watched
Many a nightingale perch giddily
On blossomy twig still swinging from the breeze,
And to that motion tune his wanton song
Like tipsy Joy that reels with tossing head.

Farewell, O Warbler! till to-morrow eve,
And you, my friends! farewell, a short farewell!
We have been loitering long and pleasantly,
And now for our dear homes.—That strain again!
Full fain it would delay me! My dear babe,
Who, capable of no articulate sound,
Mars all things with his imitative lisp,
How he would place his hand beside his ear,
His little hand, the small forefinger up,
And bid us listen! And I deem it wise
To make him Nature's play-mate. He knows well
The evening-star; and once, when he awoke
In most distressful mood (some inward pain
Had made up that strange thing, an infant's dream—)
I hurried with him to our orchard-plot,
And he beheld the moon, and, hushed at once,
Suspends his sobs, and laughs most silently,
While his fair eyes, that swam with undropped tears,
Did glitter in the yellow moon-beam! Well!—
It is a father's tale: But if that Heaven
Should give me life, his childhood shall grow up
Familiar with these songs, that with the night
He may associate joy.—Once more, farewell,
Sweet Nightingale! once more, my friends! farewell.

ROBERT SOUTHEY

On Donne's Poem 'To a Flea'·

Be proud as Spaniards! Leap for pride ye Fleas!
Henceforth in Nature's mimic World grandees.
In Phoebus' archives registered are ye,
And this your patent of Nobility.
No skip-Jacks now, nor civiller skip-Johns,
Dread Anthropophagi! specks of living bronze,
I hail you one and all, sans Pros or Cons,
Descendants from a noble race of Dons.
What tho' that great ancestral Flea be gone,
Immortal with immortalising Donne,
His earthly spots bleached off a Papist's gloze,
In purgatory fire on Bardolph's nose.

(*skip-Jack:* pert, shallow fellow.)

Fragment: "The spruce and limber yellow-hammer"

The spruce and limber yellow-hammer
In the dawn of spring and sultry summer,
In hedge or tree the hours beguiling
With notes as of one who brass is filing.

ROBERT SOUTHEY
(1774-1843)

On the Death of a Favourite Old Spaniel

And they have drown'd thee then at last! poor Phillis!
The burden of old age was heavy on thee,
And yet thou should'st have lived! What though thine
    eye
Was dim, and watch'd no more with eager joy
The wonted call that on thy dull sense sunk
With fruitless repetition, the warm Sun
Might still have cheer'd thy slumbers; thou didst love
To lick the hand that fed thee, and though past
Youth's active season, even Life itself
Was comfort. Poor old friend, how earnestly
Would I have pleaded for thee! thou hadst been
Still the companion of my boyish sports;

And as I roam'd o'er Avon's woody cliffs,
From many a day-dream has thy short quick bark
Recall'd my wandering soul. I have beguiled
Often the melancholy hours at school,
Sour'd by some little tyrant, with the thought
Of distant home, and I remember'd then
Thy faithful fondness; for not mean the joy,
Returning at the happy holydays,
I felt from thy dumb welcome. Pensively
Sometimes have I remark'd thy slow decay,
Feeling myself changed too, and musing much
On many a sad vicissitude of Life.
Ah, poor companion! when thou followedst last
Thy master's parting footsteps to the gate
Which closed for ever on him, thou didst lose
Thy truest friend, and none was left to plead
For the old age of brute fidelity.
But fare thee well! Mine is no narrow creed;
And HE who gave thee being did not frame
The mystery of life to be the sport
Of merciless Man. There is another world
For all that live and move . . a better one!
Where the proud bipeds, who would fain confine
INFINITE GOODNESS to the little bounds
Of their own charity, may envy thee.

Bristol, 1796.

To a Goose

If thou didst feed on western plains of yore;
Or waddle wide with flat and flabby feet
Over some Cambrian mountain's plashy moor;
Or find in farmer's yard a safe retreat
From gipsy thieves and foxes sly and fleet;
If thy grey quills, by lawyer guided, trace
Deeds big with ruin to some wretched race,
Or love-sick poet's sonnet, sad and sweet,
Wailing the rigour of his lady fair;
Or if, the drudge of a housemaid's daily toil,
Cobwebs and dust thy pinions white besoil,

111

Departed Goose! I neither know nor care.
But this I know, that we pronounced thee fine,
Season'd with sage and onions, and port wine.

London, 1798.

To a Spider

Spider! thou need'st not run in fear about
    To shun my curious eyes;
  I won't humanely crush thy bowels out
    Lest thou should'st eat the flies;
Nor will I roast thee with a damn'd delight
  Thy strange instinctive fortitude to see,
    For there is One who might
    One day roast me.

Thou art welcome to a Rhymer sore perplext,
    The subject of his verse;
  There's many a one who on a better text
    Perhaps might comment worse.
Then shrink not, old Free-Mason, from my view,
  But quietly like me spin out the line;
    Do thou thy work pursue
    As I will mine.

Weaver of snares, thou emblemest the ways
    Of Satan, Sire of lies;
  Hell's huge black Spider, for mankind he lays
    His toils, as thou for flies.
When Betty's busy eye runs round the room,
  Woe to that nice geometry, if seen!
    But where is He whose broom
    The earth shall clean?

Spider! of old thy flimsy webs were thought,
    And 'twas a likeness true,
To emblem laws in which the weak are caught,
    But which the strong break through:
    And if a victim in thy toils is ta'en,
  Like some poor client is that wretched fly;
    I'll warrant thee thou'lt drain
    His life-blood dry.

And is not thy weak work like human schemes
And care on earth employ'd?
Such are young hopes and Love's delightful dreams
So easily destroy'd!
So does the Statesman, whilst the Avengers sleep,
Self-deem'd secure, his wiles in secret lay,
Soon shall destruction sweep
His work away.

Thou busy labourer! one resemblance more
May yet the verse prolong,
For spider, thou art like the Poet poor,
Whom thou hast help'd in song.
Both busily our needful food to win,
We work, as Nature taught, with ceaseless pains:
Thy bowels thou dost spin,
I spin my brains.

The Dancing Bear

Recommended to the Advocates for the Slave-Trade

Rare music! I would rather hear cat-courtship
Under my bed-room window in the night,
Than this scraped catgut's screak. Rare dancing too!
Alas, poor Bruin! How he foots the pole
And waddles round it with unwieldy steps,
Swaying from side to side! . . The dancing-master
Hath had as profitless a pupil in him
As when he would have tortured my poor toes
To minuet grace, and made them move like clockwork
In musical obedience. Bruin! Bruin!
Thou art but a clumsy biped! . . And the mob
With noisy merriment mock his heavy pace,
And laugh to see him led by the nose! . . themselves
Led by the nose, embruted, and in the eye
Of Reason from their Nature's purposes
As miserably perverted.

Bruin-Bear!
Now could I sonnetize thy piteous plight,
And prove how much my sympathetic heart
Even for the miseries of a beast can feel,
In fourteen lines of sensibility.
But we are told all things were made for Man;
And I'll be sworn there's not a fellow here
Who would not swear 'twere hanging blasphemy
To doubt that truth. Therefore as thou wert born,
Bruin! for Man, and Man makes nothing of thee
In any other way, . . . most logically
It follows, thou wert born to make him sport;
That that great snout of thine was form'd on purpose
To hold a ring; and that thy fat was given thee
For an approved pomatum!

To demur
Were heresy. And politicians say,
(Wise men who in the scale of reason give
No foolish feelings weight,) that thou art here
Far happier than thy brother Bears who roam
O'er trackless snow for food; that being born
Inferior to thy leader, unto him
Rightly belongs dominion; that the compact
Was made between ye, when thy clumsy feet
First fell into the snare, and he gave up
His right to kill, conditioning thy life
Should thenceforth be his property; . . besides,
'Tis wholesome for thy morals to be brought
From savage climes into a civilized state,
Into the decencies of Christendom. . . .
Bear! Bear! it passes in the Parliament
For excellent logic this! What if we say
How barbarously Man abuses power?
Talk of thy baiting, it will be replied,
Thy welfare is thy owner's interest,
But were thou baited it would injure thee,
Therefore thou are not baited. For seven years
Hear it, O Heaven, and give ear, O Earth!
For seven long years, this precious syllogism
Hath baffled justice and humanity!

Westbury, 1799.

The Filbert

Nay, gather not that Filbert, Nicholas,
There is a maggot there, . . it is his house, . .
His castle, . . oh commit not burglary!
Strip him not naked, . . 'tis his clothes, his shell,
His bones, the case and armour of his life,
And thou shalt do no murder, Nicholas!
It were an easy thing to crack that nut
Or with thy crackers or thy double teeth,
So easily may all things be destroy'd!
But 'tis not in the power of mortal man
To mend the fracture of a filbert shell.
There were two great men once amused themselves
Watching two maggots run their wriggling race,
And wagering on their speed; but Nick, to us
It were no sport to see the pamper'd worm
Roll out and then draw in his folds of fat,
Like to some Barber's leathern powder-bag
Wherewith he feathers, frosts, or cauliflowers
Spruce Beau, or Lady fair, or Doctor grave.
Enough of dangers and of enemies
Hath Nature's wisdom for the worm ordain'd,
Increase not thou the number! Him the Mouse
Gnawing with nibbling tooth the shell's defence,
May from his native tenement eject;
Him may the Nut-hatch, piercing with strong bill,
Unwittingly destroy; or to his hoard
The Squirrel bear, at leisure to be crack'd.
Man also hath his dangers and his foes
As this poor Maggot hath; and when I muse
Upon the aches, anxieties, and fears,
The Maggot knows not, Nicholas, methinks
It were a happy metamorphosis
To be enkernell'd thus: never to hear
Of wars, and of invasions, and of plots,
Kings, Jacobines, and Tax-commissioners;
To feel no motion but the wind that shook
The Filbert Tree, and rock'd us to our rest;
And in the middle of such exquisite food
To live luxurious! The perfection this

Of snugness! it were to unite at once
Hermit retirement, Aldermanic bliss,
And Stoic independence of mankind.

Westbury, 1799.

On a Picture by J. M. Wright, Esq

[Engraved for the Keepsake of 1829.]

The sky-lark hath perceived his prison-door
    Unclosed; for liberty the captive tries:
Puss eagerly hath watched him from the floor,
    And in her grasp he flutters, pants, and dies.

Lucy's own Puss, and Lucy's own dear Bird,
    Her foster'd favourites both for many a day.
That which the tender-hearted girl preferr'd,
    She in her fondness knew not sooth to say.

For if the sky-lark's pipe were shrill and strong,
    And its rich tones the thrilling ear might please,
Yet Pussybel could breathe a fireside song
    As winning, when she lay on Lucy's knees.

Both knew her voice, and each alike would seek
    Her eye, her smile, her fondling touch to gain:
How faintly then may words her sorrow speak,
    When by the one she sees the other slain.

The flowers fall scatter'd from her lifted hands;
    A cry of grief she utters in affright;
And self-condemn'd for negligence she stands
    Aghast and helpless at the cruel sight.

Come, Lucy, let me dry those tearful eyes;
    Take thou, dear child, a lesson not unholy,
From one whom nature taught to moralize
    Both in his mirth and in his melancholy.

I will not warn thee not to set thy heart
    Too fondly upon perishable things;
In vain the earnest preacher spends his art
    Upon that theme; in vain the poet sings.

It is our nature's strong necessity,
    And this the soul's unerring instincts tell:

Therefore I say, let us love worthily,
    Dear child, and then we cannot love too well.

Better it is all losses to deplore,
    Which dutiful affection can sustain,
Than that the heart should, in its inmost core,
    Harden without it, and have lived in vain.

This love which thou hast lavish'd, and the woe
    Which makes thy lip now quiver with distress,
Are but a vent, an innocent overflow,
    From the deep springs of female tenderness.

And something I would teach thee from the grief
    That thus hath fill'd those gentle eyes with tears,
The which may be thy sober, sure relief
    When sorrow visits thee in after years.

I ask not whither is the spirit flown
    That lit the eye which there in death is seal'd;
Our Father hath not made that mystery known;
    Needless the knowledge, therefore not reveal'd.

But didst thou know in sure and sacred truth,
    It had a place assign'd in yonder skies,
There through an endless life of joyous youth,
    To warble in the bowers of Paradise;

Lucy, if then the power to thee were given
    In that cold form its life to re-engage,
Wouldst thou call back the warbler from its Heaven,
    To be again the tenant of a cage?

Only that thou might'st cherish it again,
    Wouldst thou the object of thy love recall
To mortal life, and chance, and change, and pain,
    And death, which must be suffered once by all?

Oh, no, thou say'st: oh, surely not, not so!
    I read the answer which those looks express:
For pure and true affection well I know
    Leaves in the heart no room for selfishness.

Such love of all our virtues is the gem;
    We bring with us the immortal seed at birth:
Of heaven it is, and heavenly; woe to them
    Who make it wholly earthly and of earth!

What we love perfectly, for its own sake
　We love and not our own, being ready thus
Whate'er self-sacrifice is ask'd, to make;
　That which is best for it, is best for us.

O Lucy! Treasure up that pious thought!
　It hath a balm for sorrow's deadliest darts;
And with true comfort thou wilt find it fraught,
　If grief should reach thee in thy heart of hearts.

Buckland, 1828.

WALTER SAVAGE LANDOR
(1775-1864)

To a Spaniel

No, Daisy! lift not up thy ear,
It is not she whose steps draw near.
Tuck under thee that leg, for she
Continues yet beyond the sea,
And thou may'st whimper in thy sleep
These many days, and start and weep.

Lines to a Dragon-fly

Life (priest and poet say) is but a dream;
　　I wish no happier one than to be laid
　　Beneath a cool syringa's scented shade,
Or wavy willow, by the running stream,
　　Brimful of moral, where the dragon-fly,
　　Wanders as careless and content as I.
Thanks for this fancy, insect king,
Of purple crest and filmy wing,
Who with indifference givest up
The water-lily's golden cup,

(*Brimful of moral:* allusion to Shakespeare's "books in the running brooks"?)

To come again and overlook
What I am writing in my book.
Believe me, most who read the line
Will read with hornier eyes than thine;
And yet their souls shall live for ever,
And thine drop dead into the river!
God pardon them, O insect king,
Who fancy so unjust a thing!

David Koster

The Dead Marten

My pretty Marte, my winter friend,
In these bright days ought thine to end!
When all thy kindred far away
Enjoy the genial hours of May.
How often hast thou play'd with me,
And lickt my lip to share my tea,
And run away and turn'd again
To hide my glove or crack my pen,
Until I swore, to check thy taunts,
I'd write to uncles and to aunts,
And grandmama, whom dogs pursued
But could not catch her in the wood.
Ah! I repeat the jokes we had,
Yet think me not less fond, less sad.
Julia and Charles and Walter grave
Would throw down every toy they have
To see thy joyous eyes at eve,
And feel thy feet upon the sleeve,
And tempt thy glossy teeth to bite
And almost hurt them, but not quite;
For thou didst look, and then suspend
The ivory barbs, but reprehend
With tender querulous tones, that told
Thou wert too good and we too bold.
Never was malice in thy heart,
My gentlest, dearest little Marte!
Nor grief, nor reason to repine,
As there is now in this of mine.

THOMAS CAMPBELL
(1777-1844)

The Parrot

The following incident, so strongly illustrating the power of memory and association in the lower animals, is not a fiction. I heard it many years ago in the Island of Mull, from the family to whom the bird belonged.—T.C.

The deep affections of the breast
    That Heaven to living things imparts
Are not exclusively possess'd
    By human hearts.

A parrot from the Spanish Main,
    Full young and early cag'd, came o'er
With bright wings to the bleak domain
    Of Mulla's shore.

To spicy groves where he had won
    His plumage of resplendent hue,
His native fruits and skies and sun,
    He bade adieu.

For these he changed the smoke of turf,
    A heathery land and misty sky,
And turn'd on rocks and raging surf
    His golden eye.

But, petted, in our climate cold
    He lived and chatter'd many a day;
Until with age from green and gold
    His wings grew gray.

At last, when blind and seeming dumb,
    He scolded, laughed, and spoke no more,
A Spanish stranger chanced to come
    To Mulla's shore;

He hailed the bird in Spanish speech;
    The bird in Spanish speech replied,
Flapped round his cage with joyous screech,
    Dropt down, and died.

JANE TAYLOR
(1783-1824)

The Pigs

"Do look at those pigs as they lie in the straw,"
    Said Dick to his father, one day;
"They keep eating longer than ever I saw,
    What nasty fat gluttons are they."

"I see they are feasting," his father reply'd,
    "They eat a great deal I allow;
But let us remember, before we deride,
    'Tis the nature, my dear, of a sow.

"But when a great boy, such as you, my dear Dick,
    Does nothing but eat all the day,
And keeps sucking good things till he makes himself sick,
    What a glutton! indeed, we may say.

"When plumcake and sugar for ever he picks,
    And sweetmeats, and comfits, and figs;
Pray let him get rid of his own nasty tricks,
    And then he may laugh at the pigs."

LEIGH HUNT
(1784-1859)

On Seeing a Pigeon Make Love

Is not the picture strangely like?
Doesn't the very bowing strike?
Can any art of love in fashion
Express a more prevailing passion?
That air—that sticking to her side—
That deference, ill-concealing pride,—
That seeming consciousness of coat,
And repetition of one note,—
Ducking and tossing back his head,
As if at every bow he said,
"Madam, by God",—or "Strike me dead".

And then the lady! look at her:
What bridling sense of character!
How she declines, and seems to go,
Yet still endures him to and fro;
Carrying her plumes and pretty clothings,
Blushing stare, and muttered nothings,
Body plump, and airy feet,
Like any charmer in a street.

Give him a hat beneath his wing,
And is not he the very thing?
Give her a parasol or plaything,
And is not she the very she-thing?

The Fish, the Man, and the Spirit

To a Fish

You strange, astonished-looking, angle-faced,
    Dreary-mouthed, gaping wretches of the sea,
    Gulping salt water everlastingly,
Cold-blooded, though with red your blood be graced,
And mute, though dwellers in the roaring waste;
    And you, all shapes beside, that fishy be,—
    Some round, some flat, some long, all devilry,
Legless, unloving, infamously chaste:—

O scaly, slippery, wet, swift, staring wights,
    What is't ye do? What life lead? eh, dull goggles?
How do ye vary your vile days and nights?
    How pass your Sundays? Are ye still but joggles
In ceaseless wash? Still nought but gapes, and bites,
    And drinks, and stares, diversified with boggles?

A Fish Answers

Amazing monster! that, for aught I know,
    With the first sight of thee didst make our race
    For ever stare! O flat and shocking face,
Grimly divided from the breast below!
Thou that on dry land horribly dost go
    With a split body and most ridiculous pace,
    Prong after prong, disgracer of all grace,
Long-useless-finned, haired, upright, unwet, slow!

123

R.H. BARHAM

O breather of unbreathable, sword-sharp air,
  How canst exist? How bear thyself, thou dry
And dreary sloth? What particle canst share
  Of the only blessed life, the watery?
I sometimes see of ye an actual *pair*
  Go by! linked fin by fin! most odiously.

**The Fish turns into a Man, and then into a Spirit,
and again speaks**

Indulge thy smiling scorn, if smiling still,
  O man! and loathe, but with a sort of love;
For difference must its use by difference prove,
And, in sweet clang, the spheres with music fill.
One of the spirits am I, that at his will
  Live in whate'er has life—fish, eagle, dove—
No hate, no pride, beneath nought, nor above,
A visitor of the rounds of God's sweet skill.

Man's life is warm, glad, sad, 'twixt loves and graves,
  Boundless in hope, honoured with pangs austere,
Heaven-gazing; and his angel-wings he craves:—
  The fish is swift, small-needing, vague yet clear,
A cold, sweet, silver life, wrapped in round waves,
  Quickened with touches of transporting fear.

R.H. BARHAM
(1788-1845)

The Cynotaph

> Poor Tray charmant!
> Poor Tray de mon Ami!
> Dog-bury and Vergers.

Oh! where shall I bury my poor dog Tray,
Now his fleeting breath has passed away?—
Seventeen years, I can venture to say,
Have I seen him gambol, and frolic, and play,
Evermore happy, and frisky, and gay,
As though every one of his months was May,
And the whole of his life one long holiday—
Now he's a lifeless lump of clay,
Oh! where shall I bury my faithful Tray?

R.H. BARHAM

I am almost tempted to think it hard
That it may not be there, in yon sunny churchyard,
    Where the green willows wave
    O'er the peaceful grave,
Which holds all that once was honest and brave,
Kind, and courteous, and faithful, and true;
Qualities, Tray, that were found in you.
But it may not be—yon sacred ground
By holiest feelings fenced around,
May ne'er within its hallow'd bound
Receive the dust of a soul-less hound.

I would not place him in yonder fane,
Where the mid-day sun through the storied pane
Throws on the pavement a crimson stain;
Where the banners of chivalry heavily swing
O'er the pinnacled tomb of the Warrior King,
With helmet and shield, and all that sort of thing.
    No!—come what may,
    My gentle Tray
Shan't be an intruder on bluff Harry Tudor,
Or panoplied monarchs yet earlier and ruder
    Whom you see on their backs,
    In stone or in wax,
Though the Sacristans now are "forbidden to ax"
For what Mr. Hume calls "a scandalous tax;"
While the Chartists insist they've a right to go snacks.—
No!—Tray's humble tomb would look but shabby
'Mid the sculptured shrines of that gorgeous Abbey.
    Besides, in the place
    They say there's not space
To bury what wet-nurses call "a Babby."
Even "Rare Ben Jonson," that famous wight,
I am told, is interr'd there bolt upright,
In just such a posture, beneath his bust,
As Tray used to sit in to beg for a crust.
    The epitaph, too,
    Would scarcely do:
For what could it say, but, "Here lies Tray,
A very good kind of a dog in his day?"
And satirical folks might be apt to imagine it
Meant as a quiz on the House of Plantagenet.

No! no!—The Abbey may do very well
For a feudal "Nob," or poetical "Swell,"
"Crusaders," or "Poets," or "Knights of St. John,"
Or Knights of St. John's Wood, who once went on
To the Castle of Goode Lorde Eglintonne.
Count Fiddle-fumkin, and Lord Fiddle-faddle,
"Sir Craven," "Sir Gael," and "Sir Campbell of Saddell,"
(Who, as poor Hook said, when he heard of the feat,
"Was somehow knock'd out of his family-seat:")
      The Esquires of the body
      To my Lord Tomnoddy;
"Sir Fairlie," "Sir Lamb,"
And the "Knight of the Ram,"
The "Knight of the Rose," and the "Knight of the Dragon,"
      Who, save at the flagon,
      And prog in the wagon,
The newspapers tell us did little "to brag on;"

And more, though the Muse knows but little concerning 'em,
"Sir Hopkins," "Sir Popkins," "Sir Gage," and "Sir Jerningham.

All *Preux Chevaliers*, in friendly rivalry
Who should best bring back the glory of Chi-valry.—
—(Pray be so good, for the sake of my song,
To pronounce here the ante-penultimate long;
Or some hyper-critic will certainly cry,
"The word 'Chivalry' is but a rhyme to the eye."
      And I own it is clear
      A fastidious ear
Will be, more or less, always annoy'd with you when you
Insert any rhyme that's not perfectly genuine.
      As to pleasing the "eye,"
      'Tisn't worth while to try,
Since Moore and Tom Campbell themselves admit "Spinach"
Is perfectly antiphonetic to "Greenwich.")—
But stay!—I say!
Let me pause while I may—
This digression is leading me sadly astray
From my object—A grave for my poor dog Tray!

I would not place him beneath thy walls,
And proud o'ershadowing dome, St. Paul's!
Though I've always consider'd Sir Christopher Wren,
As an architect, one of the greatest of men;

And, talking of Epitaphs,—much I admire his,
"Circumspice, si Monumentum requiris;"
Which an erudite Verger translated to me,
"If you ask for his monument, *Sir-come-spy-see!"*—
    No!—I should not know where
    To place him there;
I would not have him by surly Johnson be;—
Or that queer-looking horse that is rolling on Ponsonby;—
    Or those ugly minxes
    The sister Sphynxes,
Mix'd creatures, half lady, half lioness, *ergo*,
(Denon says,) the emblems of *Leo* and *Virgo*;
On one of the backs of which singular jumble,
Sir Ralph Abercrombie is going to tumble,
With a thump which alone were enough to dispatch him,
If the Scotchman in front shouldn't happen to catch him.

No! I'd not have him there, —nor nearer the door,
Where the man and the Angel have got Sir John Moore,
And are quietly letting him down through the floor,
By Gillespie, the one who escaped, at Vellore,
    Alone from the row;—
    Neither he, nor Lord Howe
Would like to be plagued with a little Bow-wow.
    No, Tray, we must yield,
    And go further a-field;
To lay you by Nelson were downright effront'ry;
—We'll be off from the City, and look at the country.

    It shall not be there,
    In that sepulchred square,
Where folks are interr'd for the sake of the air,
(Though, pay but the dues, they could hardly refuse
To Tray what they grant to Thuggs, and Hindoos,
Turks, Infidels, Heretics, Jumpers, and Jews,)
    Where the tombstones are placed
    In the very *best taste*,
    At the feet and the head
    Of the elegant Dead,
And no one's received who's not "buried in lead:"
For, there lie the bones of Deputy Jones,
Whom the widow's tears, and the orphan's groans
Affected as much as they do the stones
His executors laid on the Deputy's bones;

R.H. BARHAM

Little rest, poor knave!
Would Tray have in his grave;
Since Spirits, 'tis plain,
Are sent back again,
To roam round their bodies,—the bad ones in pain,—
Dragging after them sometimes a heavy jack-chain;
Whenever they met, alarm'd by its groans, his
Ghost all night long would be barking at Jones's.

Nor shall he be laid
By that cross Old Maid,
Miss Penelope Bird,—of whom it is said
All the dogs in the parish were ever afraid.
He must not be placed
By one so strait-laced
In her temper, her taste, her morals, and waist.

For, 'tis said, when she went up to Heaven, and St. Peter,
Who happened to meet her,
Came forward to greet her,
She pursed up with scorn every vinegar feature,
And bade him "Get out for a horrid Male Creature!"
So, the Saint, after looking as if he could eat her,
Not knowing, perhaps, very well how to treat her,
And not being willing—or able,— to beat her,
Sent her back to her grave till her temper grew sweeter,
With an epithet which I decline to repeat here.
No,—if Tray were interr'd
By Penelope Bird,
No dog would be e'er so be-"whelp" 'd and be-"cur" 'r'd—
All the night long her cantankerous Sprite
Would be running about in the pale moon-light,
Chasing him round, and attempting to lick
The ghost of poor Tray with the ghost of a stick.

Stay!— let me see!—
Ay—here it shall be
At the root of this gnarled and time-worn tree,
Where Tray and I
Would often lie,
And watch the bright clouds as they floated by
In the broad expanse of the clear blue sky,
When the sun was bidding the world good-bye;
And the plaintive Nightingale, warbling nigh,

Pour'd forth her mournful melody;
While the tender Wood-pigeon's cooing cry
Has made me say to myself, with a sigh,
"How nice you would eat with a steak in a pie!"

Ay, here it shall be!—far, far from the view
Of the noisy world and its maddening crew.
    Simple and few,
    Tender and true
The lines o'er his grave.—They have, some of them, too,
The advantage of being remarkably new.

Epitaph.

Affliction sore
Long time he bore,
Physicians were in vain!—
Grown blind, alas! he'd
Some Prussic Acid,
And that put him out of his pain!

Cynotaph: pun on 'cenotaph' (cyno = dog); *go snacks:* have a share
n; *prog in the wagon:* food for the journey.)

JOHN CLARE
(1793-1864)

"The badger grunting on his woodland track"

The badger grunting on his woodland track
With shaggy hide and sharp nose scrowed with black
Roots in the bushes and the woods and makes
A great hugh burrow in the ferns and brakes
With nose on ground he runs a awkard pace
And anything will beat him in the race
The shepherds dog will run him to his den
Followed and hooted by the dogs and men
The woodman when the hunting comes about
Go round at night to stop the foxes out

And hurrying through the bushes ferns and brakes
Nor sees the many hol[e]s the badger makes
And often through the bushes to the chin
Breaks the old holes and tumbles headlong in

When midnight comes a host of dogs and men
Go out and track the badger to his den
And put a sack within the hole and lye
Till the old grunting badger passes bye
He comes and hears they let the strongest loose
The old fox hears the noise and drops the goose
The poacher shoots and hurrys from the cry
And the old hare half wounded buzzes bye
They get a forked stick to bear him down
And clapt the dogs and bore him to the town
And bait him all the day with many dogs
And laugh and shout and fright the scampering hogs
He runs along and bites at all he meets
They shout and hollo down the noisey streets

He turns about to face the loud uproar
And drives the rebels to their very doors
The frequent stone is hurled where ere they go
When badgers fight and every ones a foe
The dogs are clapt and urged to join the fray
The badger turns and drives them all away
Though scarcly half as big dimute and small
He fights with dogs for hours and beats them all
The heavy mastiff savage in the fray
Lies down and licks his feet and turns away
The bull dog knows his match and waxes cold
The badger grins and never leaves his hold
He drive[s] the crowd and follows at their heels
And bites them through the drunkard swears and reels
The frighted women takes the boys away
The blackguard laughs and hurrys on the fray
He tries to reach the woods a awkard race
But sticks and cudgels quickly stop the chace
He turns agen and drives the noisey crowd
And beats the many dogs in noises loud
He drives away and beats them every one
And then they loose them all and set them on
He falls as dead and kicked by boys and men
Then starts and grins and drives the crowd agen

David Koster

Till kicked and torn and beaten out he lies
And leaves his hold and cackles groans and dies

Some keep a baited badger tame as hog
And tame him till he follows like the dog
They urge him on like dogs and show fair play
He beats and scarcely wounded goes away
Lapt up as if asleep he scorns to fly
And siezes any dog that ventures nigh
Clapt like a dog he never bites the men
But worrys dogs and hurrys to his den
They let him out and turn a harrow down
And there he fights the host of all the town
He licks the patting hand and trys to play
And never trys to bite or run away
And runs away from noise in hollow trees
Burnt by the boys to get a swarm of bees

(*scrowed:* striped; *dimute:* diminutive.)

"The martin cat long shaged of courage good"

The martin cat long shaged of courage good
Of weazle shape a dweller in the wood
With badger hair long shagged and darting eyes
And lower then the common cat in size
Small head and running on the stoop
Snuffing the ground and hind parts shouldered up
He keeps one track and hides in lonely shade
Where print of human foot is scarcely made
Save when the woods are cut the beaten track
The woodmans dog will snuff cock tailed and black
Red legged and spotted over either eye
Snuffs barks and scrats the lice and passes bye
The great brown horned owl looks down below
And sees the shaggy martin come and go

The martin hurrys through the woodland gaps
And poachers shoot and make his skin for caps
When any woodman come and pass the place
He looks at dogs and scarcely mends his pace
And gipseys often and birdnesting boys
Look in the hole and hear a hissing noise

They climb the tree such noise they never heard
And think the great owl is a foreign bird
When the grey owl her young ones cloathed in down
Seizes the boldest boy and drives him down
They try agen and pelt to start the fray
The grey owl comes and drives them all away
And leaves the martin twisting round his den
Left free from boys and dogs and noise and men

(*martin cat:* wild cat; *shaged:* shagged, rough haired.)

JOHN KEATS
(1795-1821)

"I had a dove and the sweet dove died"

I had a dove and the sweet dove died;
    And I have thought it died of grieving:
Oh, what could it grieve for? Its feet were tied,
    With a silken thread of my own hand's weaving;
Sweet little red feet! why should you die —
Why should you leave me, sweet dove! why?
You liv'd alone on the forest-tree,
Why, pretty thing! could you not live with me?
I kiss'd you oft and gave you white peas;
Why not live sweetly, as in the green trees?

On Mrs Reynolds's Cat

Cat! who hast pass'd thy grand climacteric,
    How many mice and rats hast in thy days
    Destroy'd? — How many tit bits stolen? Gaze
With those bright languid segments green, and prick
Those velvet ears — but pr'ythee do not stick
    Thy latent talons in me — and upraise
    Thy gentle mew — and tell me all thy frays
Of fish and mice, and rats and tender chick.
Nay, look not down, nor lick thy dainty wrists —
    For all the wheezy asthma, — and for all
Thy tail's tip is nick'd off — and though the fists
    Of many a maid have given thee many a maul,
Still is that fur as soft as when the lists
    In youth thou enter'dst on glass-bottled wall.

GEORGE DARLEY
(1795-1846)

"Speckle-black Toad and freckle-green Frog"
Song from *Thomas à Becket, a Dramatic Chronicle*

Speckle-black Toad and freckle-green Frog,
Hopping together from quag to bog;
From pool into puddle
Right on they huddle;
Through thick and through thin,
Without tail or fin;
Croakle goes first and *Quackle* goes after,
Plash in the flood
And plump in the mud,
With slippery heels
Vaulting over the eels,
And mouths to their middles split down
    with laughter!
    Hu! hu! hex!

HARTLEY COLERIDGE
(1796-1849)

To a Cat

Nelly, methinks, 'twixt thee and me
There is a kind of sympathy;
And could we interchange our nature,—
If I were cat, thou human creature,—

I should, like thee, be no great mouser,
And thou, like me, no great composer;
For, like thy plaintive mews, my muse
With villainous whine doth fate abuse,
Because it hath not made me sleek
As golden down on Cupid's cheek;
And yet thou canst upon the rug lie,
Stretch'd out like snail, or curl'd up snugly,
As if thou wert not lean or ugly;
And I, who in poetic flights
Sometimes complain of sleepless nights,
Regardless of the sun in heaven,
Am apt to dose till past eleven,—
The world would just the same go round
If I were hang'd and thou wert drown'd;
There is one difference, 'tis true,—
Thou dost not know it, and I do.

THOMAS HOOD
(1799-1845)

Address to Mr Cross, of Exeter 'Change On the Death of the Elephant

"Tis Greece, but living *Greece* no more" *Giaour.*

   Oh, Mr Cross!
Permit a sorry stranger to draw near,
   And shed a tear
(I've shed my shilling) for thy recent loss!
   I've been a visitor,
Of old, a sort of a Buffon inquisitor
Of thy menagerie—and knew the beast
   That is deceased!—
I was the Damon of the gentle giant,
   And oft have been,
   Like Mr Kean,
Tenderly fondled by his trunk compliant;
Whenever I approach'd, the kindly brute
Flapp'd his prodigious ears, and bent his knees,—
   It makes me freeze

To think of it!—No chums could better suit,
Exchanging grateful looks for grateful fruit,—
For so our former dearness was begun.
I bribed him with an apple, and beguiled
The beast of his affection like a child;
And well he loved me till his life was done
    (Except when he was wild):
It makes me blush for human friends—but none
I have so truly kept or cheaply won!

    Here is his pen!—
The casket,—but the jewel is away!—
The den is rifled of its denizen—
    Ah, well a day!
This fresh free air breathes nothing of his grossness,
And sets me sighing, even for its closeness.
    This light one-storey
Where, like a cloud, I used to feast my eyes on
The grandeur of his Titan-like horizon,
Tells a dark tale of its departed glory.
The very beasts lament the change, like me;
    The shaggy Bison
Leaneth his head dejected on his knee!
Th' Hyæna's laugh is hush'd, and Monkey's pout,
The Wild Cat frets in a complaining whine,
The Panther paces restlessly about,
    To walk her sorrow out;
The Lions in a deeper bass repine,—
The Kangaroo wrings its sorry short fore paws,
    Shrieks come from the Macaws;
The old bald Vulture shakes his naked head,
    And pineth for the dead,
The Boa writhes into a double knot,
    The Keeper groans
    Whilst sawing bones,
And looks askance at the deserted spot—
Brutal and rational lament his loss,
The flower of thy beastly family!
    Poor Mrs Cross
Sheds frequent tears into her daily tea,
    And weakens her Bohea!

O Mr Cross, how little it gives birth
To grief, when human greatness goes to earth;

How few lament for Czars!—
But oh the universal heart o'erflow'd
 At his high mass,
 Lighted by gas,
When, like Mark Antony, the keeper show'd
 The Elephant scars!—
 Reporters' eyes
 Were of an egg-like size,
Men that had never wept for murder'd Marrs!
Hard-hearted editors, with iron faces
 Their sluices all unclosed,—
 And discomposed
Compositors went fretting to their cases!—
 That grief has left its traces:
The poor old Beef-eater has gone much greyer
 With sheer regret,
 And the Gazette
Seems the least trouble of the beast's Purveyor!

Well! he is dead!
And there's a gap in Nature of eleven
 Feet high by seven—
Five living tons!—and I remain—nine stone
 Of skin and bone!
It is enough to make me shake my head
 And dream of the grave's brink—
 'Tis worse to think
How like the Beast's the sorry life *I've* led!—
 A sort of show
Of my poor public self and my sagacity,
 To profit the rapacity
Of certain folks in Paternoster Row,
A slavish toil to win an upper story—
 And a hard glory
Of wooden beams about my weary brow!
 Oh, Mr C.!
If ever you behold me twirl my pen
To earn a public supper, that is, eat
 In the bare street,—
Or turn about their literary den—
 Shoot *me*!

WILLIAM BARNES
(1801-1886)

Sheep in the Sheade

In zummertide, I took my road
    Vrom stile to stile, vrom ground to ground,
The while the burnen zunsheen glow'd
    On leäze an' mead, wi' grass a-brown'd,
Where slowly round a wide-bent bow
The stream did wind, that glided low,
In hopevul hours, a-gliden on,
In happiness, too soon a-gone.

An' there below the elem shroud,
    Vor coolness vrom the burnen glow,
A vlock o' panken sheep did crowd
    Within the sheäpe the sheäde did show,
A-wheelen slowly on an' on,
Till they did lie, wi' sheäde a-gone.
An' oh! that happy hours should glide
Away so soon, an' never bide.

anken: panting. The spelling throughout indicates Dorset dialect
ronunciation.)

RALPH WALDO EMERSON
(1803-1882)

The Humble-Bee

Burly, dozing humble-bee,
Where thou art is clime for me.
Let them sail for Porto Rique,
Far-off heats through seas to seek;
I will follow thee alone,
Thou animated torrid-zone!
Zigzag steerer, desert cheerer,
Let me chase thy waving lines:
Keep me nearer, me thy hearer,
Singing over shrubs and vines.

Insect lover of the sun,
Joy of thy dominion!
Sailor of the atmosphere;
Swimmer through the waves of air;
Voyager of light and noon;
Epicurean of June;
Wait, I prithee, till I come
Within earshot of thy hum,—
All without is martyrdom.

When the south wind, in May days,
With a net of shining haze
Silvers the horizon wall,
And the softness touching all,
Tints the human countenance
With a color of romance,
And infusing subtle heats,
Turns the sod to violets,
Thou, in sunny solitudes,
Rover of the underwoods,
The green silence dost displace
With thy mellow, breezy bass.

Hot midsummer's petted crone,
Sweet to me thy drowsy tone
Tells of countless sunny hours,
Long days, and solid banks of flowers;
Of gulfs of sweetness without bound
In Indian wildernesses found;
Of Syrian peace, immortal leisure,
Firmest cheer, and bird-like pleasure.

Aught unsavory or unclean
Hath my insect never seen;
But violets and bilberry bells,
Maple-sap and daffodels,
Grass with green flag half-mast high,
Succory to match the sky.
Columbine with horn of honey,
Scented fern, and agrimony,

Clover, catchfly, adder's-tongue
And brier-roses, dwelt among;
All beside was unknown waste,
All was picture as he passed.

Wiser far than human seer,
Yellow-breeched philosopher!
Seeing only what is fair,
Sipping only what is sweet,
Thou dost mock at fate and care,
Leave the chaff, and take the wheat.
When the fierce northwestern blast
Cools sea and land so far and fast,
Thou already slumberest deep;
Woe and want thou canst outsleep;
Want and woe, which torture us,
Thy sleep makes ridiculous.

The Miracle

I have trod this path a hundred times
With idle footsteps, crooning rhymes.
I know each nest and web-worm's tent,
The fox-hole which the woodchucks rent,
Maple and oak, the old Divan
Self-planted twice, like the banian.
I know not why I came again
Unless to learn it ten times ten.
To read the sense the woods impart
You must bring the throbbing heart.
Love is aye the counterforce,—
Terror and Hope and wild Remorse,
Newest knowledge, fiery thought,
Or Duty to grand purpose wrought.
    Wandering yester morn the brake,
I reached this heath beside the lake,
And oh, the wonder of the power,
The deeper secret of the hour!
Nature, the supplement of man,
His hidden sense interpret can;—
What friend to friend cannot convey
Shall the dumb bird instructed say.

Passing yonder oak, I heard
Sharp accents of my woodland bird;
I watched the singer with delight,—
But mark what changed my joy to fright,—
When that bird sang, I gave the theme,
That wood-bird sang my last night's dream,
A brown wren was the Daniel
That pierced my trance its drift to tell,
Knew my quarrel, how and why,
Published it to lake and sky,
Told every word and syllable
In his flippant chirping babble,
All my wrath and all my shames,
Nay, God is witness, gave the names.

Limits

Who knows this or that?
Hark in the wall to the rat:
Since the world was, he has gnawed;
Of his wisdom, of his fraud
What dost thou know?
In the wretched little beast
Is life and heart,
Child and parent,
Not without relation
To fruitful field and sun and moon.
What art thou? His wicked eye
Is cruel to thy cruelty.

THOMAS LOVELL BEDDOES
(1803-1849)

"Hard by the lilied Nile I saw"

(Fragment from a play)

Hard by the lilied Nile I saw
A duskish river-dragon stretched along,
The brown habergeon of his limbs enamelled
With sanguine almandines and rainy pearl:
And on his back there lay a young one sleeping,

David Koster

No bigger than a mouse; with eyes like beads,
And a small fragment of its speckled egg
Remaining on its harmless, pulpy snout;
A thing to laugh at, as it gaped to catch
The baulking merry flies. In the iron jaws
Of the great devil-beast, like a pale soul
Fluttering in rocky hell, lightsomely flew
A snowy trochilus, with roseate beak
Tearing the hairy leeches from his throat.

Sonnet

To Tartar, a Terrier Beauty.

Snowdrop of dogs, with ear of brownest dye,
Like the last orphan leaf of naked tree
Which shudders in bleak autumn; though by thee,
Of hearing careless and untutored eye,
Not understood articulate speech of men,
Nor marked the artificial mind of books,
—The mortal's voice eternized by the pen,—
Yet hast thou thought and language all unknown
To Babel's scholars; oft intensest looks,
Long scrutiny o'er some dark-veined stone
Dost thou bestow, learning dead mysteries
Of the world's birth-day, oft in eager tone
With quick-tailed fellows bandiest prompt replies,
Solicitudes canine, four-footed amities.

ELIZABETH BARRETT BROWNING (1806-1861)

Flush or Faunus

You see this dog; it was but yesterday
I mused forgetful of his presence here,
Till thought on thought drew downward tear on tear:
When from the pillow where wet-cheeked I lay,
A head as hairy as Faunus thrust its way
Right sudden against my face, two golden-clear
Great eyes astonished mine, a drooping ear

Did flap me on either cheek to dry the spray!
I started first as some Arcadian
Amazed by goatly god in twilight grove:
But as the bearded vision closelier ran
My tears off, I knew Flush, and rose above
Surprise and sadness, — thanking the true PAN
Who by low creatures leads to heights of love.

HENRY WADSWORTH LONGFELLOW
(1807-1882)

From *The Song of Hiawatha*

When he heard the owls at midnight,
Hooting, laughing in the forest,
"What is that?" he cried in terror;
"What is that?" he said, "Nokomis?"
And the good Nokomis answered:
"That is but the owl and owlet,
Talking in their native language,
Talking, scolding at each other."
Then the little Hiawatha
Learned of every bird its language,
Learned their names and all their secrets,
How they built their nests in Summer,
Where they hid themselves in Winter,
Talked with them whene'er he met them,
Called them "Hiawatha's Chickens."
Of all beasts he learned the language,
Learned their names and all their secrets,
How the beavers built their lodges,
Where the squirrels hid their acorns,
How the reindeer ran so swiftly,
Why the rabbit was so timid,
Talked with them whene'er he met them,
Called them "Hiawatha's Brothers."
Then Iagoo, the great boaster,
He the marvellous story-teller,
He the traveller and the talker,
He the friend of old Nokomis,

Made a bow for Hiawatha;
From a branch of ash he made it,
From an oak-bough made the arrows,
Tipped with flint, and winged with feathers,
And the cord he made of deer-skin.
Then he said to Hiawatha:
"Go, my son, into the forest,
Where the red deer herd together,
Kill for us a famous roebuck,
Kill for us a deer with antlers!"
Forth into the forest straightway
All alone walked Hiawatha
Proudly, with his bow and arrows;
And the birds sang round him, o'er him,
"Do not shoot us, Hiawatha!"
Sang the robin, the Opechee,
Sang the bluebird, the Owaissa,
"Do not shoot us, Hiawatha!"
Up the oak-tree, close beside him,
Sprang the squirrel, Adjidaumo,
In and out among the branches,
Coughed and chattered from the oak-tree,
Laughed and said between his laughing,
"Do not shoot me, Hiawatha!"
And the rabbit from his pathway
Leaped aside, and at a distance
Sat erect upon his haunches,
Half in fear and half in frolic,
Saying to the little hunter,
"Do not shoot me, Hiawatha!"
But he heeded not, or heard them,
For his thoughts were with the red deer;
On their tracks his eyes were fastened,
Leading downward to the river,
To the ford across the river,
And as one in slumber walked he.
Hidden in the alder-bushes,
There he waited till the deer came,
Till he saw two antlers lifted,
Saw two eyes look from the thicket,
Saw two nostrils point to windward,
And a deer came down the pathway,
Flecked with leafy light and shadow.

And his heart within him fluttered,
Trembled like the leaves above him,
Like the birch-leaf palpitated,
As the deer came down the pathway.
    Then, upon one knee uprising,
Hiawatha aimed an arrow;
Scarce a twig moved with his motion,
Scarce a leaf was stirred or rustled;
But the wary roebuck started,
Stamped with all his hoofs together,
Listened with one foot uplifted,
Leaped as if to meet the arrow;
Ah! the singing, fatal arrow,
Like a wasp it buzzed and stung him!
    Dead he lay there in the forest,
By the ford across the river;
Beat his timid heart no longer,
But the heart of Hiawatha
Throbbed and shouted and exulted,
As he bore the red deer homeward,
And Iagoo and Nokomis
Hailed his coming with applauses.
    From the red deer's hide Nokomis
Made a cloak for Hiawatha,
From the red deer's flesh Nokomis
Made a banquet in his honour.
All the village came and feasted,
All the guests praised Hiawatha,
Called him Strong-Heart, Soan-ge-taha!
Called him Loon-Heart, Mahn-go-taysee!

CHARLES TENNYSON TURNER
(1808-1879)

The Lion's Skeleton

How long, O lion, hast thou fleshless lain?
What rapt thy fierce and thirsty eyes away?
First came the vulture: worms, heat, wind, and rain
Ensued, and ardors of the tropic day.

I know not—if they spared it thee—how long
The canker sate within thy monstrous mane,
Till it fell piecemeal, and bestrew'd the plain;
Or, shredded by the storming sands, was flung
Again to earth; but now thine ample front,
Whereon the great frowns gather'd, is laid bare;
The thunders of thy throat, which erst were wont
To scare the desert, are no longer there;
Thy claws remain, but worms, wind, rain, and heat
Have sifted out the substance of thy feet.

The Vacant Cage

Our little bird in his full day of health
With his gold-coated beauty made us glad,
But when disease approach'd with cruel stealth,
A sadder interest our smiles forbad.
How oft we watch'd him, when the night hours came,
His poor head buried near his bursting heart,
Which beat within a puft and troubled frame;
But he has gone at last, and play'd his part:
The seed-glass, slighted by his sickening taste,
The little moulted feathers, saffron-tipt,
The fountain, where his fever'd bill was dipt,
The perches, which his failing feet embraced,
All these remain—not even his bath removed—
But where's the spray and flutter that we loved?

He shall not be cast out like wild-wood things!
We will not spurn those delicate remains;
No heat shall blanch his plumes, nor soaking rains
Shall wash the saffron from his little wings;
Nor shall he be inearth'd—but in his cage
Stand, with his innocent beauty unimpair'd;
And all the skilled'st hand can do, to assuage
Poor Dora's grief, by more than Dora shared,
Shall here be done. What though these orbs of glass
Will feebly represent his merry look
Of recognition, when he saw her pass,
Or from her palm the melting cherry took—
Yet the artist's kindly craft shall not retain
The filming eye, and beak that gasp'd with pain.

CHARLES TENNYSON TURNER

Minnie and her Dove

Two days she miss'd her dove, and then alas!
A knot of soft gray feathers met her view,
So light, their stirring hardly broke the dew
That hung on the blue violets and the grass;
A kite had struck her fondling as he pass'd;
And o'er that fleeting, downy, epitaph
The poor child linger'd, weeping; her gay laugh
Was mute that day, her little heart o'ercast.
Ah! Minnie, if thou livest, thou wilt prove
Intenser pangs—less tearful, though less brief;
Thou'lt weep for dearer death and sweeter love,
And spiritual woe, of woes the chief,
Until the full-grown wings of human grief
Eclipse thy memory of the kite and dove.

Maggie's Star

*To the White Star on the forehead of a
favourite old Mare.*

White star! that travellest at old Maggie's pace
About my field, where'er a wandering mouth,
And foot, that slowly shifts from place to place,
Conduct thee,—East or West, or North or South;
A loving eye is my best chart to find
Thy whereabouts at dawn or dusk; but when
She dreams at noon, with heel a-tilt behind,
And pendent lip, I mark thee fairest then;
I see thee dip and vanish, when she rolls
On earth, supine; then with one rousing shake
Reculminate; but, most, thou lovest to take
A quiet onward course—Heaven's law controls
The mild, progressive motion thou dost make,
Albeit thy path is scarce above the mole's.

A Summer Night in the Beehive

The little bee returns with evening's gloom,
To join her comrades in the braided hive,
Where, housed beside their mighty honeycomb,
They dream their polity shall long survive.
Still falls the summer night—the browsing horse
Fills the low portal with a grassy sound
From the near paddock, while the water-course
Sends them sweet murmurs from the meadow-ground;
None but such peaceful noises break the hush,
Save Pussy, growling, in the thyme and sage,
Over the thievish mouse, in happy rage:
At last, the flowers against the threshold brush
In morning airs—fair shines the uprisen sun
Another day of honey has begun!

The Bee-wisp

Our window-panes enthral our summer bees;
(To insect woes I give this little page)—
We hear them threshing in their idle rage
Those crystal floors of famine, while, at ease,
Their outdoor comrades probe the nectaries
Of flowers, and into all sweet blossoms dive;
Then home, at sundown, to the happy hive,
On forward wing, straight through the dancing flies:
For such poor strays a full-plumed wisp I keep,
And when I see them pining, worn, and vext,
I brush them softly with a downward sweep
To the raised sash—all anger'd and perplext:
So man, the insect, stands on his defence
Against the very hand of Providence.

On Finding a Small Fly Crushed in a Book

Some hand, that never meant to do thee hurt,
Has crush'd thee here between these pages pent;
But thou has left thine own fair monument,
Thy wings gleam out and tell me what thou wert:
Oh! that the memories, which survive us here,
Were half as lovely as these wings of thine!
Pure relics of a blameless life, that shine

Now thou art gone. Our doom is ever near;
The peril is beside us day by day;
The book will close upon us, it may be,
Just as we lift ourselves to soar away
Upon the summer-airs. But, unlike thee,
The closing book may stop our vital breath,
Yet leave no lustre on our page of death.

On Some Humming-birds in a Glass Case

For vacant song behold a shining theme!
The dumb-struck flutterers from Indian land,
The colour on whose crests, sweet Nature's hand,
Fulfils our richest thought of crimson gleam;
Whose wings, thus spread and balanced forth, might seem
Slender as serpent's tongue or fairy's wand—
And, as with vantage of the sun we stand,
Each glossy bosom kindles in his beam;
Ah me! how soon does human death impair
The tender beauty of the fairest face,
Whatever balms and unguents we prepare!
While these resplendent creatures bear no trace,
Bright-bosom'd and bright-crested as they are,
No soil, nor token of the tomb's disgrace!

Julius Cæsar and the Honey-bee

Poring on Cæsar's death with earnest eye,
I heard a fretful buzzing in the pane:
"Poor bee!" I cried, "I'll help thee by-and-by;"
Then dropp'd mine eyes upon the page again.
Alas! I did not rise; I help'd him not:
In the great voice of Roman history
I lost the pleading of the window-bee,
And all his woes and troubles were forgot.
In pity for the mighty chief, who bled
Beside his rival's statue, I delay'd
To serve the little insect's present need;
And so he died for lack of human aid.
I could not change the Roman's destiny;
I might have set the honey-maker free.

CHARLES TENNYSON TURNER

On Shooting a Swallow in Early Youth

I hoard a little spring of secret tears,
For thee, poor bird; thy death-blow was my crime:
From the far past it has flow'd on for years;
It never dries; it brims at swallow-time.
No kindly voice within me took thy part,
Till I stood o'er thy last faint flutterings;
Since then, methinks, I have a gentler heart,
And gaze with pity on all wounded wings.
Full oft the vision of thy fallen head,
Twittering in highway dust, appeals to me;
Thy helpless form, as when I struck thee dead,
Drops out from every swallow-flight I see.
I would not have thine airy spirit laid,
I seem to love the little ghost I made.

Calvus to a Fly

Ah! little fly, alighting fitfully
In the dim dawn on this bare head of mine,
Which spreads a white and gleaming track for thee,
When chairs and dusky wardrobes cease to shine.
Though thou art irksome, let me not complain;
Thy foolish passion for my hairless head
Will spend itself, when these dark hours are sped,
And thou shalt seek the sunlight on the pane.
But still beware! thou art on dangerous ground:
An angry sonnet, or a hasty hand,
May slander thee, or crush thee: thy shrill sound
And constant touch may shake my self-command:
And thou mayst perish in that moment's spite,
And die a martyr to thy love of light.

Cowper's Three Hares

They know not of their mission from above,
These little hares, that through the coppice stray;
Nor how they will take rank, some future day,
As friends of sorrow, and allies of love.
To their wild haunts a friendly thief shall come,

And take them hence, no more to rove at will,
Till those three gentle hearts grow gentler still,
And ready for the mourning poet's home.
Hail, little triad, peeping from the fern,
Ye have a place to fill, a name to earn!
Far from the copse your tender mission lies,—
To soothe a soul, too sad for trust and prayer,
To gambol round a woe ye cannot share,
And mix your woodland breath with Cowper's sighs.

ALFRED, LORD TENNYSON
(1809-1892)

"She took the dappled partridge fleckt with blood"

She took the dappled partridge fleckt with blood,
    And in her hand the drooping pheasant bare,
    And by his feet she held the woolly hare,
And like a master-painting where she stood,
Lookt some new Goddess of an English wood.
    Nor could I find an imperfection there,
    Nor blame the wanton act that showed so fair—
To me whatever freak she plays is good.
Hers is the fairest Life that breathes with breath,
    And *their* still plumes and azure eyelids closed
        Made quiet Death so beautiful to see
That Death lent grace to Life and Life to Death
    And in one image Life and Death reposed,
        To make my love an Immortality.

The Blackbird

O blackbird! sing me something well:
    While all the neighbours shoot thee round,
    I keep smooth plats of fruitful ground,
Where thou mayst warble, eat and dwell.

The espaliers and the standards all
    Are thine; the range of lawn and park:
    The unnetted black-hearts ripen dark,
All thine, against the garden wall.

Yet, though I spared thee all the spring,
    Thy sole delight is, sitting still,
    With that gold dagger of thy bill
To fret the summer jenneting.

A golden bill! the silver tongue,
    Cold February loved, is dry:
    Plenty corrupts the melody
That made thee famous once, when young:

And in the sultry garden-squares,
    Now thy flute-notes are changed to coarse,
    I hear thee not at all, or hoarse
As when a hawker hawks his wares.

Take warning! he that will not sing
    While yon sun prospers in the blue,
    Shall sing for want, ere leaves are new,
Caught in the frozen palms of Spring.

(*black-hearts:* cherries; *jenneting:* an early apple.)

The Eagle
(Fragment)

He clasps the crag with crooked hands;
Close to the sun in lonely lands,
Ring'd with the azure world, he stands.

The wrinkled sea beneath him crawls;
He watches from his mountain walls,
And like a thunderbolt he falls.

WILLIAM BELL SCOTT
(1811-1890)

The Robin

Crumbs for the robin; well he knew
 The click of that old garden gate.
Among the leaves he somewhere flew,
 Nor came to breakfast ever late.

From twig to twig he ventures near,
 With sidelong bright dark eye he comes,
Not for the poems but the crumbs,
 We take good care he need not fear.

Is that the garden gate again?
 Comes the maid to gather peas?
It is the gardener, well-known swain,
 Our robin likes old friends like these.

But hark! that click once more, we see
 A caller feathered for the day,
He knows as well, it seems, as we
 The time is come to fly away.

ROBERT BROWNING
(1812-1889)

Tray

Sing me a hero! Quench my thirst
Of soul, ye bards!
    Quoth Bard the first:
"Sir Olaf, the good knight, did don
His helm and eke his habergeon . . ."
Sir Olaf and his bard—!

"That sin-scathed brow" (quoth Bard the second)
"That eye wide ope as though Fate beckoned
My hero to some steep, beneath
Which precipice smiled tempting death . . ."
You too without your host have reckoned!

156

"A beggar-child" (let's hear this third!)
"Sat on a quay's edge: like a bird
Sang to herself at careless play,
And fell into the stream. 'Dismay!
Help, you the standers-by!' None stirred.

"Bystanders reason, think of wives
And children ere they risk their lives.
Over the balustrade has bounced
A mere instinctive dog, and pounced
Plumb on the prize. 'How well he dives!

" 'Up he comes with the child, see, tight
In mouth, alive too, clutched from quite
A depth of ten feet—twelve, I bet!
Good dog! What, off again? There's yet
Another child to save? All right!

" 'How strange we saw no other fall!
It's instinct in the animal.
Good dog! But he's a long while under:
If he got drowned I should not wonder—
Strong current, that against the wall!

" 'Here he comes, holds in mouth this time
—What may the thing be? Well, that's prime!
Now, did you ever? Reason reigns
In man alone, since all Tray's pains
Have fished—the child's doll from the slime!'

"And so, amid the laughter gay,
Trotted my hero off,—old Tray,—
Till somebody, prerogatived
With reason, reasoned: 'Why he dived,
His brain would show us, I should say.

" 'John, go and catch—or, if needs be,
Purchase—that animal for me!
By vivisection, at expense
Of half-an-hour and eighteenpence,
How brain secretes dog's soul, we'll see!' "

FREDERICK WILLIAM FABER
(1814-1863)
The Dog

Grief for her absent master in her wrought,
So I in pity took her out with me,
Though I would fain have walked alone, to be
Less hindered in the current of my thought:
And then I threw her sticks for which she ran;—
Who would not cheer a sorrow when he can?
After some miles we met at twilight pale
A neighbor of her master's passing by,
And, with blythe demonstration in her eye,
She turned and followed him along the vale.
So I walked on, companioned by the moon,
Well pleased that even a casual form or feature
Of the old times was dearer to the creature
Than the new friend of one bright afternoon.

JOHN RUSKIN
(1819-1900)

("The Needless Alarm" was written by Ruskin in January 1826, before he was seven, and is printed as he copied it into a notebook, with no punctuation and no capitals except for the initial word. "My Dog Dash" was written at the age of eleven.)

The Needless Alarm

Among the rushes lived a mouse
with a pretty little house
made of rushes tall and high
that to the skies were heard to sigh
while one night while she was sleeping
comes a dog that then was peeping
and had found her out in spite
of her good wall for then his sight
was better than our mouses
so
she was obliged to yield to foe

when frightened was the dog just then
at the scratching of a hen
so of[f] he ran and little mouse
was left in safety with her house.

My Dog Dash

I have a dog of Blenheim birth,
With fine long ears, and full of mirth;
And sometimes, running o'er the plain,
   He tumbles on his nose:
But, quickly jumping up again,
   Like lightning on he goes!
'Tis queer to watch his gambols gay;
He's very loving—in his way:
He even wants to lick your face,
But that is somewhat out of place.
'Tis well enough your hand to kiss;
But Dash is not content with this!
Howe'er, let all his faults be past,
I'll praise him to the very last.

WALT WHITMAN
(1819-1892)

To the Man-of-War-Bird

Thou who hast slept all night upon the storm,
Waking renew'd on thy prodigious pinions,
(Burst the wild storm? above it thou ascended'st,
And rested on the sky, thy slave that cradled thee,)
Now a blue point, far, far in heaven floating,
As to the light emerging here on deck I watch thee,
(Myself a speck, a point on the world's floating vast.)

Far, far at sea,

After the night's fierce drifts have strewn the shore with wrecks,
With re-appearing day as now so happy and serene,
The rosy and elastic dawn, the flashing sun,
The limpid spread of air cerulean,
Thou also re-appearest.

Thou born to match the gale, (thou art all wings,)
To cope with heaven and earth and sea and hurricane,
Thou ship of air that never furl'st thy sails,
Days, even weeks untired and onward, through spaces, realms
    gyrating,
At dusk that look'st on Senegal, at morn America,
That sport'st amid the lightning-flash and thunder-cloud,
In them, in thy experiences, had'st thou my soul,
What joys! what joys were thine!

The Dalliance of the Eagles

Skirting the river road, (my forenoon walk, my rest,)
Skyward in air a sudden muffled sound, the dalliance of the
    eagles,
The rushing amorous contact high in space together,
The clinching interlocking claws, a living, fierce, gyrating
    wheel,
Four beating wings, two beaks, a swirling mass tight grap-
    pling,
In tumbling, turning clustering loops, straight downward
    falling,
Till o'er the river pois'd, the twain yet one, a moment's lull,
A motionless still balance in the air, then parting, talons
    loosing,
Upward again on slow-firm pinions slanting, their separate
    diverse flight,
She hers, he his, pursuing.

From "Song of Myself"

Oxen that rattle the yoke and chain or halt in the leafy
    shade, what is that you express in your eyes?
It seems to me more than all the print I have read in my life.

My tread scares the wood-drake and wood-duck on my
    distant and day-long ramble,
They rise together, they slowly circle around.

I believe in those wing'd purposes,
And acknowledge red, yellow, white, playing within me,

And consider green and violet and the tufted crown
    intentional,
And do not call the tortoise unworthy because she is not
    something else,
And the jay in the woods never studied the gamut, yet trills
    pretty well to me,
And the look of the bay mare shames silliness out of me.

The wild gander leads his flock through the cool night,
Ya-honk he says, and sounds it down to me like an invitation,
The pert may suppose it meaningless, but I listening close,
Find its purpose and place up there toward the wintry sky.

The sharp-hoof'd moose of the north, the cat on the
    house-sill, the chickadee, the prairie-dog,
The litter of the grunting sow as they tug at her teats,
The brood of the turkey-hen and she with her half-spread
    wings,
I see in them and myself the same old law.

*   *   *

I believe a leaf of grass is no less than the journey-work of
    the stars,
And the pismire is equally perfect, and a grain of sand,
    and the egg of the wren,
And the tree-toad is a chef-d'oeuvre for the highest,
And the running blackberry would adorn the parlors of
    heaven,
And the narrowest hinge in my hand puts to scorn all
    machinery,
And the cow crunching with depress'd head surpasses any
    statue,
And a mouse is miracle enough to stagger sextillions of
    infidels.
I find I incorporate gneiss, coal, long-threaded moss, fruits,
    grains, esculent roots,
And am stucco'd with quadrupeds and birds all over,
And have distanced what is behind me for good reasons,
But call any thing back again when I desire it.

In vain the speeding or shyness,
In vain the plutonic rocks send their old heat against my
    approach,

In vain the mastodon retreats beneath its own powder'd
bones,
In vain objects stand leagues off and assume manifold
shapes,
In vain the ocean settling in hollows and the great monsters
lying low,
In vain the buzzard houses herself with the sky,
In vain the snake slides through the creepers and logs,
In vain the elk takes to the inner passes of the woods,
In vain the razor-bill'd auk sails far north to Labrador,
I follow quickly, I ascend to the nest in the fissure of the
cliff.

I think I could turn and live with animals, they are so placid
and self-contain'd,
I stand and look at them long and long.

They do not sweat and whine about their condition,
They do not lie awake in the dark and weep for their sins,
They do not make me sick discussing their duty to God,
Not one is dissatisfied, not one is demented with the mania
of owning things,
Not one kneels to another, nor to his kind that lived
thousands of years ago,
Not one is respectable or unhappy over the whole earth.

So they show their relations to me and I accept them,
They bring me tokens of myself, they evince them plainly in
their possession.
I wonder where they get those tokens,
Did I pass that way huge times ago and negligently drop
them?

Myself moving forward then and now and forever,
Gathering and showing more always and with velocity,
Infinite and omnigenous, and the like of these among them,
Not too exclusive toward the reachers of my remembrancers,
Picking out here one that I love, and now go with him on
brotherly terms.

A gigantic beauty of a stallion, fresh and responsive to my
caresses,
Head high in the forehead, wide between the ears,
Limbs glossy and supple, tail dusting the ground,

Eyes full of sparkling wickedness, ears finely cut, flexibly
    moving.

His nostrils dilate as my heels embrace him,
His well-built limbs tremble with pleasure as we race
    around and return.

I but use you a minute, then I resign you, stallion,
Why do I need your paces when I myself out-gallop them?
Even as I stand or sit passing faster than you.

The World Below the Brine

The world below the brine,
Forests at the bottom of the sea, the branches and leaves,
Sea-lettuce, vast lichens, strange flowers and seeds, the thick
    tangle, openings, and pink turf,
Different colors, pale gray and green, purple, white, and gold,
    the play of light through the water,
Dumb swimmers there among the rocks, coral, gluten, grass,
    rushes, and the aliment of the swimmers,
Sluggish existences grazing there suspended, or slowly crawl-
    ing close to the bottom,
The sperm-whale at the surface blowing air and spray, or
    disporting with his flukes,
The leaden-eyed shark, the walrus, the turtle, the hairy sea-
    leopard, and the sting-ray,
Passions there, wars, pursuits, tribes, sight in those ocean-
    depths, breathing that thick-breathing air, as so many
    do,
The change thence to the sight here, and to the subtle air
    breathed by beings like us who walk this sphere,
The change onward from ours to that of beings who walk
    other spheres.

JEAN INGELOW
(1820-1897)

Introduction to *"Songs on the Voices of Birds"*

Child and Boatman

"Martin, I wonder who makes all the songs."
"You do, sir?"
                    "Yes, I wonder how they come."
"Well, boy, I wonder what you'll wonder next!"
"But somebody must make them?"
                    "Sure enough."
"Does your wife know?"
                    "She never said she did."
"You told me that she knew so many things."
"I said she was a London woman, sir,
And a fine scholar, but I never said
She knew about the songs."
                    "I wish she did."
"And I wish no such thing; she knows enough,
She knows too much already. Look you now,
This vessel's off the stocks, a tidy craft."
"A schooner, Martin?"
                    "No, boy, no; a brig
Only she's schooner-rigged—a lovely craft."
"Is she for me? O, thank you, Martin dear.
What shall I call her?"
                    "Well, sir, what you please."
"Then write on her 'The Eagle.' "
                    "Bless the child!
Eagle! why, you know nought of eagles, you.
When we lay off the coast, up Canada way,
And chanced to be ashore when twilight fell,
That was the place for eagles; bald they were,
With eyes as yellow as gold."
                    "O, Martin dear,
Tell me about them."
                    "Tell! there's nought to tell,
Only they snored o' nights and frighted us."
"Snored?"
                    "Ay, I tell you, snored; they slept upright
In the great oaks by scores; as true as time,

If I'd had aught upon my mind just then,
I wouldn't have walked that wood for unknown gold;
It was most awful. When the moon was full,
I've seen them fish at night, in the middle watch,
When she got low. I've seen them plunge like stones,

And come up fighting with a fish as long,
Ay, longer than my arm; and they would sail—
When they had struck its life out— they would sail
Over the deck, and show their fell, fierce eyes,
And croon for pleasure, hug the prey, and speed
Grand as a frigate on a wind."
                          "My ship,
She must be called 'The Eagle' after these.
Martin, you'll ask your wife about the songs
When you go in at dinner-time?"
                                "Not I."

FREDERICK GODDARD TUCKERMAN
(1821-1873)

The Cricket

I

The humming bee purrs softly o'er his flower;
    From lawn and thicket
The dogday locust singeth in the sun
    From hour to hour:
Each has his bard, and thou, ere day be done,
    Shalt have no wrong.
So bright that murmur mid the insect crowd,
Muffled and lost in bottom-grass, or loud
    By pale and picket:
Shall I not take to help me in my song
    A little cooing cricket?

II

The afternoon is sleepy; let us lie
Beneath these branches whilst the burdened brook,
Muttering and moaning to himself, goes by;
And mark our minstrel's carol whilst we look

165

Toward the faint horizon swooning blue.
    Or in a garden bower,
Trellised and trammeled with deep drapery
    Of hanging green,
    Light glimmering through—
There let the dull hop be,
Let bloom, with poppy's dark refreshing flower:
Let the dead fragrance round our temples beat,
Stunning the sense to slumber, whilst between
The falling water and fluttering wind
    Mingle and meet
    Murmur and mix,
No few faint pipings from the glades behind,
    Or alder-thicks:
But louder as the day declines,
From tingling tassel, blade, and sheath,
Rising from nets of river vines,
    Winrows and ricks,
    Above, beneath,
    At every breath,
At hand, around, illimitably
Rising and falling like the sea,
    Acres of cricks!

III

Dear to the child who hears thy rustling voice
Cease at his footstep, though he hears thee still,
Cease and resume with vibrance crisp and shrill,
Thou sittest in the sunshine to rejoice.
Night lover too; bringer of all things dark
And rest and silence; yet thou bringest to me
Always that burthen of the unresting Sea,
The moaning cliffs, the low rocks blackly stark;
These upland inland fields no more I view,
But the long flat seaside beach, the wild seamew,
    And the overturning wave!
Thou bringest too, dim accents from the grave
To him who walketh when the day is dim,
Dreaming of those who dream no more of him,
With edged remembrances of joy and pain;
And heyday looks and laughter come again:

Forms that in happy sunshine lie and leap,
With faces where but now a gap must be,
Renunciations, and partitions deep
And perfect tears, and crowning vacancy!
And to thy poet at the twilight's hush,
No chirping touch of lips with laugh and blush,
But wringing arms, hearts wild with love and woe,
Closed eyes, and kisses that would not let go!

IV

So wert thou loved in that old graceful time
    When Greece was fair,
While god and hero hearkened to thy chime;
    Softly astir
Where the long grasses fringed Caÿster's lip;
Long-drawn, with glimmering sails of swan and ship,
    And ship and swan;
    Or where
    Reedy Eurotas ran.
Did that low warble teach thy tender flute
    Xenaphyle?
Its breathings mild? say! did the grasshopper
Sit golden in thy purple hair
    O Psammathe?
    Or wert thou mute,
Grieving for Pan amid the alders there?
And by the water and along the hill
That thirsty tinkle in the herbage still,
Though the lost forest wailed to horns of Arcady?

V

Like the Enchanter old—
Who sought mid the dead water's weeds and scum
For evil growths beneath the moonbeam cold,
    Or mandrake or dorcynium;
And touched the leaf that opened both his ears,
So that articulate voices now he hears
In cry of beast, or bird, or insect's hum,—
Might I but find thy knowledge in thy song!
    That twittering tongue,
Ancient as light, returning like the years.

So might I be,
Unwise to sing, thy true interpreter
Through denser stillness and in sounder dark,
Than ere thy notes have pierced to harrow me.
　So might I stir
　The world to hark
　To thee my lord and lawgiver,
　And cease my quest:
Content to bring thy wisdom to the world;
Content to gain at last some low applause,
　Now low, now lost
Like thine from mossy stone, amid the stems and straws,
　Or garden gravemound tricked and dressed—
　Powdered and pearled
　By stealing frost—
In dusky rainbow beauty of euphorbias!
For larger would be less indeed, and like
The ceaseless simmer in the summer grass
To him who toileth in the windy field,
　Or where the sunbeams strike,
Naught in innumerable numerousness.
　So might I much possess,
　So much must yield;
But failing this, the dell and grassy dike,
The water and the waste shall still be dear,
And all the pleasant plots and places
　Where thou hast sung, and I have hung
　To ignorantly hear.
Then Cricket, sing thy song! or answer mine!
Thine whispers blame, but mine has naught but praises.
It matters not. Behold! the autumn goes,
　The shadow grows,
The moments take hold of eternity;
Even while we stop to wrangle or repine
　Our lives are gone—
　Like thinnest mist,
Like yon escaping color in the tree;
Rejoice! rejoice! whilst yet the hours exist—
Rejoice or mourn, and let the world swing on
Unmoved by cricket song of thee or me.

MATTHEW ARNOLD
(1822-1888)

Geist's Grave

Four years!—and didst thou stay above
The ground, which hides thee now, but four?
And all that life, and all that love,
Were crowded, Geist! into no more?

Only four years those winning ways,
Which make me for thy presence yearn,
Called us to pet thee or to praise,
Dear little friend! at every turn?

That loving heart, that patient soul,
Had they indeed no longer span,
To run their course, and reach their goal,
And read their homily to man?

That liquid, melancholy eye,
From whose pathetic, soul-fed springs
Seemed surging the Virgilian cry,
The sense of tears in mortal things—

That steadfast, mournful strain, consoled
By spirits gloriously gay,
And temper of heroic mould—
What, was four years their whole short day?

Yes, only four!—and not the course
Of all the centuries yet to come,
And not the infinite resource
Of Nature, with her countless sum

Of figures, with her fullness vast
Of new creation evermore,
Can ever quite repeat the past,
Or just thy little self restore.

Stern law of every mortal lot!
Which man, proud man, finds hard to bear,
And builds himself I know not what
Of second life I know not where.

But thou, when struck thine hour to go,
On us, who stood despondent by,
A meek last glance of love didst throw,
And humbly lay thee down to die.

Yet would we keep thee in our heart—
Would fix our favourite on the scene,
Nor let thee utterly depart
And be as if thou ne'er hadst been.

And so there rise these lines of verse
On lips that rarely form them now;
While to each other we rehearse:
Such ways, such arts, such looks hadst thou!

We stroke thy broad brown paws again,
We bid thee to thy vacant chair,
We greet thee by the window-pane,
We hear thy scuffle on the stair.

We see the flaps of thy large ears
Quick raised to ask which way we go;
Crossing the frozen lake, appears
Thy small black figure on the snow!

Nor to us only art thou dear
Who mourn thee in thine English home;
Thou hast thine absent master's tear,
Dropped by the far Australian foam.

Thy memory lasts both here and there,
And thou shalt live as long as we.
And after that—thou dost not care!
In us was all the world to thee.

Yet, fondly zealous for thy fame,
Even to a date beyond our own
We strive to carry down thy name,
By mounded turf, and graven stone.

We lay thee, close within our reach,
Here, where the grass is smooth and warm,
Between the holly and the beech,
Where oft we watched thy couchant form,

Asleep, yet lending half an ear
To travellers on the Portsmouth road;
There build we thee, O guardian dear,
Marked with a stone, thy last abode.

Then some, who through this garden pass,
When we too, like thyself, are clay,
Shall see thy grave upon the grass,
And stop before the stone, and say:

People who lived here long ago
Did by this stone, it seems, intend
To name for future times to know
The dachs-hound, Geist, their little friend.

(*Geist:* a dachshund belonging to Arnold's son, then in Australia.)

Poor Matthias

Poor Matthias!—Found him lying
Fall'n beneath his perch and dying?
Found him stiff, you say, though warm—
All convulsed his little form?
Poor canary! many a year
Well he knew his mistress dear;
Now in vain you call his name,
Vainly raise his rigid frame,
Vainly warm him in your breast,
Vainly kiss his golden crest,
Smooth his ruffled plumage fine,
Touch his trembling beak with wine.
One more gasp—it is the end!
Dead and mute our tiny friend!
—Songster thou of many a year,
Now thy mistress brings thee here,
Says, it fits that I rehearse,
Tribute due to thee, a verse,
Meed for daily song of yore
Silent now for evermore.

Poor Matthias! Wouldst thou have
More than pity? claim'st a stave?
—Friends more near us than a bird
We dismissed without a word.

Rover, with the good brown head,
Great Atossa, they are dead;
Dead, and neither prose nor rhyme
Tells the praises of their prime.
Thou didst know them old and grey,
Know them in their sad decay.
Thou hast seen Atossa sage
Sit for hours beside thy cage;
Thou wouldst chirp, thou foolish bird,
Flutter, chirp—she never stirred!
What were now these toys to her?
Down she sank amid her fur;
Eyed thee with a soul resigned—
And thou deemedst cats were kind!
—Cruel, but composed and bland,
Dumb, inscrutable and grand,
So Tiberius might have sat,
Had Tiberius been a cat.

Rover died—Atossa too.
Less than they to us are you!
Nearer human were their powers,
Closer knit their life with ours.
Hands had stroked them, which are cold,
Now for years, in churchyard mould;
Comrades of our past were they,
Of that unreturning day.
Changed and aging, they and we
Dwelt, it seemed, in sympathy.
Alway from their presence broke
Somewhat which remembrance woke
Of the loved, the lost, the young—
Yet they died, and died unsung.

Geist came next, our little friend;
Geist had verse to mourn his end.
Yes, but that enforcement strong
Which compelled for Geist a song—
All that gay courageous cheer,
All that human pathos dear;
Soul-fed eyes with suffering worn,
Pain heroically borne,
Faithful love in depth divine—
Poor Matthias, were they thine?

MATTHEW ARNOLD

Max and Kaiser we to-day
Greet upon the lawn at play;
Max a dachshound without blot—
Kaiser should be, but is not.
Max, with shining yellow coat,
Prinking ears and dewlap throat—
Kaiser, with his collie face,
Penitent for want of race.
—Which may be the first to die,
Vain to augur, they or I?
But, as age comes on, I know,
Poet's fire gets faint and low;
If so be that travel they
First the inevitable way,
Much I doubt if they shall have
Dirge from me to crown their grave.

Yet, poor bird, thy tiny corse
Moves me, somehow, to remorse;
Something haunts my conscience, brings
Sad, compunctious visitings.
Other favourites, dwelling here,
Open lived to us, and near;
Well we knew when they were glad,
Plain we saw if they were sad,
Joyed with them when they were gay,
Soothed them in their last decay;
Sympathy could feel and show
Both in weal of theirs and woe.

Birds, companions more unknown,
Live beside us, but alone;
Finding not, do all they can,
Passage from their souls to man.
Kindness we bestow, and praise,
Laud their plumage, greet their lays;
Still beneath their feathered breast,
Stirs a history unexpressed.
Wishes there, and feelings strong,
Incommunicably throng;
What they want, we cannot guess,
Fail to track their deep distress—
Dull look on when death is nigh,
Note no change, and let them die.

Poor Matthias! couldst thou speak,
What a tale of thy last week!
Every morning did we pay
Stupid salutations gay,
Suited well to health, but how
Mocking, how incongrous now!
Cake we offered, sugar, seed,
Never doubtful of thy need;
Praised, perhaps, thy courteous eye,
Praised thy golden livery.
Gravely thou the while, poor dear!
Sat'st upon thy perch to hear,
Fixing with a mute regard
Us, thy human keepers hard,
Troubling, with our chatter vain,
Ebb of life, and mortal pain—
Us, unable to divine
Our companion's dying sign,
Or o'erpass the severing sea
Set betwixt ourselves and thee,
Till the sand thy feathers smirch
Fallen dying off thy perch!

Was it, as the Grecian sings,
Birds were born the first of things,
Before the sun, before the wind,
Before the gods, before mankind,
Airy, ante-mundane throng—
Witness their unworldly song!
Proof they give, too, primal powers,
Of a prescience more than ours—
Teach us, while they come and go,
When to sail, and when to sow.
Cuckoo calling from the hill,
Swallow skimming by the mill,
Swallows trooping in the sedge,
Starlings swirling from the hedge,
Mark the seasons, map our year,
As they show and disappear.
But, with all this travail sage
Brought from that anterior age,
Goes an unreversed decree
Whereby strange are they and we,

Making want of theirs, and plan,
Indiscernible by man.

No, away with tales like these
Stol'n from Aristophanes!
Does it, if we miss your mind,
Prove us so remote in kind?
Birds! we but repeat on you
What amongst ourselves we do.
Somewhat more or somewhat less,
'Tis the same unskilfulness.
What you feel, escapes our ken—
Know we more our fellow men?
Human suffering at our side,
Ah, like yours is undescried!
Human longings, human fears,
Miss our eyes and miss our ears.
Little helping, wounding much,
Dull of heart, and hard of touch,
Brother man's despairing sign
Who may trust us to divine?
Who assure us, sundering powers
Stand nor 'twixt his soul and ours?
Poor Matthias! See, thy end
What a lesson doth it lend!
For that lesson thou shalt have,
Dead canary bird, a stave!
Telling how, one stormy day,
Stress of gale and showers of spray
Drove my daughter small and me
Inland from the rocks and sea.
Driv'n inshore, we follow down
Ancient streets of Hastings town—
Slowly thread them — when behold,
French canary-merchant old
Shepherding his flock of gold
In a low dim-lighted pen
Scanned of tramps and fishermen!
There a bird, high-coloured, fat,
Proud of port, though something squat—
Pursy, played-out Philistine—
Dazzled Nelly's youthful eyne,

But, far in, obscure, there stirred
On his perch a sprightlier bird,
Courteous-eyed, erect and slim;
And I whispered: "Fix on *him*!"
Home we brought him, young and fair,
Songs to trill in Surrey air.
Here Matthias sang his fill,
Saw the cedars of Pains Hill;
Here he poured his little soul,
Heard the murmur of the Mole.
Eight in number now the years
He hath pleased our eyes and ears;
Other favourites he hath known
Go, and now himself is gone.
—Fare thee well, companion dear!
Fare for ever well, nor fear,
Tiny though thou art, to stray
Down the uncompanioned way!
We without thee, little friend,
Many years have not to spend;
What are left, will hardly be
Better than we spent with thee.

(*his mistress:* Arnold's daughter Nelly.)

Kaiser Dead
April 6, 1887

What, Kaiser dead? The heavy news
Post-haste to Cobham calls the Muse,
From where in Farringford she brews
    The ode sublime,
Or with Pen-bryn's bold bard pursues,
    A rival rhyme.

Kai's bracelet tail, Kai's busy feet,
Were known to all the village-street.
"What, poor Kai dead?" say all I meet;
    "A loss indeed!"
O for the croon pathetic, sweet,
    Of Robin's reed!

MATTHEW ARNOLD

Six years ago I brought him down,
A baby dog, from London town;
Round his small throat of black and brown
    A ribbon blue,
And vouched by glorious renown
    A dachshound true.

His mother, most majestic dame,
Of blood-unmixed, from Potsdam came;
And Kaiser's race we deemed the same—
    No lineage higher.
And so he bore, the imperial name.
    But ah, his sire!

Soon, soon the days conviction bring.
The collie hair, the collie swing,
The tail's indomitable ring,
    The eye's unrest —
The case was clear; a mongrel thing
    Kai stood confessed.

But all those virtues, which commend
The humbler sort who serve and tend,
Were thine in store, thou faithful friend.
    What, sense, what cheer!
To us, declining tow'rds our end,
    A mate how dear!

For Max, thy brother-dog, began
To flag, and feel his narrowing span.
And cold, besides, his blue blood ran,
    Since, 'gainst the classes,
He heard, of late, the Grand Old Man
    Incite the masses.

Yes, Max and we grew slow and sad;
But Kai, a tireless shepherd-lad,
Teeming with plans, alert, and glad
    In work or play,
Like sunshine went and came, and bade
    Live out the day!

Still, still I see the figure smart —
Trophy in mouth, agog to start,
Then, home returned, once more depart;
 Or pressed together
Against thy mistress, loving heart,
 In wintry weather.

I see the tail, like bracelet twirled,
In moments of disgrace uncurled,
Then at a pardoning word re-furled,
 A conquering sign;
Crying, "Come on, and range the world,
 And never pine."

Thine eye was bright, thy coat it shone;
Thou hadst thine errands, off and on;
In joy thy last morn flew; anon,
 A fit! All's over;
And thou art gone where Geist hath gone,
 And Toss, and Rover.

Poor Max, with downcast, reverent head,
Regards his brother's form outspread;
Full well Max knows the friend is dead
 Whose cordial talk,
And jokes in doggish language said,
 Beguiled his walk.

And Glory, stretched at Burwood gate,
Thy passing by doth vainly wait;
And jealous Jock, thy only hate,
 The chiel from Skye,
Lets from his shaggy Highland pate
 Thy memory die.

Well, fetch his graven collar fine,
And rub the steel, and make it shine,
And leave it round thy neck to twine,
 Kai, in thy grave.
There of thy master keep that sign.
 And this plain stave.

(*Kaiser:* Arnold's mongrel dachshund; *Farringford and Pen-bryn:*
respective homes of the poets Tennyson and Lewis Morris.)

WILLIAM ALLINGHAM
(1824-1889)

The Lion and the Wave

A haughty Lion, from his burning sand
And palmtree-shaded wells, found ocean-strand,
And glared upon the limitless blue plain.
A huge Wave rose, rush'd on with flying mane,
Plunged at him, crashing down with furious roar:
Whereat, with broken growl of terror and wrath
He bounded back, and fled; the milky froth
Filling his footprints on the lone sea-shore.
 No peer in his wild kingdom did he brook,
All living creatures quail'd beneath his look,
And at his thunderous voice the desert shook:
But now his heart knew fear; the matchless pride
And courage wither'd; Serpent, Elephant,
Gorilla, Crocodile, had power to daunt.
Restless he roamed and dwindled, and the Wave
Disturb'd his dreams. At last into his cave
This Lion cowering crept, lay down, and died.

GEORGE MEREDITH
(1828-1909)

(This epitaph was on Meredith's pet dachshund, Islet. The last line
characterises a dachshund's appearance.)

Islet the Dachs

Our Islet out of Helgoland, dismissed
From his quaint tenement, quits hates and loves.
There lived with us a wagging humourist
In that hound's arch dwarf-legged on boxing-gloves.

DANTE GABRIEL ROSSETTI
(1828-1882)

Beauty and the Bird

She fluted with her mouth as when one sips,
  And gently waved her golden head, inclin'd
  Outside his cage close to the window-blind;
Till her fond bird, with little turns and dips,
Piped low to her of sweet companionships.
  And when he made an end, some seed took she
  And fed him from her tongue, which rosily
Peeped as a piercing bud between her lips.

And like the child in Chaucer, on whose tongue
  The Blessed Mary laid, when he was dead,
A grain,—who straightway praised her name in song:
  Even so, when she, a little lightly red,
Now turned on me and laughed, I heard the throng
  Of inner voices praise her golden head.

Sunset Wings

To-night this sunset spreads two golden wings
  Cleaving the western sky;
Winged too with wind it is, and winnowings
Of birds; as if the day's last hour in rings
  Of strenuous flight must die.

Sun-steeped in fire, the homeward pinions sway
  Above the dovecote-tops;
And clouds of starlings, ere they rest with day,
Sink, clamorous like mill-waters, at wild play,
  By turns in every copse:

Each tree heart-deep the wrangling rout receives,—
  Save for the whirr within,
You could not tell the starlings from the leaves;
Then one great puff of wings, and the swarm heaves
  Away with all its din.

Even thus Hope's hours, in ever-eddying flight,
    To many a refuge tend;
With the first light she laughed, and the last light
Glows round her still; who natheless in the night
    At length must make an end.

And now the mustering rooks innumerable
    Together sail and soar,
While for the day's death, like a tolling knell,
Unto the heart they seem to cry, Farewell,
    No more, farewell, no more!

Is Hope not plumed, as 'twere a fiery dart?
    And oh! thou dying day,
Even as thou goest must she too depart,
And Sorrow fold such pinions on the heart
    As will not fly away?

Fragment: *"At her step the water-hen"*

    At her step the water-hen
Springs from her nook, and skimming the clear stream,
Ripples its waters in a sinuous curve,
And dives again in safety.

CHRISTINA ROSSETTI
(1830-1894)

Eve

"While I sit at the door,
Sick to gaze within,
Mine eye weepeth sore
For sorrow and sin:
As a tree my sin stands
To darken all lands;
Death is the fruit it bore.

"How have Eden bowers grown
Without Adam to bend them?
How have Eden flowers blown,
Squandering their sweet breath,
Without me to tend them?
The Tree of Life was ours,
Tree twelvefold-fruited,
Most lofty tree that flowers,
Most deeply rooted:
I chose the Tree of Death.

"Hadst thou but said me nay,
   Adam my brother,
I might have pined away —
   I, but none other:
God might have let thee stay
Safe in our garden,
By putting me away
Beyond all pardon.

"I, Eve, sad mother
Of all who must live,
I, not another,
Plucked bitterest fruit to give
My friend, husband, lover.
O wanton eyes, run over!
Who but I should grieve?
Cain hath slain his brother:
Of all who must die mother,
Miserable Eve!"

Thus she sat weeping,
Thus Eve our mother,
Where one lay sleeping
Slain by his brother.
Greatest and least
Each piteous beast
To hear her voice
Forgot his joys
And set aside his feast.

The mouse paused in his walk
And dropped his wheaten stalk;
Grave cattle wagged their heads
In rumination;
The eagle gave a cry
From his cloud station:
Larks on thyme beds
Forbore to mount or sing;
Bees dropped upon the wing;
The raven perched on high
Forgot his ration;
The conies in their rock,
A feeble nation,
Quaked sympathetical;
The mocking-bird left off to mock;
Huge camels knelt as if
In deprecation;
The kind hart's tears were falling;
Chattered the wistful stork;
Dove-voices with a dying fall
Cooed desolation,
Answering grief by grief.

Only the serpent in the dust,
Wriggling and crawling,
Grinned an evil grin and thrust
His tongue out with its fork.

Freaks of Fashion

Such a hubbub in the nests,
    Such a bustle and squeak!
Nestlings, guiltless of a feather,
    Learning just to speak,
Ask—"And how about the fashions?"
    From a cavernous beak.

Perched on bushes, perched on hedges,
    Perched on firm hahas,
Perched on anything that holds them,
    Gay papas and grave mammas
Teach the knowledge-thirsty nestlings:
    Hear the gay papas.

Robin says: "A scarlet waistcoat
    Will be all the wear,
Snug, and also cheerful-looking
    For the frostiest air,
Comfortable for the chest too
    When one comes to plume and pair."

"Neat grey hoods will be in vogue,"
    Quoth a Jackdaw: "glossy grey,
Setting close, yet setting easy,
    Nothing fly-away;
Suited to our misty mornings,
    À la négligée."

Flushing salmon, flushing sulphur,
    Haughty Cockatoos
Answer—"Hoods may do for mornings,
    But for evenings choose
High head-dresses, curved like crescents
    Such as well-bred persons use."

"Top-knots, yes; yet more essential
    Still, a train or tail,"
Screamed the Peacock: "gemmed and lustrous,
    Not too stiff, and not too frail;
Those are best which rearrange as
    Fans, and spread or trail."

Spoke the Swan, entrenched behind
    An inimitable neck:
"After all, there's nothing sweeter
    For the lawn or lake
Than simple white, if fine and flaky
    And absolutely free from speck."

"Yellow," hinted a Canary,
  "Warmer, not less *distingué.*"
"Peach colour," put in a Lory,
  "Cannot look *outré.*"
"All the colours are in fashion,
  And are right," the Parrots say.

"Very well. But do contrast
  Tints harmonious,"
Piped a Blackbird, justly proud
  Of bill aurigerous;
"Half the world may learn a lesson
  As to that from us."

Then a Stork took up the word:
  "Aim at height and *chic*:
Not high heels, they're common; somehow,
  Stilted legs, not thick,
Nor yet thin:" he just glanced downward
  And snapped-to his beak.

Here a rustling and a whirring,
  As of fans outspread,
Hinted that mammas felt anxious
  Lest the next thing said
Might prove less than quite judicious,
  Or even underbred.

So a mother Auk resumed
  The broken thread of speech:
"Let colours sort themselves, my dears,
  Yellow, or red, or peach;
The main points, as it seems to me,
  We mothers have to teach,

"Are form and texture, elegance,
  And air reserved, sublime;
The mode of wearing what we wear
  With due regard to month and clime.
But now, let's all compose ourselves,
  It's almost breakfast-time."

A hubbub, a squeak, a bustle!
   Who cares to chatter or sing
With delightful breakfast coming?
   Yet they whisper under the wing:
"So we may wear whatever we like,
   Anything, everything!"

The Lambs of Grasmere, 1860

The upland flocks grew starved and thinned:
   Their shepherds scarce could feed the lambs
Whose milkless mothers butted them,
   Or who were orphaned of their dams.
The lambs athirst for mother's milk
   Filled all the place with piteous sounds:
Their mothers' bones made white for miles
   The pastureless wet pasture grounds.

Day after day, night after night,
   From lamb to lamb the shepherds went,
With teapots for the bleating mouths
   Instead of nature's nourishment.
The little shivering gaping things
   Soon knew the step that brought them aid,
And fondled the protecting hand,
   And rubbed it with a woolly head.

Then as the days waxed on to weeks,
   It was a pretty sight to see
These lambs with frisky heads and tails
   Skipping and leaping on the lea,
Bleating in tender, trustful tones,
   Resting on rocky crag or mound.
And following the beloved feet
   That once had sought for them and found.

These very shepherds of their flocks,
   These loving lambs so meek to please,
Are worthy of recording words
   And honour in their due degrees:
So I might live a hundred years,
   And roam from strand to foreign strand,
Yet not forget this flooded spring
   And scarce-saved lambs of Westmoreland.

EMILY DICKINSON

Three poems from Sing-Song:
A Nursery Rhyme Book

When fishes set umbrellas up
   If the rain-drops run,
Lizards will want their parasols
   To shade them from the sun.

O sailor, come ashore,
   What have you brought for me?
Red coral, white coral,
   Coral from the sea.

I did not dig it from the ground,
   Nor pluck it from a tree;
Feeble insects made it
   In the stormy sea.

Hurt no living thing:
   Ladybird, nor butterfly,
Nor moth with dusty wing,
   Nor cricket chirping cheerily,
Nor grasshopper so light of leap,
   Nor dancing gnat, nor beetle fat,
Nor harmless worms that creep.

EMILY DICKINSON
(1830-1886)

"Papa above"

Papa above!
Regard a Mouse
O'erpowered by the Cat!
Reserve within thy kingdom
A "Mansion" for the Rat!

Snug in seraphic Cupboards
To nibble all the day,
While unsuspecting Cycles
Wheel solemnly away!

"If I should'nt be alive"

If I should'nt be alive
When the Robins come,
Give the one in Red Cravat,
A Memorial crumb.

If I could'nt thank you,
Being fast asleep,
You will know I'm trying
With my Granite lip!

"A Bird came down the Walk"

A Bird came down the Walk—
He did not know I saw—
He bit an Angleworm in halves
And ate the fellow, raw,

And then he drank a Dew
From a convenient Grass—
And then hopped sidewise to the Wall
To let a Beetle pass—

He glanced with rapid eyes
That hurried all around—
They looked like frightened Beads, I thought—
He stirred his Velvet Head

Like one in danger, Cautious,
I offered him a Crumb
And he unrolled his feathers
And rowed him softer home—

Than Oars divide the Ocean,
Too silver for a seam—
Or Butterflies, off Banks of Noon
Leap, plashless as they swim.

EMILY DICKINSON

"The Spider holds a Silver Ball"

The Spider holds a Silver Ball
In unperceived Hands —
And dancing softly to Himself
His Yarn of Pearl — unwinds —

He plies from Nought to Nought —
In unsubstantial Trade —
Supplants our Tapestries with His —
In half the period —

An Hour to rear supreme
His Continents of Light —
Then dangle from the Housewife's Broom —
His Boundaries — forgot —

"The Bat is dun, with wrinkled Wings"

The Bat is dun, with wrinkled Wings —
Like fallow Article —
And not a song pervade his Lips —
Or none perceptible.

His small Umbrella quaintly halved
Describing in the Air
An Arc alike inscrutable
Elate Philosopher.

Deputed from what Firmament —
Of what Astute Abode —
Empowered with what Malignity
Auspiciously withheld —

To his adroit Creator
Ascribe no less the praise —
Beneficent, believe me,
His Eccentricities —

"A narrow Fellow in the Grass"

A narrow Fellow in the Grass
Occasionally rides —
You may have met Him — did you not
His notice sudden is —

The Grass divides as with a Comb —
A spotted shaft is seen —
And then it closes at your feet
And opens further on —

He likes a Boggy Acre
A Floor too cool for Corn —
Yet when a Boy, and Barefoot —
I more than once at Noon
Have passed, I thought, a Whip lash
Unbraiding in the Sun
When stooping to secure it
It wrinkled, and was gone —

C.S. CALVERLEY

Several of Nature's People
I know, and they know me —
I feel for them a transport
Of cordiality —

But never met this Fellow
Attended, or alone
Without a tighter breathing
And Zero at the Bone —

C.S. CALVERLEY
(1831-1884)

Sad Memories

They tell me I am beautiful: they praise my silken hair,
My little feet that silently slip on from stair to stair:
They praise my pretty trustful face and innocent grey eye;
Fond hands caress me oftentimes, yet would that I might die!

Why was I born to be abhorred of man and bird and beast?
The bullfinch marks me stealing by, and straight his song hath
    ceased;
The shrewmouse eyes me shudderingly, then flees; and,
    worse than that,
The housedog he flees after me — why was I born a cat?

Men prize the heartless hound who quits dry-eyed his native land;
Who wags a mercenary tail and licks a tyrant hand.
The leal true cat they prize not, that if e'er compelled to roam
Still flies, when let out of the bag, precipitately home.

They call me cruel. Do I know if mouse or song-bird feels?
I only know they make me light and salutary meals:
And if, as 'tis my nature to, ere I devour I tease 'em,
Why should a low-bred gardener's boy pursue me with a besom?

Should china fall or chandeliers, or anything but stocks —
Nay stocks, when they're in flowerpots — the cat expects hard knocks:
Should ever anything be missed — milk, coals, umbrellas, brandy —
The cat's pitched into with a boot or any thing that's handy.

"I remember, I remember," how one night I "fleeted by,"
And gained the blessed tiles and gazed into the cold clear sky.
"I remember, I remember, how my little lovers came;"
And there, beneath the crescent moon, played many a little game.

They fought — by good St. Catherine, 'twas a fearsome sight to see
The coal-black crest, the glowering orbs, of one gigantic He.
Like bow by some tall bowman bent at Hastings or Poictiers,
His huge back curved, till none observed a vestige of his ears:

He stood, an ebon crescent, flouting that ivory moon;
Then raised the pibroch of his race, the Song without a Tune;
Gleamed his white teeth, his mammoth tail waved darkly to and fro,
As with one complex yell he burst, all claws, upon the foe.

It thrills me now, that final Miaow — that weird unearthly din:
Lone maidens heard it far away, and leaped out of their skin.
A potboy from his den o'erhead peeped with a scared wan face;
Then sent a random brickbat down, which knocked me into space.

Nine days I fell, or thereabouts: and, had we not nine lives,
I wis I ne'er had seen again thy sausage-shop, St. Ives!
Had I, as some cats have, nine tails, how gladly I would lick
The hand, and person generally, of him who heaved that brick!

For me they fill the milkbowl up, and cull the choice sardine:
But ah! I nevermore shall be the cat I once have been!
The memories of that fatal night they haunt me even now:
In dreams I see that rampant He, and tremble at that Miaow.

Disaster

'Twas ever thus from childhood's hour!
    My fondest hopes would not decay:
I never loved a tree or flower
    Which was the first to fade away!
The garden, where I used to delve
    Short-frocked, still yields me pinks in plenty:
The peartree that I climbed at twelve
    I see still blossoming, at twenty.

C.S. CALVERLEY

I never nursed a dear gazelle;
    But I was given a parroquet —
(How I did nurse him if unwell!—
    He's imbecile, but lingers yet.
He's green, with an enchanting tuft;
    He melts me with his small black eye:
He'd look inimitable stuffed,
    And knows it — but he will not die!

I had a kitten — I was rich
    In pets — but all too soon my kitten
Became a full-sized cat, by which
    I've more than once been scratched and bitten.
And when for sleep her limbs she curled
    One day beside her untouched plateful,
And glided calmly from the world,
    I freely own that I was grateful.

And then I bought a dog — a queen!
    Ah Tiny, dear departing pug!
She lives, but she is past sixteen
    And scarce can crawl across the rug.
I loved her beautiful and kind;
    Delighted in her pert Bow-wow:
But now she snaps if you don't mind;
    'Twere lunacy to love her now.

I used to think, should e'er mishap
    Betide my crumple-visaged Ti,
In shape of prowling thief, or trap,
    Or coarse bull-terrier — I should die.
But ah! disasters have their use;
    And life might e'en be too sunshiny:
Nor would I make myself a goose,
    If some big dog should swallow Tiny.

Motherhood

She laid it where the sunbeams fall
Unscanned upon the broken wall.
Without a tear, without a groan,
She laid it near a mighty stone,

Which some rude swain had haply cast
Thither in sport, long ages past,
And Time with mosses had o'erlaid,
And fenced with many a tall grassblade,
And all about bid roses bloom
And violets shed their soft perfume.
There, in its cool and quiet bed,
She set her burden down and fled:
Nor flung, all eager to escape,
One glance upon the perfect shape
That lay, still warm and fresh and fair,
But motionless and soundless there.

No human eye had marked her pass
Across the linden-shadowed grass
Ere yet the minster clock chimed seven:
Only the innocent birds of heaven —
The magpie, and the rook whose nest
Swings as the elmtree waves his crest —
And the lithe cricket, and the hoar
And huge-limbed hound that guards the door,
Looked on when, as a summer wind
That, passing, leaves no trace behind,
All unapparelled, barefoot all,
She ran to that old ruined wall,
To leave upon the chill dank earth
(For ah! she never knew its worth)
'Mid hemlock rank, and fern, and ling,
And dews of night, that precious thing!

And there it might have lain forlorn
From morn till eve, from eve to morn:
But that, by some wild impulse led,
The mother, ere she turned and fled,
One moment stood erect and high;
Then poured into the silent sky
A cry so jubilant, so strange,
That Alice — as she strove to range
Her rebel ringlets at her glass —
Sprang up and gazed across the grass;
Shook back those curls so fair to see,
Clapped her soft hands in childish glee,
And shrieked — her sweet face all aglow,

Her very limbs with rapture shaking —
"My hen has laid an egg, I know;
And only hear the noise she's making!"

LORD DE TABLEY
(1835-1895)

Lines to a Lady-bird

Cow-lady, or sweet lady-bird,
Of thee a song is seldom heard.
What record of thy humble days
Almost ignored in poets' lays,
Salutes thy advent? Oversung
Is Philomel by many lyres;
And how the lark to heaven aspires,
Is rumoured with abundant fame,
While dim oblivion wraps thy name.
Hail! then, thou unpresuming thing,
A bright mosaic of the spring,
Enamelled brooch upon the breast
Of the rich-bosomed rose caressed.
Thy wings the balmy zephyrs bear
When woods unfold in vernal air,
When crumpled buds around expand,
Thou lightest on our very hand.
Red as a robin thou dost come,
Confiding, in entreaty dumb.
Who would impede thy harmless track,
Or crush thy wing or burnished back?
'Tis said, thy lighting and thy stay
Bring luck: and few would brush away
The small unbidden crawling guest,
But let thee sheathe thy wings in rest,
And take thy voluntary flight
Uninjured to some flower's delight.
For there is nothing nature through,
Lovely and curious as you:
A little dome-shaped insect round,
With five black dots on a carmine ground.

What art thou? I can hardly tell.
A little tortoise of the dell
With carapace or vaulted shell
Of shining crimson? Or again,
I picture thee, in fancy plain,
A little spotted elfin cow,
Of whose sweet milk a milkmaid fairy
Makes syllabub in Oberon's dairy.
Thou hast a legend-pedigree
That gives thy race a high degree
From the shed blood of Venus sweet,
Thorn-wounded in her pearly feet,
As thro' the dewy woods she went,
Love-lorn, in utter discontent,
Listening afar the echoing horn
Of coy Adonis, in whose scorn
The Love-queen languished, love-forlorn.
He burned to hunt the boar at bay,
And loathed the lover's idle play;
So Venus followed in the chase
And from her wounded heel a trace
Of blood-drip tinged the dewy mead,
And, from the ichor she did bleed,
From Aphrodite's precious blood,
Arose the lady-birds, a brood
As gentle as the hurt of love,
That gave them birth and parentage
In legends of the golden age.
But, coming to our modern day,
Thee peevish children scare away,
And speed thy flight with evil rhyme,
Waving an idle hand meantime,
To make thee spread thy wings in fear
With rumours of disaster near,
And tidings of thy home in flames,
And all thy burning children's names,
How all are scorched but Ann alone
Who safely crept inside a stone;
With many an old unlettered fable
Of churlish lips inhospitable.
And when these fancies all are past,
I see thee as thou art at last,

A welcome sign of genial spring,
Awaited as a swallow's wing,
The cuckoo's call, the drone of bee,
The small gnat's dancing minstrelsy.
Ere hawthorn buds are sweetly stirred
I bid thee hail, bright lady-bird!

August 21st 1895

THOMAS HARDY
(1840-1928)

Last Words to a Dumb Friend

Pet was never mourned as you,
Purrer of the spotless hue,
Plumy tail, and wistful gaze
While you humoured our queer ways,
Or outshrilled your morning call
Up the stairs and through the hall —
Foot suspended in its fall —
While, expectant, you would stand
Arched, to meet the stroking hand;
Till your way you chose to wend
Yonder, to your tragic end.

Never another pet for me!
Let your place all vacant be;
Better blankness day by day
Than companion torn away.
Better bid his memory fade,
Better blot each mark he made,
Selfishly escape distress
By contrived forgetfulness,
Than preserve his prints to make
Every morn and eve an ache.

From the chair whereon he sat
Sweep his fur, nor wince thereat;
Rake his little pathways out
Mid the bushes roundabout,
Smooth away his talons' mark
From the claw-worn pine-tree bark,
Where he climbed as dusk embrowned,
Waiting us who loitered round.

Strange it is this speechless thing,
Subject to our mastering,
Subject for his life and food
To our gift, and time, and mood;
Timid pensioner of us Powers,
His existence ruled by ours,
Should — by crossing at a breath
Into safe and shielded death,
By the merely taking hence
Of his insignificance —
Loom as largened to the sense,
Shape as part, above man's will,
Of the Imperturbable.

As a prisoner, flight debarred,
Exercising in a yard,
Still retain I, troubled, shaken,
Mean estate, by him forsaken;
And this home, which scarcely took
Impress from his little look,
By his faring to the Dim
Grows all eloquent of him.

Housemate, I can think you still
Bounding to the window-sill,
Over which I vaguely see
Your small mound beneath the tree,
Showing in the autumn shade
That you moulder where you played.

2 October 1904

A Bird-Scene at a Rural Dwelling

When the inmate stirs, the birds retire discreetly
From the window-ledge, whereon they whistled sweetly
    And on the step of the door,
      In the misty morning hoar;
   But now the dweller is up they flee
   To the crooked neighbouring codlin-tree;
And when he comes fully forth they seek the garden,
And call from the lofty costard, as pleading pardon
    For shouting so near before
      In their joy at being alive:—
Meanwhile the hammering clock within goes five.

I know a domicile of brown and green,
Where for a hundred summers there have been
Just such enactments, just such daybreaks seen.

Compassion

An Ode

**In Celebration of the Centenary of the Royal Society
for the Prevention of Cruelty to Animals**

I

   Backward among the dusky years
   A lonesome lamp is seen arise,
   Lit by a few fain pioneers
      Before incredulous eyes. —
   We read the legend that it lights:
"Wherefore beholds this land of historied rights
Mild creatures, despot-doomed, bewildered, plead
Their often hunger, thirst, pangs, prisonment,
    In deep dumb gaze more eloquent
      Than tongues of widest heed?"

II

What was faint-written, read in a breath
In that year — ten times ten away —
A larger louder conscience saith
    More sturdily to-day. —
But still those innocents are thralls
To throbless hearts, near, far, that hear no calls
Of honour towards their too-dependent frail,
And from Columbia Cape to Ind we see
    How helplessness breeds tyranny
        In power above assail.

III

Cries still are heard in secret nooks,
Till hushed with gag or slit or thud;
And hideous dens whereon none looks
    Are sprayed with needless blood.
But here, in battlings, patients, slow,
Much has been won — more, maybe, than we know —
And on we labour hopeful. "Ailinon!"
A mighty voice calls: "But may the good prevail!"
    And "Blessed are the merciful!"
        Calls a yet mightier one.

22 January 1924

Horses Aboard

Horses in horsecloths stand in a row
On board the huge ship that at last lets go:
Whither are they sailing? They do not know,
Nor what for, nor how. —
                    They are horses of war,
And are going to where there is fighting afar;
But they gaze through their eye-holes unwitting they are,
And that in some wilderness, gaunt and ghast,
Their bones will bleach ere a year has passed,
And the item be as "war-waste" classed. —
And when the band booms, and the folk say "Good-bye!"
And the shore slides astern, they appear wrenched awry
From the scheme Nature planned for them, — wondering why.

Why She Moved House

(The Dog Muses)

Why she moved house, without a word,
    I cannot understand;
She'd mirrors, flowers, she'd book and bird,
    And callers in a band.

And where she is she gets no sun,
    No flowers, no book, no glass;
Of callers I am the only one,
    And I but pause and pass.

Bags of Meat

"Here's a fine bag of meat,"
Says the master-auctioneer,
As the timid, quivering steer,
Starting a couple of feet
At the prod of a drover's stick,
And trotting lightly and quick,
A ticket stuck on his rump,
Enters with a bewildered jump.

"Where he's lived lately, friends,
I'd live till lifetime ends:
They've a whole life everyday
Down there in the Vale, have they!
He'd be worth the money to kill
And give away Christmas for good-will."

"Now here's a heifer — worth more
Than bid, were she bone-poor;
Yet she's round as a barrel of beer;"
"She's a plum," said the second auctioneer.

"Now this young bull — for thirty pound?
    Worth that to manure your ground!"
"Or to stand," chimed the second one,
    "And have his picter done!"
The beast was rapped on the horns and snout
    To make him turn about.
"Well," cried a buyer, "another crown —
Since I've dragged here from Taunton Town!"

    "That calf, she sucked three cows,
    Which is not matched for bouse
    In the nurseries of high life
By the first-born of a nobleman's wife!"
The stick falls, meaning, "A true tale's told,"
On the buttock of the creature sold,
    And the buyer leans over and snips
His mark on one of the animal's hips.

    Each beast, when driven in,
Looks round at the ring of bidders there
With a much-amazed reproachful stare,
    As at unnatural kin,
For bringing him to a sinister scene
So strange, unhomelike, hungry, mean;
His fate the while suspended between
    A butcher, to kill out of hand,
    And a farmer, to keep on the land;
One can fancy a tear runs down his face
When the butcher wins, and he's driven from the place.

A Popular Personage at Home

    "I live here: 'Wessex' is my name:
    I am a dog known rather well:
    I guard the house; but how that came
    To be my whim I cannot tell.

    "With a leap and a heart elate I go
    At the end of an hour's expectancy
    To take a walk of a mile or so
    With the folk I let live here with me.

202

"Along the path, amid the grass
I sniff, and find out rarest smells
For rolling over as I pass
The open fields towards the dells.

"No doubt I shall always cross this sill,
And turn the corner, and stand steady,
Gazing back for my mistress till
She reaches where I have run already,

"And that this meadow with its brook,
And bulrush, even as it appears
As I plunge by with hasty look,
Will stay the same a thousand years."

Thus "Wessex". But a dubious ray
At times informs his steadfast eye,
Just for a trice, as though to say,
"Yet, will this pass, and pass shall I?"

1924

Dead "Wessex" the Dog to the Household

Do you think of me at all,
    Wistful ones?
Do you think of me at all
    As if nigh?
Do you think of me at all
At the creep of evenfall,
Or when the sky-birds call
    As they fly?

Do you look for me at times,
    Wistful ones?
Do you look for me at times,
    Strained and still?
Do you look for me at times,
When the hour for walking chimes,
On that grassy path that climbs
    Up the hill?

You may hear a jump or trot,
    Wistful ones,
You may hear a jump or trot —
    Mine, as 'twere —
You may hear a jump or trot
On the stair or path or plot;
But I shall cause it not,
    Be not there.

Should you call as when I knew you,
    Wistful ones,
Should you call as when I knew you,
    Shared your home;
Should you call as when I knew you,
I shall not turn to view you,
I shall not listen to you,
    Shall not come.

MATHILDE BLIND
(1841-1896)

Internal Firesides

Bewilderingly, from wildly shaken cloud,
    Invisible hands, deft moving everywhere,
    Have woven a winding sheet of velvet air,
And laid the dead earth in her downy shroud.
And more and more, in white confusion, crowd
    Wan, whirling flakes, while o'er the icy glare
    Blue heaven that was glooms blackening through
        the bare
Tree skeletons, to ruthless tempest bowed.

Nay, let the outer world be winter-locked;
    Beside the hearth of glowing memories
I warm my life. Once more our boat is rocked,
    As on a cradle by the palm-fringed Nile;
And, sharp-cut silhouettes, in single file,
    Lank camels lounge against transparent skies.

On a Forsaken Lark's Nest

Lo, where left 'mid the sheaves, cut down by the iron-
    fanged reaper,
Eating its way as it clangs fast through the wavering
    wheat,
Lies the nest of a lark, whose little brown eggs could
    not keep her
As she, affrighted and scared, fled from the harvester's
    feet.

Ah, what a heartful of song that now will never awaken,
Closely packed in the shell, awaited love's fostering,
That should have quickened to life what, now a-cold and
    forsaken,
Never, enamoured of light, will meet the dawn on the
    wing.

Ah, what pæans of joy, what raptures no mortal can
    measure,
Sweet as honey that's sealed in the cells of the honey-
    comb,
Would have ascended on high in jets of mellifluous
    pleasure,
Would have dropped from the clouds to nest in its gold-
    curtained home.

Poor, pathetic brown eggs! Oh, pulses that never will
    quicken
Music mute in the shell that hath been turned to a
    tomb!
Many a sweet human singer, chilled and adversity-
    stricken,
Withers benumbed in a world his joy might have helped
    to illume.

ROBERT BUCHANAN
(1841-1901)

The Starling

The little lame tailor
    Sat stitching and snarling—
Who in the world
    Was the tailor's darling?
To none of his kind
Was he well-inclined,
    But he doted on Jack the starling.

For the bird had a tongue,
    And of words good store,
And his cage was hung
    Just over the door.
And he saw the people,
    And heard the roar,—
Folk coming and going
    Evermore,—
And he look'd at the tailor,—
    And swore.

From a country lad
    The tailor bought him,—
His training was bad,
    For tramps had taught him;
On alehouse benches
    His cage had been,
While louts and wenches
    Made jests obscene,—
But he learn'd, no doubt,
    His oaths from fellows
Who travel about
    With kettle and bellows,
And three or four,
    The roundest by far
That ever he swore,
    Were taught by a tar.
And the tailor heard—
    "We'll be friends!" said he,
"You're a clever bird,
    And our tastes agree —

We both are old,
  And esteem life base,
The whole world cold,
  Things out of place,
And we're lonely too,
  And full of care—
So what can we do
  But swear?

"The devil take you,
  How you mutter!—
Yet there's much to make you
  Swear and flutter.
You want the fresh air
  And the sunlight, lad,
And your prison there
  Feels dreary and sad,
And here I frown
  In a prison as dreary,
Hating the town,
  And feeling weary:
We're too confined, Jack,
  And we want to fly,
And you blame mankind, Jack,
  And so do I!
And then, again
  By chance as it were,,
We learn'd from men
  How to grumble and swear;
You let your throat
  By the scamps be guided,
And swore by rote—
  All just as I did!
And without beseeching,
  Relief is brought us—
For we turn the teaching
  On those who taught us!"

A haggard and ruffled
  Old fellow was Jack,
With a grim face muffled
  In ragged black,
And his coat was rusty
  And never neat,

And his wings were dusty
   With grime of the street,
And he sidelong peer'd,
   With eyes of soot,
And scowl'd and sneer'd,—
   And was lame of a foot!
And he long'd to go
   From whence he came;—
And the tailor, you know,
   Was just the same.

All kinds of weather
   They felt confined,
And swore together
   At all mankind;
For their mirth was done,
   And they felt like brothers,
And the swearing of one
   Meant no more than the other's;
'Twas just a way
   They had learn'd, you see,—
Each one wanted to say
   Only this—"Woe's me!
I'm a poor old fellow,
   And I'm prison'd so,
While the sun shines mellow,
And the corn waves yellow,
   And the fresh winds blow,—
And the folk don't care
   If I live or die,
But I long for air,
   And I wish to fly!"
Yet unable to utter it,
   And too wild to bear,
They could only mutter it,
   And swear.

Many a year
   They dwelt in the city,
In their prisons drear,
   And none felt pity,
And few were sparing
   Of censure and coldness,
To hear them swearing

With such plain boldness;
But at last, by the Lord,
    Their noise was stopt,—
For down on his board
    The tailor dropt,
And they found him dead,
    And done with snarling,
And over his head
    Still grumbled the Starling;
But when an old Jew
    Claim'd the goods of the tailor,
And with eye askew
    Eyed the feathery railer,
And, with a frown
    At the dirt and rust,
Took the old cage down,
    In a shower of dust,—
Jack, with heart aching,
    Felt life past bearing,
And shivering, quaking,
All hope forsaking,
    Died, swearing.

The Blind Linnet

τί γὰρ ἔδει μ' ὁρᾶν,
ὅτῳ γ' ὁρῶντι μηδὲν ἦν ἰδεῖν γλυκύ;
                    SOPH. ŒD. TYR.

The sempstress's linnet sings
    At the window opposite me;—
It feels the sun on its wings,
    Though it cannot see.
Can a bird have thoughts? May be.

The sempstress is sitting,
    High o'er the humming street,
The little blind linnet is flitting
    Between the sun and her seat.

All day long
   She stitches wearily there,
And I know she is not young,
   And I know she is not fair;
For I watch her head bent down
   Throughout the dreary day,
And the thin meek hair o' brown
   Is threaded with silver gray;
And now and then, with a start
At the fluttering of her heart,
   She lifts her eyes to the bird,
And I see in the dreary place
The gleam of a thin white face.
   And my heart is stirr'd.

Loud and long
The linnet pipes his song!
For he cannot see
   The smoky street all round,
But loud in the sun sings he,
   Though he hears the murmurous sound,
For his poor, blind eyeballs blink,
   While the yellow sunlights fall,
And he thinks (if a bird can think)
   He hears a waterfall,
Or the broad and beautiful river
   Washing fields of corn,
Flowing for ever
   Through the woods where he was born;
And his voice grows stronger,
   While he thinks that he is there,
And louder and longer
   Falls his song on the dusky air,
And oft, in the gloaming still,
   Perhaps (for who can tell?)
   The musk and the muskatel,
That grow on the window sill,
   Cheat him with their smell.

But the sempstress can see
How dark things be;
How black through the town

The stream is flowing;
And tears fall down
  Upon her sewing.
So at times she tries,
  When her trouble is stirr'd
To close her eyes,
  And be blind like the bird.
And *then*, for a minute,
  As sweet things seem,
As to the linnet
  Piping in his dream!
For she feels on her brow
  The sunlight glowing,
And hears nought now
  But a river flowing—
A broad and beautiful river,
  Washing fields of corn.
Flowing for ever
  Through the woods where she was born—
And a wild bird winging
Over her head, and singing!
And she can smell
The musk and muskatel
  That beside her grow,
And, unaware,
She murmurs an old air
  That she used to know!

GERARD MANLEY HOPKINS
(1844-1889)

Fragment: "Mark you how the peacock's eye'"

Mark you how the peacock's eye
Winks away its ring of green,
Barter'd for an azure dye,
And the piece that's like a bean,
The pupil, plays its liquid jet
To win a look of violet.

The Sea and the Skylark

On ear and ear two noises too old to end
   Trench — right, the tide that ramps against the shore;
   With a flood or a fall, low lull-off or all roar,
Frequenting there while moon shall wear and wend.

Left hand, off land, I hear the lark ascend,
   His rash-fresh re-winded new-skeined score
   In crisps of curl off wild winch whirl, and pour
And pelt music, till none's to spill nor spend.

How these two shame this shallow and frail town!
   How ring right out our sordid turbid time,
Being pure! We, life's pride and cared-for crown,

   Have lost that cheer and charm of earth's past prime:
Our make and making break, are breaking, down
   To man's last dust, drain fast towards man's first slime.

The Caged Skylark

As a dare-gale skylark scanted in a dull cage
   Man's mounting spirit in his bone-house, mean house, dwells—
   That bird beyond the remembering his free fells;
This in drudgery, day-labouring-out life's age.

Though aloft on turf or perch or poor low stage,
   Both sing sometimes the sweetest, sweetest spells,
   Yet both droop deadly sometimes in their cells
Or wring their barriers in bursts of fear or rage.

Not that the sweet-fowl, song-fowl, needs no rest—
Why, hear him, hear him babble and dropdown to his nest,
   But his own nest, wild nest, no prison.

Man's spirit will be flesh-bound when found at best,
But uncumbered: meadow-down is not distressed
   For a rainbow footing it nor he for his bónes rísen.

ROBERT BRIDGES

Fragment: "Repeat that, repeat"

Repeat that, repeat,
Cuckoo, bird, and open ear wells, heart-springs, delightfully sweet,
With a ballad, with a ballad, a rebound
Off trundled timber and scoops of the hillside ground, hollow
    hollow hollow ground:
The whole landscape flushes on a sudden at a sound.

ROBERT BRIDGES
(1844-1930)

From *Epistle II: To a Socialist in London*

(In line 1 "this merciless outrage" is the domination by money of "the weak
ones,/Those ill-fated, opprest, unfortun'd needy.")

And what if all Nature ratify this merciless outrage?
If her wonder of arch-wonders, her fair animal life,
Her generate creatures, her motion'd warmblooded offspring,
Haunters of the forest & royal country, her antler'd
Mild-gazers, that keep silvan sabbath idly without end;
Her herded galopers, sleeksided stately careerers
Of trembling nostril; her coy unapproachable estrays,
Stealthy treaders, climbers; her leapers furry, lissom-limb'd;
Her timorous burrowers, and grangers thrifty, the sandy
Playmates of the warren; her clumsy-footed, shaggy roamers;
Her soarers, the feather'd fast-fliers, loftily floating
Sky-sailers, exiles of high solitudinous eyries;
Her perching carolers, twitterers & sweetly singing birds:
All ocean's finny clans, mute mouthers, watery breathers,
Furtive arrow-darters, and fan-tail'd easy balancers,
Silvery-scale, gilt-head, thorn-back, frill'd harlequinading
Globe and slimy ribbon: Shell-builders of many-chamber'd
Pearly dwellings, soft shapes mosslike or starry, adorning
With rich floral fancy the gay rock-garden of ebb-tide:
All life, from the massive-bulkt, ivory-tusht, elephantine
Centenarian, acknowledging with crouching obeisance
Man's will, ev'n to the least petty whiffling ephemeral insect,
Which in a hot sunbeam engend'ring, when summer is high,
Vaunteth an hour his speck of tinsely gaudiness and dies:

Ah! what if all & each of Nature's favorite offspring,
'Mong many distinctions, have this portentous agreement,
MOUTH, STOMACH, INTESTINE? Question that brute appa-
ratus,
So manifoldly devis'd, set alert with furious instinct:
What doth it interpret but this, that LIFE LIVETH ON LIFE?
That the select creatures, who inherit earth's domination,
Whose happy existence is Nature's intelligent smile,
Are bloody survivors of a mortal combat, a-tweenwhiles
Chanting a brief pæan for victory on the battlefield?
Since that of all their kinds most owe their prosperous estate
Unto the art, whereby they more successfully destroy'd
Their weaker brethren, more insatiably devour'd them;
And all fine qualities, their forms pictorial, admired,
Their symmetries, their grace, & beauty, the loveliness of ther
Were by Murder evolv'd, to 'scape from it or to effect it.

*   *   *

Know you the story of our hive-bees, the yellow honey-
makers,
Whose images from of old have haunted Poetry, settling
On the blossoms of man's dream-garden, as on the summer-
flow'rs,
Pictures of happy toil, sunny glances, gendering always
Such sweet thoughts, as be by slumbrous music awaken'd?
How all their outward happiness,—that fairy demeanour
Of busy contentment, singing at their work,—is an inborn
Empty habit, the relics of a time when considerate joy
Truly possest their tiny bodies; when golden abundance
Was not a State-kept hoard; when feasts were plentiful
indulg'd
With wine well-fermented, or old-stored spicy metheglin:
For they died not then miserably within the second moon
Forgotten, unrespected of all; but slept many winters,
Saw many springs, liv'd, lov'd like men, consciously rejoicing
In Nature's promises, with like hopes and recollections.
Intelligence had brought them Science, Genius enter'd;
Seers and sages arose, great Bees, perfecting among them
Copious inventions, with man's art worthily compared.
Then was a time when that, which haps not in ages of ages,
Strangely befel: they stole from Nature's secrecy one key,

Found the hidden motive which works to variety of kind;
And thus came wondrously possest of pow'r to determine
Their children's qualities, habitudes, yea their specialized
    form
Masculine or feminine to produce, or asexual offspring
Redow'rd and differenced with such alternative organs
As they chose, to whate'er preferential function adapted,
Wax-pocket or honey-bag, with an instinct rightly acordant.
  We know well the result, but not what causes effected
Their decision to prefer so blindly the race to the unit,
As to renounce happiness for a problem, a vain abstraction;
Making home and kingdom a vast egg-factory, wherein
Food and life are stor'd up alike, and strictly proportion'd
In loveless labour with mean anxiety. Wondrous
Their reason'd motive, their altruistic obedience
Unto a self-impos'd life-sentence of prison or toil.
Wonder wisely! then ask if these ingenious insects,
(Who made Natur' against her will their activ' acomplice,
And, methodizing anew her heartless system, averted
From their house the torrent of whelming natural increase,)
Are blood-guiltless among their own-born progeny: What
    skill
Keeps their peace, or what price buys it? Alack! 'tis murder,
Murder again. No worst Oriental despot, assuring
'Gainst birthright or faction or envy his ill-gotten empire,
So decimates his kin, as do these rown-bodied egg-queens
Surprise competitors, and stab their slumbering infants,
Into the wax-cradles replunging their double-edged stings.
Or what a deed of blood some high-day, when the summer
    hath
Their clammy cells o'erbrim'd, and already ripening orchards
And late flow'rs proclaim that starving winter approacheth,
Nor will again any queen lead forth her swarm, dispeopling
Their strawbuilt citadel; then watch how these busy workers
Cease for awhile from toil; how crowding upon the devoted
Drones they fall; those easy fellows gave some provocation;
Yet 'tis a foul massacre, cold murder of unsuspecting
Life-long companions; and done bloodthirstily:— is not
Exercise of pow'r a delight? have you not a doctrine
That calls duty pleasure? What an if they make merry, saying
"Lazy-livers, runagates, evil beasts, greedy devourers,
"Too happy and too long ye've liv'd, unashamed to have outliv'd

"Your breeders, feeders, warmers and toiling attendants;
"Had-ye ever been worthy a public good to accomplish,
"Each had nobly perish'd long-ago. Unneeded, obese ones,
"Impious encumbrance, whose hope of service is over,
"Who did not, now can not, assist the community, YE DIE!"

EUGENE LEE-HAMILTON
(1845-1907)

(Both the following sonnets allude to the poet's long years of being bed-ridden
through cerebro-spinal disease.)

A Snail's Derby

Once, in this Tuscan garden, noon's huge ball
   So slowly crossed the sky above my head,
   As I lay idle on my dull wheeled bed,
That, sick of Day's inexorable crawl,

I set some snails a-racing on the wall,
   With their striped shells upon their backs, instead
   Of motley jockeys—black, white, yellow, red,
And watched them till the twilight's tardy fall.

And such my life, as years go one by one:
   A garden where I lie beyond the flowers,
And where the snails outrace the creeping sun.

For me there are no pinions to the hours;
   Compared with them, the snails like racers run:
Wait but Death's night, and, lo! the great ball lowers.

To my Tortoise Chronos

Thou vague dumb crawler with the groping head,
   As listless to the sun as to the showers,
   Thou very image of the wingless hours
Now creeping past me with their feet of lead;

For thee and me the same small garden bed
   Is the whole world; the same half life is ours;
   And year by year, as Fate restricts my powers,
I grow more like thee, and the soul grows dead.

"MICHAEL FIELD"

No, Tortoise: from thy like in days of old
  Was made the living lyre; and mighty strings
Spanned thy green shell with pure vibrating gold.

The notes soared up, on strong but trembling wings,
  Through ether's lower zones; then growing bold,
Spurned earth for ever and its wingless things.

"MICHAEL FIELD"

(KATHERINE BRADLEY, 1846-1914 and EDITH COOPER, 1862-1913)

(Miss Bradley and Miss Cooper were aunt and niece respectively who together
wrote under the pseudonym Michael Field. Whym Chow was a pet dog.)

Whym Chow

Nay, thou art my eternal attribute:
Not as Saint Agnes in loose arms her lamb --
The very essence of the thing I am:
And, as the lion, at Saint Jerome's suit,
Stood ever at his right hand, scanning mute
The hollows of the fountainous earth, whence swam
Emergent from the welter, sire and dam:
While Jerome with no knowledge of the brute
Beside him, wrote of later times, of curse,
Bloodshed, and bitter exile, verse on verse
Murmuring above the manuscript [*in awe*
The lion watched his lord, the Vulgate grew] ,
So it was wont to be betwixt us two --
How still thou lay'st deep-nosing on thy paw!

A Dying Viper

The lethargy of evil in her eyes --
As blue snow is the substance of a mere
Where the dead waters of a glacier drear
Stand open and behold -- a viper lies.

Brooding upon her hatreds: dying thus
Wounded and broken, helpless with her fangs,
She dies of her sealed curse, yea, of her pangs
At God's first ban that made her infamous.

Yet, by that old curse frozen in her wreath,
She, like a star, hath central gravity
That draws and fascinates the soul to death;

While round her stark and terrible repose,
Vaults for its hour a glittering sapphire fly,
Mocking the charm of death. O God, it knows!

ALICE MEYNELL
(1847-1922)

The Poet to the Birds

You bid me hold my peace,
    Or so I think, you birds; you'll not forgive
My kill-joy song that makes the wild song cease,
    Silent or fugitive.

Yon thrush stopt in mid-phrase
    At my mere footfall; and a longer note
Took wing and fled afield, and went its ways
    Within the blackbird's throat.

Hereditary song,
    Illyrian lark and Paduan nightingale,
Is yours, unchangeable the ages long;
    Assyria heard your tale;

Therefore you do not die.
    But single, local, lonely, mortal, new,
Unlike, and thus like all my race, am I,
    Preluding my adieu.

My human song must be
    My human thought. Be patient till 'tis done.
I shall not hold my little peace; for me
    There is no peace but one.

GEORGE J. ROMANES
(1848-1894)

The Sloth

Thou most absurd of all absurdities,
  Thou living irony of Nature's law,
  No wonder that in thee old Cuvier saw
Grim signs of humour in an otherwise
Not over-witty god: with ears and eyes
  Inverted, and each serviceable paw
  Transformed into a wretched hanging claw,
Thou hast turned topsy-turvy earth and skies.

"O 'paragon of animals,' why jeer
  At one who gazes with inverted eye?
The 'change of attitude' thou findest here
  Is my attempt to follow thine, and try
What benefit arises in this sphere
  By twisting all one's being towards the sky."

(*Cuvier:* George Cuvier, French naturalist, 1769-1832.)

ROBERT LOUIS STEVENSON
(1850-1894)

Nest Eggs

Birds all the sunny day
  Flutter and quarrel
Here in the arbour-like
  Tent of the laurel.

Here in the fork
  The brown nest is seated;
Four little blue eggs
  The mother keeps heated.

While we stand watching her,
  Staring like gabies,
Safe in each egg are the
  Birds' little babies.

Soon the frail eggs they shall
   Chip, and upspringing
Make all the April woods
   Merry with singing.

Younger than we are,
   O children, and frailer,
Soon in blue air they'll be.
   Singer and sailor.

We, so much older,
   Taller and stronger,
We shall look down on the
   Birdies no longer.

They shall go flying
   With musical speeches
High overhead in the
   Tops of the beeches.

In spite of our wisdom
   And sensible talking,
We on our feet must go
   Plodding and walking.

A Visit from the Sea

Far from the loud sea beaches
   Where he goes fishing and crying,
Here in the inland garden
   Why is the sea-gull flying?

Here are no fish to dive for;
   Here is the corn and lea;
Here are the green trees rustling.
   Hie away home to sea!

Fresh is the river water
   And quiet among the rushes;
This is no home for the sea-gull
   But for the rooks and thrushes.

Pity the bird that has wandered!
　　Pity the sailor ashore!
Hurry him home to the ocean,
　　Let him come here no more!

High on the sea-cliff ledges
　　The white gulls are trooping and crying,
Here among rooks and roses,
　　Why is the sea-gull flying?

ROBERT LOUIS STEVENSON

"My house, I say. But hark to the sunny doves"

My house, I say. But hark to the sunny doves
That make my roof the arena of their loves,
That gyre about the gable all day long
And fill the chimneys with their murmurous song:
Our house, they say; and *mine*, the cat declares
And spreads his golden fleece upon the chairs;
And *mine* the dog, and rises stiff with wrath
If any alien foot profane the path.
So too the buck that trimmed my terraces,
Our whilome gardener, called the garden his;
Who now, deposed, surveys my plain abode
And his late kingdom, only from the road.

The Cow

The friendly cow all red and white,
    I love with all my heart:
She gives me cream with all her might,
    To eat with apple-tart.

She wanders lowing here and there,
    And yet she cannot stray,
All in the pleasant open air,
    The pleasant light of day;

And blown by all the winds that pass
    And wet with all the showers,
She walks among the meadow grass
    And eats the meadow flowers.

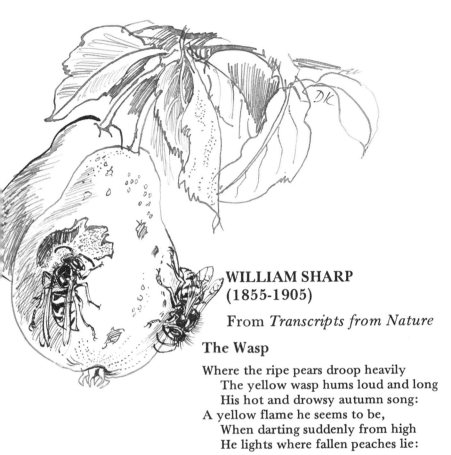

WILLIAM SHARP
(1855-1905)

From *Transcripts from Nature*

The Wasp

Where the ripe pears droop heavily
 The yellow wasp hums loud and long
 His hot and drowsy autumn song:
A yellow flame he seems to be,
 When darting suddenly from high
 He lights where fallen peaches lie:

Yellow and black, this tiny thing's
A tiger-soul on elfin wings.

WILLIAM SHARP

The Rookery at Sunrise

The lofty elm-trees darkly dream
    Against the steel-blue sky; till far
    I' the twilit east a golden star
O'erbrims the dusk in one vast stream
    Of yellow light, and lo! a cry
    Breaks from the windy nest — the sky

Is filled with wheeling rooks — they sway
In one black phalanx towards the day.

Fireflies

Softly sailing emerald lights
    Above the cornfields come and go,
    Listlessly wandering to and fro:
The magic of these July nights
    Has surely even pierced down deep
    Where the earth's jewels unharmed sleep,

And filled with fire the emeralds there
And raised them thus to the outer air.

The Eagle

Between two mighty hills a sheer
    Abyss—far down in the ravine
    A thread-like torrent and a screen
Of oaks like shrubs — and one doth rear
    A dry scarp'd peak above all sound
    Save windy voices wailing round:

At sunrise here, in proud disdain
The eagle scans his vast domain.

WILLIAM SHARP

From *Australian Transcripts*

V. Mid-noon in January

Upon a fibry fern-tree bough
A huge iguana lies alow,
Bright yellow in the noonday glow
With bars of black,—it watcheth now
A gorgeous insect hover high
Till suddenly its lance doth fly
    And catch the prey—but still no sound
    Breathes 'mid the green fern-spaces round.

IX. The Bell-Bird

The stillness of the Austral noon
Is broken by no single sound—
No lizards even on the ground
Rustle amongst dry leaves—no tune
The lyre-bird sings—yet hush! I hear
A soft bell tolling, silvery clear!
    Low soft aerial chimes, unknown
    Save 'mid these silences alone.

X. The Wood-Swallows*

(Sunrise)

The lightning-stricken giant gum
Stands leafless, dead—a giant still
But heedless of this sunrise-thrill:
What stir is this where all was dumb?—
What seem like old dead leaves break swift;
And lo, a hundred wings uplift
    A cloud of birds that to and fro
    Dart joyous midst the sunrise-glow.

*The wood-swallows of Australia have the singular habit of clustering like bees or bats on the boughs of a dead tree.

JOHN DAVIDSON
(1857-1909)

Two Dogs

Two dogs on Bournemouth beach: a mongrel, one,
With spaniel plainest on the palimpsest,
The blur of muddled stock; the other, bred,
With tapering muzzle, rising brow, strong jaw—
A terrier to the tail's expressive tip,
Magnetic, nimble, endlessly alert.

The mongrel, wet and shivering, at my feet
Deposited a wedge of half-inch board,
A foot in length and splintered at the butt;
Withdrew a yard and crouched in act to spring,
While to and fro between his wedge and me
The glancing shuttle of his eager look
A purpose wove. The terrier, ears a-cock,
And neck one curve of sheer intelligence,
Stood sentinel: no sound, no movement, save
The mongrel's telepathic eyes, bespoke
The object of the canine pantomine.

I stooped to grasp the wedge, knowing the game;
But like a thing uncoiled the mongrel snapped
It off, and promptly set it out again,
The terrier at his quarters, every nerve
Waltzing inside his lithe rigidity.

"More complex than I thought!" Again I made
To seize the wedge; again the mongrel won,
Whipped off the jack, relaid it, crouched and watched,
The terrier at attention all the time.
I won the third bout: ere the mongrel snapped
His toy, I stayed my hand; he halted, half
Across the neutral ground, and in his pause
Of doubt I seized the prize. A vanquished yelp
From both; and then intensest vigilance.

Together, when I tossed the wedge, they plunged
Before it reached the sea. The mongrel, out
Among the waves, and standing to them, meant
Heroic business; but the terrier dodged
Behind adroitly scouting in the surf,
And seized the wedge, rebutted by the tide,
In shallow water, while the mongrel searched
The English Channel on his hind-legs poised.
The terrier laid the trophy at my feet;
And neither dog protested when I took
The wedge: the overture of their marine
Diversion had been played out once for all.

A second match the reckless mongrel won,
Vanishing twice under the heavy surf,
Before he found and brought the prize to land.
Then for an hour the aquatic sport went on,
And still the mongrel took the heroic rôle,
The terrier hanging deftly in the rear.
Sometimes the terrier when the mongrel found
Betrayed a jealous scorn, as who should say,
"Your hero's always a vulgarian! Pah!"
But when the mongrel missed, after a fight
With such a sea of troubles, and saw the prize
Grabbed by the terrier in an inch of surf,
He seemed entirely satisfied, and watched
With more pathetic vigilance the cast
That followed.
            "Once a passion, mongrel, this
Retrieving of a stick," I told the brute,
"Has now become a vice with you. Go home!
Wet to the marrow and palsied with the cold,
You won't give in; and, good or bad, you've earned
My admiration. Go home now and get warm,
And the best bone in the pantry." As I talked
I stripped the water from his hybrid coat,
Laughed and made much of him — which mortified
The funking terrier.

"I'm despised, it seems!"
The terrier thought. "My cleverness (my feet
Are barely wet!) beside the mongrel's zeal
Appears timidity. This biped's mad
To pet the stupid brute. Yap! Yah!" He seized
The wedge and went; and at his heels at once,
Without a thought of me, the mongrel trudged.

Along the beach, smokers of cigarettes,
All sixpenny-novel-readers to a man,
Attracted Master Terrier. Again the wedge,
Passed to the loyal mongrel, was teed with care;
Again the fateful overture began.
Upon the fourth attempt, and not before,
And by a feint at that, the challenged youth
(Most equable, be sure, of all the group:
Allow the veriest dog to measure men!)
Secured the soaked and splintered scrap of deal.
Thereafter, as with me, the game progressed,
The breathless, shivering mongrel, rushing out
Into the heavy surf, there to be tossed
And tumbled like a floating bunch of kelp,
While gingerly the terrier picked his steps
Strategic in the rear, and snapped the prize
Oftener than his more adventurous, more
Romantic, more devoted rival did.

The uncomfortable moral glares at one!
And, further, in the mongrel's wistful mind
A primitive idea darkly wrought:
Having once lost the prize in the overture
With his bipedal rival, he felt himself
In honour and in conscience bound to plunge
For ever after it at the winner's will.
But the smart terrier was an Overdog,
And knew a trick worth two of that. He thought —
If canine cerebration works like ours,
And I interpret canine mind aright —
"Let men and mongrels worry and wet their coats!
I use my brains and choose the better part.
Quick-witted ease and self-approval lift
Me miles above this anxious cur, absorbed,
Body and soul, in playing a game I win
Without an effort. And yet the mongrel seems

The happier dog. How's that? Belike, the old
Compensatory principle again:
I have pre-eminence and conscious worth;
And he his power to fling himself away
For anything or nothing. Men and dogs,
What an unfathomable world it is!''

The Wasp

Once as I went by rail to Epping Street,
Both windows being open, a wasp flew in;
Through the compartment swung and almost out
Scarce seen, scarce heard; but dead against the pane
Entitled "Smoking," did the train's career
Arrest her passage. Such a wonderful
Impervious transparency, before
That palpitating moment, had never yet
Her airy voyage thwarted. Undismayed,
With diligence incomparable, she sought
An exit, till the letters like a snare
Entangled her; or else the frosted glass
And signature indelible appeared
The key to all the mystery: there she groped,
And flirted petulant wings, and fiercely sang
A counter-spell against the sorcery,
The sheer enchantment that inhibited
Her access to the world — her birthright, there!
So visible, and so beyond her reach!
Baffled and raging like a tragic queen,
She left at last the stencilled tablet; roamed
The pane a while to cool her regal ire,
Then tentatively touched the window-frame:
Sure footing still, though rougher than the glass;
Dissimilar in texture, and so obscure!

Perplexed now by opacity with foot and wing
She coasted up and down the wood, and worked
Her wrath to passion-point again. Then from the frame
She slipped by chance into the open space
Left by the lowered sash — the world once more
In sight! She paused; she closed her wings, and felt

The air with learned antennæ for the smooth
Resistance that she knew now must belong
To such mysterious transparencies.
No foothold? Down she fell — six inches down! —
Hovered a second, dazed and dubious still;
Then soared away a captive queen set free.

A Runnable Stag

When the pods went pop on the broom, green broom,
　And apples began to be golden-skinn'd,
We harbour'd a stag in the Priory coomb,
　And we feather'd his trail up-wind, up-wind,
　We feather'd his trail up-wind—
　　A stag of warrant, a stag, a stag,
　　A runnable stag, a kingly crop,
　　Brow, bay and tray and three on top,
　　A stag, a runnable stag.

Then the huntsman's horn rang yap, yap yap,
　And "Forwards" we heard the harbourer shout;
But 'twas only a brocket that broke a gap
　In the beechen underwood, driven out.
　From the underwood antler'd out
　　By warrant and might of the stag, the stag,
　　The runnable stag, whose lordly mind
　　Was bent on sleep, though beam'd and tined
　　He stood, a runnable stag.

So we tufted the covert till afternoon
　With Tinkerman's Pup and Bell-of-the-North;
And hunters were sulky and hounds out of tune
　Before we tufted the right stag forth,
　Before we tufted him forth,
　　The stag of warrant, the wily stag,
　　The runnable stag with his kingly crop,
　　Brow, bay and tray and three on top,
　　The royal and runnable stag.

It was Bell-of-the-North and Tinkerman's Pup
    That stuck to the scent till the copse was drawn.
"Tally ho! tally ho!" and the hunt was up,
    The tufters whipp'd and the pack laid on,
    The resolute pack laid on,
        And the stag of warrant away at last,
        The runnable stag, the same, the same,
        His hoofs on fire, his horns like flame,
        A stag, a runnable stag.

"Let your gelding be: if you check or chide
    He stumbles at once and you're out of the hunt,
For three hundred gentlemen, able to ride,
    On hunters accustom'd to bear the brunt,
    Accustom'd to bear the brunt,
        Are after the runnable stag, the stag,
        The runnable stag with his kingly crop,
        Brow, bay and tray and three on top,
        The right, the runnable stag."

By perilous paths in coomb and dell,
    The heather, the rocks, and the river-bed,
The pace grew hot, for the scent lay well,
    And a runnable stag goes right ahead,
    The quarry went right ahead—
        Ahead, ahead, and fast and far,
        His antler'd crest, his cloven hoof,
        Brow, bay and tray and three aloof,
        The stag, the runnable stag.

For a matter of twenty miles and more,
    By the densest hedge and the highest wall,
Through herds of bullocks he baffled the lore,
    Of harbourer, huntsman, hounds and all,
    Of harbourer, hounds and all—
        The stag of warrant, the wily stag,
        For twenty miles, and five and five,
        He ran, and he never was caught alive,
        This stag, this runnable stag.

When he turn'd at bay in the leafy gloom,
  In the emerald gloom where the brook ran deep
He heard in the distance the rollers boom,
  And he saw in a vision of peaceful sleep
  In a wonderful vision of sleep,
    A stag of warrant, a stag, a stag,
    A runnable stag in a jewell'd bed,
    Under the sheltering ocean dead,
    A stag, a runnable stag.

So a fateful hope lit up his eye,
  And he open'd his nostrils wide again,
And he toss'd his branching antlers high
  As he headed the hunt down the Charlock glen,
  As he raced down the echoing glen—
    For five miles more, the stag, the stag,
    For twenty miles, and five and five,
    Not to be caught now, dead or alive,
    The stag, the runnable stag.

Three hundred gentlemen, able to ride,
  Three hundred horses as gallant and free,
Beheld his escape on the evening tide,
  Far out till he sank in the Severn Sea,
  Till he sank in the depths of the sea—
    The stag, the buoyant stag, the stag
    That slept at last in a jewell'd bed
    Under the sheltering ocean spread,
    The stag, the runnable stag.

W. B. YEATS
(1865-1939)

The Wild Swans at Coole

The trees are in their autumn beauty
The woodland paths are dry,
Under the October twilight the water
Mirrors a still sky;
Upon the brimming water among the stones
Are nine-and-fifty swans.

The nineteenth autumn has come upon me
Since I first made my count;
I saw, before I had well finished,
All suddenly mount
And scatter wheeling in great broken rings
Upon their clamorous wings.

I have looked upon those brilliant creatures,
And now my heart is sore,
All's changed since I, hearing at twilight,
The first time on this shore,
The bell-beat of their wings above my head,
Trod with a lighter tread.

Unwearied still, lover by lover,
They paddle in the cold
Companionable streams or climb the air;
Their hearts have not grown old;
Passion or conquest, wander where they will,
Attend upon them still.

But now they drift on the still water,
Mysterious, beautiful;
Among what rushes will they build,
By what lake's edge or pool
Delight men's eyes when I awake some day
To find they have flown away?

(*Coole:* Coole Park, Lady Gregory's Irish house.)

To a Squirrel at Kyle-Na-No

Come play with me;
Why should you run
Through the shaking tree
As though I'd a gun
To strike you dead?
When all I would do
Is to scratch your head
And let you go.

(*Kyle-Na-No:* a wood at Coole Park.)

233

RUDYARD KIPLING
(1865-1936)

The Undertaker's Horse

'To-tschin-shu is condemned to death. How can he drink
  tea with the Executioner?' — *Japanese Proverb.*

The eldest son bestrides him,
And the pretty daughter rides him,
And I meet him oft o' mornings on the Course;
And there wakens in my bosom
An emotion chill and gruesome
As I canter past the Undertaker's Horse.

Neither shies he nor is restive,
But a hideously suggestive
Trot, professional and placid, he affects;
And the cadence of his hoof-beats
To my mind this grim reproof beats:
"Mind your pace, my friend, I'm coming. Who's the next?

Ah! stud-bred of ill-omen,
I have watched the strongest go — men
Of pith and might and muscle — at your heels,
Down the plantain-bordered highway,
(Heaven send it ne'er be my way!)
In a lacquered box and jetty upon wheels.

Answer, sombre beast and dreary,
Where is Brown, the young, the cheery,
Smith, the pride of all his friends and half the Force?
You were at that last dread *dak*
We must cover at a walk,
Bring them back to me, O Undertaker's Horse!

With your mane unhogged and flowing,
And your curious way of going,
And that businesslike black crimping of your tail,

E'en with Beauty on your back, Sir,
Pacing as a lady's hack, Sir,
What wonder when I meet you I turn pale?

It may be you wait your time, Beast,
Till I write my last bad rhyme, Beast —
Quit the sunlight, cut the rhyming, drop the glass —
Follow after with the others,
Where some dusky heathen smothers
Us with marigolds in lieu of English grass.

Or, perchance, in years to follow,
I shall watch your plump sides hollow,
See Carnifex (gone lame) become a corse —
See old age at last o'erpower you,
And the Station Pack devour you,
I shall chuckle then, O Undertaker's Horse!

But to insult, jibe, and quest, I've
Still the hideously suggestive
Trot that hammers out the grim and warning text,
And I hear it hard behind me
In what place soe'er I find me:—
"Sure to catch you sooner or later. Who's the next?"

EDGAR LEE MASTERS
(1868-1950)

My Dog Ponto

If I say to you "Come, Ponto, want some meat?"
You laugh in your dog-way and bark your "Yes."
And if I say "Shall we go walking" or
"Stand up, nice Ponto," then you stand up, or
If I say to you "Lie down" you lie down.
You know what meat is, what it is to walk.
You see the meat perhaps or get an image
Of scampering on the street or chasing dogs
While sniffing in fresh air, exploring bushes.
Upon these levels our minds meet at once,
As if they were the same stuff for such thoughts.
But if I look into your eye and say:
I'll read to you a chapter on harmonics,
Here's mad Spinoza's close wrought demonstration

235

Of God as substance, here is Isaac Newton's
Great book on gravitation, here's a thesis
Upon the logos, of the word made man.
Or if I say let's talk about my soul —
Since I have talked to yours in terms of meat —
Which sails out like a spider on its thread
Through mathematics, music — look at you
You merely lie there with half open eye,
And thump your tail quite feebly just because,
And for no other reason save I'm talking,
And I'm your master and you're fond of me,
And through affection would no doubt be glad
To know what I am saying, as 'twere meat
I might be saying. But I know a way
To make you howl for things not understood:
It makes you howl to hear my new Victrola
With a Beethoven record, why is this?
Perhaps this is to you a maddening token
Of realms that lie above the realms of meat,
And torture you because they have suggestions
Of things beyond you.
                But in any case,
Dear Ponto, if you were an infidel
You might say "What's harmonics? they're a joke."
"And who's Spinoza, Newton, they are myths."
"And mathematics, music, can you eat them,"
"For what you cannot eat has no existence."
Deny them as you will these spheres of thought
Lie as the steps of mountains over you.
They wait for you to gain them, you can find them
By rising to them, then how real they are!
As real as scampering when I take a walk.
But are they all? How do I know what spheres
Of life lie all around me and above me,
Just waiting not for me, but till I climb
And rest awhile and take their meaning in.
How do I know what hand plays a Victrola
With records greater than Beethoven's song,
Which make me howl as piteously as you?
But here again our minds meet on a level:
I know no more than you do why I howl;

Nor what it is that makes me howl, nor why,
Though not content with meat, I want to know,
And keep as all my own this higher music.

HILAIRE BELLOC
(1870-1954)

The Song called
"His Hide is Covered with Hair"

The dog is a faithful, intelligent friend,
    But his hide is covered with hair;
The cat will inhabit the house to the end,
    But *her* hide is covered with hair.

The hide of the mammoth was covered with wool,
The hide of the porpoise is sleek and cool,
But you'll find, if you look at that gambolling fool,
    That his hide is covered with hair.

Oh, I thank my God for this at least,
I was born in the West and not in the East,
And He made me a human instead of a beast,
    Whose hide is covered with hair!

The cow in the pasture that chews the cud,
    Her hide is covered with hair.
And even a horse of the Barbary blood,
    His hide is covered with hair!

The camel excels in a number of ways,
And travellers give him unlimited praise —
He can go without drinking for several days —
    But his hide is covered with hair.

The bear of the forest that lives in a pit,
    His hide is covered with hair;
The laughing hyena in spite of his wit,
    His hide is covered with hair!

The Barbary ape and the chimpanzee,
And the lion of Africa, verily he,
With his head like a wig, and the tuft on his knee,
    His hide . . .

A. STODART-WALKER
(d. 1934)

"I had a Duck"

(The piece that follows comes from *The Moxford Book of English Verse 1340-1913*, "presented by" A. Stodart-Walker — a book of parodies. See under Keats in the present collection for the poem parodied.)

I had a duck and the young duck died;
And I have thought it died of strangling:
O, who did it strangle? Its feet were tied,
From this ball of string I'm disentangling;
Why should I sell you, duckling. Why?
You quacked so long in the farmyard free
Why dainty thing, are you not trussed for me?
I fed you oft; and the buyer agrees
You will taste sweetly, served with green peas.

J.M. SYNGE
(1871-1909)

In Glencullen

Thrush, linnet, stare, and wren,
Brown lark beside the sun,
Take thought of kestrel, sparrow-hawk,
Birdlime and roving gun.

You great-great-grandchildren
Of birds I've listened to,
I think I robbed your ancestors
When I was young as you.

W.H. DAVIES
(1871-1940)

Eyes

The owl has come
    Right into my house;
He comes down the chimney,
    To look for a mouse —
And he sits on the rim of my old black table.

Lord , since I see
    Those wonderful eyes,
As big as a man's
    Or a maiden's in size —
Have I not proved his wisdom is no fable?

The Last Years

A dog, that has ten years of breath,
Can count the number left to me,
    To reach my seventy as a man.
In five years' time a bird is born,
Whose shorter life is then my own,
    Reducing still the human span.

Soon after that, a butterfly,
Who lives for but a year or less,
    Reminds me that the end is near;
And that, when I have lived his life,
A shorter life is still to come —
    Which brings the Summer's insect here.

And when at last that insect comes,
That lives for but a single day,
    He makes my life his very own:
Man, dog, and bird and butterfly
And insect yield their separate lives —
    And Death takes all of us as one.

To a Butterfly

We have met,
    You and I;
Loving man,
    Lovely Fly.

If I thought
    You saw me,
And love made
    You so free

To come close —
    I'd not move
Till you tired
    Of my love.

WALTER DE LA MARE
(1873-1956)

Summer Evening

The sandy cat by the Farmer's chair
Mews at his knee for dainty fare;
Old Rover in his moss-greened house
Mumbles a bone, and barks at a mouse.
In the dewy fields the cattle lie
Chewing the cud 'neath a fading sky;
Dobbin at manger pulls his hay:
Gone is another summer's day.

The Tomtit

Twilight had fallen, austere and grey,
The ashes of a wasted day,
When, tapping at the window-pane,
My visitor had come again,
To peck late supper at his ease —
A morsel of suspended cheese.

What ancient code, what Morse knew he —
This eager little mystery —
That, as I watched, from lamp-lit room,
Called on some inmate of my heart to come
Out of its shadows — filled me then
With love, delight, grief, pining, pain,
Scarce less than had he angel been?

Suppose, such countenance as that,
Inhuman, deathless, delicate,
Had gazed this winter moment in —
Eyes of an ardour and beauty no
Star, no Sirius could show!

Well, it were best for such as I
To shun direct divinity;
Yet not stay heedless when I heard
The tip-tap nothings of a tiny bird.

Tat for Tit

Shrill, glass-clear notes — "Titmouse!" I sighed, enchanted;
Then looked for the singer ere its song should cease:
A wild-eyed gipsy pushing an old go-cart,
    Its wheels in need of grease.

EDWARD THOMAS
(1878-1917)

The Combe

The Combe was ever dark, ancient and dark.
Its mouth is stopped with bramble, thorn, and briar;
And no one scrambles over the sliding chalk
By beech and yew and perishing juniper
Down the half precipices of its sides, with roots
And rabbit holes for steps. The sun of Winter,
The moon of Summer, and all the singing birds
Except the missel-thrush that loves juniper,

Are quite shut out. But far more ancient and dark
The Combe looks since they killed the badger there,
Dug him out and gave him to the hounds,
That most ancient Briton of English beasts.

Two Pewits

Under the after-sunset sky
Two pewits sport and cry,
More white than is the moon on high
Riding the dark surge silently;
More black than earth. Their cry
Is the one sound under the sky.
They alone move, now low, now high,
And merrily they cry
To the mischievous Spring sky,
Plunging earthward, tossing high,
Over the ghost who wonders why
So merrily they cry and fly,
Nor choose 'twixt earth and sky,
While the moon's quarter silently
Rides, and earth rests as silently.

Thaw

Over the land freckled with snow half-thawed
The speculating rooks at their nests cawed
And saw from elm-tops, delicate as flower of grass,
What we below could not see, Winter pass.

[Man and Dog]

" 'Twill take some getting." "Sir, I think 'twill so."
The old man stared up at the mistletoe
That hung too high in the poplar's crest for plunder
Of any climber, though not for kissing under:
Then he went on against the north-east wind—
Straight but lame, leaning on a staff new-skinned,
Carrying a brolly, flag-basket, and old coat,—
Towards Alton, ten miles off. And he had not

Done less from Chilgrove where he pulled up docks.
'Twere best, if he had had "a money-box",
To have waited there till the sheep cleared a field
For what a half-week's flint-picking would yield.
His mind was running on the work he had done
Since he left Christchurch in the New Forest, one
Spring in the 'seventies,—navvying on dock and line
From Southampton to Newcastle-on-Tyne,—
In 'seventy-four a year of soldiering
With the Berkshires,—hoeing and harvesting
In half the shires where corn and couch will grow.
His sons, three sons, were fighting, but the hoe
And reap-hook he liked, or anything to do with trees.
He fell once from a poplar tall as these:
The Flying Man they called him in hospital.
"If I flew now, to another world I'd fall."
He laughed and whistled to the small brown bitch
With spots of blue that hunted in the ditch.
Her foxy Welsh grandfather must have paired
Beneath him. He kept sheep in Wales and scared
Strangers, I will warrant, with his pearl eye
And trick of shrinking off as he were shy,
Then following close in silence for—for what?
"No rabbit, never fear, she ever got,
Yet always hunts. Today she nearly had one:
She would and she wouldn't. 'Twas like that. The bad one!
She's not much use, but still she's company,
Though I'm not. She goes everywhere with me.
So Alton I must reach tonight somehow:
I'll get no shakedown with that bedfellow
From farmers. Many a man sleeps worse tonight
Than I shall." "In the trenches." "Yes, that's right.
But they'll be out of that—I hope they be—
This weather, marching after the enemy."
"And so I hope. Good luck." And there I nodded
"Good-night. You keep straight on." Stiffly he plodded;
And at his heels the crisp leaves scurried fast,
And the leaf-coloured robin watched. They passed,
The robin till next day, the man for good,
Together in the twilight of the wood.

EDWARD THOMAS

The Gallows

There was a weasel lived in the sun
With all his family,
Till a keeper shot him with his gun
And hung him up on a tree,
Where he swings in the wind and rain,
In the sun and in the snow,
Without pleasure, without pain,
On the dead oak tree bough.

There was a crow who was no sleeper,
But a thief and a murderer
Till a very late hour; and this keeper
Made him one of the things that were,
To hang and flap in rain and wind,
In the sun and in the snow.
There are no more sins to be sinned
On the dead oak tree bough.

There was a magpie, too,
Had a long tongue and a long tail;
He could both talk and do—
But what did that avail?
He, too, flaps in the wind and rain
Alongside weasel and crow,
Without pleasure, without pain,
On the dead oak tree bough.

And many other beasts
And birds, skin, bone and feather,
Have been taken from their feasts
And hung up there together,
To swing and have endless leisure
In the sun and in the snow,
Without pain, without pleasure,
On the dead oak tree bough.

J.C. SQUIRE
(1884-1958)

To a Bull-dog
(W.H.S., Capt. [Acting Major] R.F.A.; killed April 12, 1917)

We shan't see Willy any more, Mamie,
    He won't be coming any more:
He came back once and again and again,
    But he won't get leave any more.

We looked from the window and there was his cab,
    And we ran downstairs like a streak,
And he said "Hullo, you bad dog," and you crouched
      to the floor,
    Paralysed to hear him speak.

And then let fly at his face and his chest
    Till I had to hold you down,
While he took off his cap and his gloves and his coat,
    And his bag and his thonged Sam Browne.

We went upstairs to the studio,
    The three of us, just as of old,
And you lay down and I sat and talked to him
    As round the room he strolled.

Here in the room where, years ago
    Before the old life stopped,
He worked all day with his slippers and his pipe,
    He would pick up the threads he'd dropped,

Fondling all the drawings he had left behind,
    Glad to find them all still the same,
And opening the cupboards to look at his belongings
    . . . Every time he came.

But now I know what a dog doesn't know,
    Though you'll thrust your head on my knee,
And try to draw me from the absent-mindedness
    That you find so dull in me.

And all your life you will never know
    What I wouldn't tell you even if I could,
That the last time we waved him away
    Willy went for good.

But sometimes as you lie on the hearthrug
   Sleeping in the warmth of the stove,
Even through your muddled old canine brain
   Shapes from the past may rove.

You'll scarcely remember, even in a dream,
   How we brought home a silly little pup,
With a big square head and little crooked legs
   That could scarcely bear him up,

But your tail will tap at the memory
   Of a man whose friend you were,
Who was always kind though he called you a naughty
      dog
   When he found you on his chair;

Who'd make you face a reproving finger
   And solemnly lecture you
Till your head hung downwards and you looked very
      sheepish!
   And you'll dream of your triumphs too.

Of summer evening chases in the garden
   When you dodged us all about with a bone:
We were three boys, and you were the cleverest,
   But now we're two alone.

When summer comes again,
   And the long sunsets fade,
We shall have to go on playing the feeble game for two
   That since the war we've played.

And though you run expectant as you always do
   To the uniforms we meet,
You'll never find Willy among all the soldiers
   In even the longest street,

Nor in any crowd; yet, strange and bitter thought,
   Even now were the old words said,
If I tried the old trick and said "Where's Willy?"
   You would quiver and lift your head,

And your brown eyes would look to ask if I were serious,
   And wait for the word to spring.
Sleep undisturbed: I shan't say *that* again,
   You innocent old thing.

I must sit, not speaking, on the sofa,
  While you lie asleep on the floor;
For he's suffered a thing that dogs couldn't dream of,
  And he won't be coming here any more.

A Dog's Death

The loose earth falls in the grave like a peaceful regular
    breathing;
  Too like, for I was deceived a moment by the sound:
It has covered the heap of bracken that the gardener laid
    above him;
  Quiet the spade wings: there we have now his mound.

A patch of fresh earth on the floor of the wood's renewing
    chamber:
  All around is grass and moss and the hyacinth's dark
    green sprouts:
And oaks are above that were old when his fiftieth sire was
    a puppy:
  And far away in the garden I hear the children's shouts.

Their joy is remote as a dream. It is strange how we buy
    our sorrow
  For the touch of perishing things, idly, with open eyes;
How we give our hearts to brutes that will die in a few
    seasons,
  Nor trouble what we do when we do it; nor would have
    it otherwise.

ANDREW YOUNG
(1885-1971)

The Dead Bird

Ah, that was but the wind
Your soft down stirred,
O bird, lying with sidelong head;
These open eyes are blind,
I cannot frighten you away;
You are so very dead
I almost say
"You are not a dead *bird*."

The Dead Sheep

There was a blacksmith in my breast,
That worked the bellows of my chest
   And hammer of my heart,
As up the heavy scree I pressed,
   Making the loose stones scream, crag-echoes start.

Rocks, rising, showed that they were sheep,
But one remained as though asleep,
   And how it was I saw,
When loath to leave the huddled heap
   A hoodie crow rose up with angry craw.

Though stiller than a stone it lay,
The face with skin half-flayed away
   And precious jewels gone,
The eye-pits darted a dark ray
   That searched me to my shadowy skeleton.

The Dead Crab

A rosy shield upon its back,
That not the hardest storm could crack,
From whose sharp edge projected out
Black pinpoint eyes staring about;
Beneath, the well-knit cote-armure
That gave to its weak belly power;
The clustered legs with plated joints
That ended in stiletto points;
The claws like mouths it held outside:
I cannot think this creature died
By storm or fish or sea-fowl harmed
Walking the sea so heavily armed;
Or does it make for death to be
Oneself a living armoury?

(*cote-armure:* coat of mail.)

A Dead Mole

Strong-shouldered mole,
That so much lived below the ground,
Dug, fought and loved, hunted and fed,
For you to raise a mound
Was as for us to make a hole;
What wonder now that being dead
Your body lies here stout and square
Buried within the blue vault of the air?

The Young Martins

None but the mouse-brown wren
That runs and hides from men—
Though for a moment now
Clinging with fine claws to a bough
One watches me askance,
Who dimly sit where the loose sunbeams dance—
Trills in these trees today;
All other birds seem flown away,
Though when I scrambled up
Through the thick covert of the combe's wide cup
Shaking down the last dog-rose petals,
My hand kissed by the angry nettles
And clawed by the lean thistles,
Blackbird and thrush flew off with startled whistles.

I see the hillside crossed
By a black flying ghost,
Rook's passing shadow, and beyond
Like skaters cutting figures on a pond
High swifts that curve on tilted wings are drawing
Vanishing circles; but save for the rooks' cawing
And trill of the small wren
Lost in the green again
No birds are singing anywhere,
As though the hot midsummer air
Hanging like blue smoke through the holt
Had driven all birds to sit apart and moult.

Yet when I came up through the farm
Where the stacked hay smelt keen and warm
Heads of young martins, one or two,
Black and white-cheeked, were peeping through
The small holes of their houses;
There where all day the sunlight drowses
They looked out from the cool
Dark shade of eaves and saw the pool
Where white duck feathers raised a storm of foam,
The cock that stood with crimson comb
Among his scraping hens,
The short-legged bull behind the fence,
The line-hung sheets that cracked and curled,
All the sun-laden dusty world;
And nodding each to each
They kept up a small twittering speech,
As though they ready were
To launch out on the air
And from their nests of clay
Like disembodied spirits suddenly fly away.

D.H. LAWRENCE
(1885-1930)

Tortoise Shell

The Cross, the Cross
Goes deeper in than we know,
Deeper into life;
Right into the marrow
And through the bone.

Along the back of the baby tortoise
The scales are locked in an arch like a bridge,
Scale-lapping, like a lobster's sections
Or a bee's.

Then crossways down his sides
Tiger-stripes and wasp-bands.
Five, and five again, and five again,
And round the edges twenty-five little ones,
The sections of the baby tortoise shell.

Four, and a keystone;
Four, and a keystone;
Four, and a keystone;
Then twenty-four, and a tiny little keystone.

It needed Pythagoras to see life playing with counters on
    the living back
Of the baby tortoise;
Life establishing the first eternal mathematical tablet,
Not in stone, like the Judean Lord, or bronze, but in life-
    clouded, life-rosy tortoise shell.

The first little mathematical gentleman
Stepping, wee mite, in his loose trousers
Under all the eternal dome of mathematical law.

Fives, and tens,
Threes and fours, and twelves,
All the *volte face* of decimals,
The whirligig of dozens and the pinnacle of seven.

Turn him on his back,
The kicking little beetle,
And there again, on his shell-tender, earth-touching belly,
The long cleavage of division, upright of the eternal cross
And on either side count five,
On each side, two above, on each side, two below
The dark bar horizontal.

The Cross!
It goes right through him, the sprottling insect,
Through his cross-wise cloven psyche,
Through his five-fold complex-nature.

So turn him over on his toes again;
Four pin-point toes, and a problematical thumb-piece,
Four rowing limbs, and one wedge-balancing head,
Four and one makes five, which is the clue to all mathematics.

The Lord wrote it all down on the little slate
Of the baby tortoise.
Outward and visible indication of the plan within,
The complex, manifold involvedness of an individual creature
Plotted out
On this small bird, this rudiment,
This little dome, this pediment
Of all creation,
This slow one.

The Blue Jay

The blue jay with a crest on his head
Comes round the cabin in the snow.
He runs in the snow like a bit of blue metal,
Turning his back on everything.

From the pine-tree that towers and hisses like a pillar of shaggy
    cloud
Immense above the cabin
Comes a strident laugh as we approach, this little black dog
    and I.
So halts the little black bitch on four spread paws in the snow
And looks up inquiringly into the pillar of cloud,
With a tinge of misgiving.
Ca-u-a! comes the scrape of ridicule out of the tree.

What voice of the Lord is that, from the tree of smoke?

Oh, Bibbles, little black bitch in the snow,
With a pinch of snow in the groove of your silly snub nose,
What do you look at *me* for?
What do you look at me for, with such misgiving?

It's the blue jay laughing at us.
It's the blue jay jeering at us, Bibs.

Every day since the snow is here
The blue jay paces round the cabin, very busy, picking up bits,
Turning his back on us all,
And bobbing his thick dark crest about the snow, as if darkly
    saying:
I ignore those folk who look out.

You acid-blue metallic bird,
You thick bird with a strong crest,
Who are you?
Whose boss are you, with all your bully way?
You copper-sulphate blue bird!

Lobo.

FRANCES CORNFORD
(1886-1960)

Night Song

On moony nights the dogs bark shrill
Down the valley and up the hill.

There's one is angry to behold
The moon so unafraid and cold,
That makes the earth as bright as day,
But yet unhappy, dead, and grey.

Another in his strawy lair
Says: "Who's a-howling over there?
By heavens I will stop him soon
From interfering with the moon."

So back he barks, with throat upthrown:
"You leave our moon, our moon alone."
And other distant dogs respond
Beyond the fields, beyond, beyond.

Daybreak

I heard an ancient sound: a cock that crew
    In graying light as I lay warm in bed.
A long metallic cry of dung and dew
    And the unearthly dead.

The Herd

How calmly cows move to the milking sheds,
How slowly, hieratically along,
How humbly with their moon-surmounted heads,
Though fly-pursued and stained, they pass me by
As gravely as the clouds across the sky,
They being, like the stars "preserved from wrong".

(The reference in the last line is to Wordsworth's "Ode to Duty".)

ROBINSON JEFFERS
(1887-1962)

Pelicans

Four pelicans went over the house,
Sculled their worn oars over the courtyard: I saw that un-
    gainliness
Magnifies the idea of strength.
A lifting gale of sea-gulls followed them; slim yachts of the
    element,
Natural growths of the sky, no wonder
Light wings to leave sea; but those grave weights toil, and
    are powerful,
And the wings torn with old storms remember
The cone that the oldest redwood dropped from, the tilting
    of continents,
The dinosaur's day, the lift of new sea-lines.
The omnisecular spirit keeps the old with the new also.
Nothing at all has suffered erasure.
There is life not of our time. He calls ungainly bodies
As beautiful as the grace of horses.
He is weary of nothing; he watches air-planes; he watches
    pelicans.

RUPERT BROOKE
(1887-1915)

The Fish

In a cool curving world he lies
And ripples with dark ecstasies.
The kind luxurious lapse and steal
Shapes all his universe to feel
And know and be; the clinging stream
Closes his memory, glooms his dream,
Who lips the roots o' the shore, and glides
Superb on unreturning tides.
Those silent waters weave for him
A fluctuant mutable world and dim,
Where wavering masses bulge and gape
Mysterious, and shape to shape
Dies momently through whorl and hollow,
And form and line and solid follow
Solid and line and form to dream
Fantastic down the eternal stream;
An obscure world, a shifting world,
Bulbous, or pulled to thin, or curled,
Or serpentine, or driving arrows,
Or serene slidings, or March narrows.
There slipping wave and shore are one,
And weed and mud. No ray of sun,
But glow to glow fades down the deep
(As dream to unknown dream in sleep);
Shaken translucency illumes
The hyaline of drifting glooms;
The strange soft-handed depth subdues
Drowned colour there, but black to hues,
As death to living, decomposes—
Red darkness of the heart of roses,
Blue brilliant from dead starless skies,
And gold that lies behind the eyes,
The unknown unnameable sightless white
That is the essential flame of night,
Lustreless purple, hooded green,
The myriad hues that lie between
Darkness and darkness! . . .

                              And all's one
Gentle, embracing, quiet, dun,
The world he rests in, world he knows,
Perpetual curving. Only—grows
An eddy in that ordered falling,
A knowledge from the gloom, a calling
Weed in the wave, gleam in the mud—
The dark fire leaps along his blood;
Dateless and deathless, blind and still,
The intricate impulse works its will;
His woven world drops back; and he,
Sans providence, sans memory,
Unconscious and directly driven,
Fades to some dank sufficient heaven.

O world of lips, O world of laughter,
Where hope is fleet and thought flies after,
Of lights in the clear night, of cries
That drift along the wave and rise
Thin to the glittering stars above,
You know the hands, the eyes of love!
The strife of limbs, the sightless clinging,
The infinite distance, and the singing
Blown by the wind, a flame of sound,
The gleam, the flowers, and vast around
The horizon, and the heights above—
You know the sigh, the song of love!

But there the night is close, and there
Darkness is cold and strange and bare;
And the secret deeps are whisperless;
And rhythm is all deliciousness;
And joy is in the throbbing tide,
Whose intricate fingers beat and glide
In felt bewildering harmonies
Of trembling touch; and music is
The exquisite knocking of the blood.
Space is no more, under the mud;
His bliss is older than the sun.
Silent and straight the waters run.
The lights, the cries, the willows dim,
And the dark tide are one with him.

Munich, March 1911

MARIANNE MOORE
(1887-1972)

Bird-witted

With innocent wide penguin eyes, three
    large fledgling mockingbirds below
the pussy-willow tree,
    stand in a row,
wings touching, feebly solemn,
till they see
       their no longer larger
       mother bringing
something which will partially
feed one of them.

Toward the high-keyed intermittent squeak
    of broken carriage springs, made by
the three similar, meek-
    coated bird's-eye
freckled forms she comes; and when
from the beak
       of one, the still living
       beetle has dropped
out, she picks it up and puts
it in again.

Standing in the shade till they have dressed
    their thickly filamented, pale
pussy-willow-surfaced
    coats, they spread tail
and wings, showing one by one,
the modest
       white stripe lengthwise on the
       tail and crosswise
underneath the wing, and the
accordion

is closed again. What delightful note
    with rapid unexpected flute
sounds leaping from the throat
    of the astute
grown bird, comes back to one from
the remote

unenergetic sun-
lit air before
the brood was here? How harsh
the bird's voice has become.

A piebald cat observing them,
    is slowing creeping toward the trim
trio on the tree stem.
    Unused to him
the three make room—uneasy
new problem.
        A dangling foot that missed
        its grasp, is raised
and finds the twig on which it
planned to perch. The

parent darting down, nerved by what chills
    the blood, and by hope rewarded—
of toil—since nothing fills
    squeaking unfed
mouths, wages deadly combat,
and half kills
        with bayonet beak and
        cruel wings, the
intellectual cautious-
ly creeping cat.

From *The Fables of La Fontaine*

The Wolf and the Stork

        Wolves can outeat anyone;
        Indeed at a festivity,
        Such gluttony second to none
        Almost ended fatally
When a bone choked a wolf as he gulped what he ate;
But happily since he was inarticulate,
        A stork chanced to hear him groan,
        Was besought by frowns to run and peer,
And ah, had soon relieved the beast of the bone;
Then, having done him a service, had no fear,
        So asked him how compensate her.
        "Compensate?" he inquired with bared teeth,
        "A humorist, I infer!
        You should be glad that you draw breath.

Thrust your beak down my throat and you somehow
escaped death?
Be off. You are unappreciative;
Shun my paws if you care to live."

The Fox and the Grapes

A fox of Gascon, though some say of Norman descent,
When starved till faint gazed up at a trellis to which grapes were
tied—
Matured till they glowed with a purplish tint
As though there were gems inside.
Now grapes were what our adventurer on strained haunches
chanced to crave,
But because he could not reach the vine
He said, "These grapes are sour; I'll leave them for some knave."

Better, I think, than an embittered whine.

T.S. ELIOT
(1888-1965)

(The poet's opening line (and similar subsequent references) alludes to the
previous poems in his *Old Possum's Book of Practical Cats*, but may reason-
ably be read here apropos of the cats in these pages.)

The Ad-dressing of Cats

You've read of several kinds of Cat,
And my opinion now is that
You should need no interpreter
To understand their character.
You now have learned enough to see
That Cats are much like you and me
And other people whom we find
Possessed of various types of mind.
For some are sane and some are mad
And some are good and some are bad
And some are better, some are worse—
But all may be described in verse.

You've seen them both at work and games,
And learnt about their proper names,
Their habits and their habitat:
But
How would you ad-dress a Cat?

So first, your memory I'll jog,
And say: A CAT IS NOT A DOG.

Now Dogs pretend they like to fight;
They often bark, more seldom bite;
But yet a Dog is, on the whole,
What you would call a simple soul.
Of course I'm not including Pekes,
And such fantastic canine freaks.
The usual Dog about the Town
Is much inclined to play the clown,
And far from showing too much pride
Is frequently undignified.
He's very easily taken in—
Just chuck him underneath the chin
Or slap his back or shake his paw,
And he will gambol and guffaw.
He's such an easy-going lout,
He'll answer any hail or shout.

Again I must remind you that
A Dog's a Dog — A CAT'S A CAT.

With Cats, some say, one rule is true:
Don't speak till you are spoken to.
Myself, I do not hold with that —
I say, you should ad-dress a Cat.
But always keep in mind that he
Resents familiarity.
I bow, and taking off my hat,
Ad-dress him in this form: O CAT!
But if he is the Cat next door,
Whom I have often met before
(He comes to see me in my flat)
I greet him with an OOPSA CAT!
I think I've heard them call him James —
But we've not got so far as names.
Before a Cat will condescend
To treat you as a trusted friend,

Some little token of esteem
Is needed, like a dish of cream;
And you might now and then supply
Some caviare, or Strassburg Pie,
Some potted grouse, or salmon paste —
He's sure to have his personal taste.
(I know a Cat, who makes a habit
Of eating nothing else but rabbit,
And when he's finished, licks his paws
So's not to waste the onion sauce.)
A Cat's entitled to expect
These evidences of respect.
And so in time you reach your aim,
And finally call him by his NAME.

So this is this, and that is that:
And there's how you AD-DRESS A CAT.

LOUISE BOGAN
(1897-1970)

Variation on a Sentence

There are few or no bluish animals. . . .
Thoreau's Journals, Feb. 21, 1855

Of white and tawny, black as ink,
Yellow, and undefined, and pink,
And piebald, there are droves, I think.

(Buff kine in herd, gray whales in pod,
Brown woodchucks, colored like the sod,
All creatures from the hand of God.)

And many of a hellish hue;
But, for some reason hard to view,
Earth's bluish animals are few.

LOUISE BOGAN

Animal, Vegetable and Mineral

Glass Flowers from the Ware Collection in the Botanical Museum of Harvard University. Insect Pollination Series, with Sixteen Color Plates, by Fritz Kredel. New York: Harcourt, Brace and Company. 58 pages. $1.50.

Dieu ne croit pas à notre Dieu.   JULES RENARD

On gypsum slabs of preternatural whiteness
In Cambridge (Mass.) on Oxford Street is laid
One craft wherein great Nature needs no aid
From man's Abstracts and Concretes, Wrong and
    Rightness:
Cross-pollination's fixed there and displayed.

Interdependence of the seed and hive!
Astounding extraverted bee and flower!
Mixture of styles! Intensity of drive!
Both Gothic and Baroque blooms flaunt their power.
The classic *Empire* bees within them strive.

The flower is to bee a kind of arrow;
Nectar is pointed out by spot and line.
Corollas may be shaped both wide and narrow;
Mechanics vary, though the play is fine,
And bee-adapted (not for crow or sparrow).

Bush-bean and butterwort keep bee in mind;
Chamisso too (which has no common name);
Red larkspur, devil's-bit scabious are aligned
With garden violet in this bee-ish claim
(*Impatiens Roylei Walpers* acts the same).

Expectancy is constant; means are shifting.
One flower has black cloven glands that pinch
The bee's foot (on the stigma these are lifting);
Anthers with cell-hid pollen wait the clinch.
Think well on this, who think that Life is Drifting . . .

Eager quickly to free its sticky foot
The bee stamps briskly just where stamp is needed:
Motion and power attendant on this boot
Extract *pollinia*. (Here the mind's exceeded;
Wild intimations through the fibers shoot.)

Self-fertile flowers are feeble and need priming.
Nature is for this priming, it appears.
Some flowers, like water-clocks, have perfect timing:
Pistil and anthers rise, as though on gears;
One's up and when t'other's down; one falls; one's climbing.

Charles Darwin saw the primrose, and took thought.
Later, he watched the orchids. There, the bees
Enter in, one way; then, with pollen fraught,
Have to climb out another, on their knees.
The stigma profits, and the plant's at ease.

The dyer's greenwood waits the bee in tension.
Petals are pressed down: then the stamens spring
(The pistils, too) into a new dimension,
Hitting the bee's back between wing and wing.
Who thought this out? It passes comprehension.

For forty million years this has gone on
(So Baltic amber shows, and can it lie?)
The bee's back, feet, head, belly have been drawn
Into the flower's plan for history.
Nectar's been yielded for the hexagon.

Then think of Blaschkas (*père et fils*), who spent
Full fifty years in delicate adjusting,
Glass-blowing, molding, skill with instrument,
While many other crafts were merely rusting.
Two Yankee Wares (*mère, fille*) the money lent.

Cynics who think all this *bijouterie*
Certainly lack a Deepening Sense of Awe.
Here Darwin, Flora, Blaschkas and the bee
Fight something out that ends in a close draw.
Above the cases howls loud mystery.

What is the chain, then ask, and what the links?
Are these acts sad or droll? From what derived?
Within the floret's disk the insect drinks.
Next summer there's more honey to be hived.

What Artist laughs? What clever Daemon thinks?

RUTH PITTER
(1897-   )

The Bat

Lightless, unholy, eldritch thing,
Whose murky and erratic wing
Swoops so sickeningly, and whose
Aspect to the female Muse
Is a demon's, made of stuff
Like tattered, sooty waterproof,
Looking dirty, clammy, cold.

DK

Wicked, poisonous, and old:
I have maligned thee! . . . for the Cat
Lately caught a little bat,
Seized it softly, bore it in.
On the carpet, dark as sin
In the lamplight, painfully
It limped about, and could not fly.

Even fear must yield to love,
And Pity makes the depths to move.
Though sick with horror, I must stoop,
Grasp it gently, take it up,
And carry it, and place it where
It could resume the twilight air.

Strange revelation! warm as milk,
Clean as a flower, smooth as silk!
O what a piteous face appears,
What great fine thin translucent ears!
What chestnut down and crapy wings,
Finer than any lady's things—
And O a little one that clings!

Warm, clean, and lovely, though not fair,
And burdened with a mother's care:
Go hunt the hurtful fly, and bear
My blessing to your kind in air.

Dun Colour

Subtle almost beyond thought are these dim colours,
The mixed, the all-including, the pervasive,
Earth's own delightful livery, banqueting
The eye with dimness that includes all brightness;
Complexity which the mind sorts out, as the sunlight
Resolves into many purities the mingled
Dun fleeces of the moorland; the quartz sparkles,
The rosy heath glows, the mineral-like mosses
And the heathbells and the myriad lichens
Start each into the eye a separate splendour:
So in the mind's sun bloom the dim dun-colours.

RUTH PITTER

The dry vermilion glow of familiar redbreast
Is not his real glory: that is the greenish,
Light-toned, light-dissembling, eye-deceiving
Dun of his smooth-sloped back, and on his belly
The whitish dun is laid to deceive the shadow:
In the dear linnet the olive-dun is lovely,
And the primrose-duns in the yellowhammer: but most
    beguiling,
Perhaps because of the perfect shape, is the ash-dun,
That quietest, most urbane, unprofaneable colour
Reserved as her livery of beauty to the hedge-sparrow.
There is a royal azure in her blood,
As her eggs prove, and in her nature gold,
For her children's throats are kingcups; but she veils them,
Mingled and blended, in her rare dun-colour.

For the rose-duns, and the blue-duns, look to the finches:
For the clear clear brown-duns, to the fallow deer
(How the sudden tear smarts in the eye wearied of cities)
And for all these and more to the many toadstools
Which alone have the violet-dun, livid yet lovely:
But the most delicate duns are seen in the gentle
Monkeys from the great forests, the silvan spirits:
Wonderful! that these, almost our brothers,
Should be dressed so rarely, in sulphurous-dun and greenish;
O that a man had grassy hair like these dryads!
O that I too were attired in such dun colours!

Index of first lines of poems and extracts

269

INDEX

INDEX

INDEX

INDEX